BLIND

MATTHEW FARRER ONCE again brings his dazzling talent to bear on the Shira Calpurnia series. The fast-paced, intelligent action takes place in the great Imperial fortress system of Hydraphur, where Adeptus Arbites officer Shira Calpurnia enforces the law.

Now she is investigating the murder of a blind astropath – psychic humans who use their gifts to communicate across the vast reaches of the galaxy – and she fears that the killer will strike again.

A WARHAMMER 40,000 NOVEL

Shira Calpurnia

BLIND

Matthew Farrer

For B&B

Thanks to Philip Sibbering and Jon Green, for suggestions; to Lindsey Priestley, for patience; to Dan Abnett, James Swallow and Stephen King for trailblazing.

Special thanks to Kim Newman and the Reverend Anthony William Jago, for inspiration.

A BLACK LIBRARY PUBLICATION

First published in Great Britain in 2006 by
BL Publishing,
Games Workshop Ltd.,
Willow Road, Nottingham,
NG7 2WS, UK.

10 9 8 7 6 5 4 3 2 1

Cover illustration by Clint Langley.

A CIP record for this book is available from the British Library.

ISBN 13: 978 1 84416 373 1
ISBN 10: 1 84416 373 3

Distributed in the US by Simon & Schuster
1230 Avenue of the Americas, New York, NY 10020, US.

Printed and bound in Great Britain by
Bookmarque, Surrey, UK.

See the Black Library on the Internet at
www.blacklibrary.com

Find out more about Games Workshop
and the world of Warhammer 40,000 at
www.games-workshop.com

IT IS THE 41st millennium. For more than a hundred centuries the Emperor has sat immobile on the Golden Throne of Earth. He is the master of mankind by the will of the gods, and master of a million worlds by the might of his inexhaustible armies. He is a rotting carcass writhing invisibly with power from the Dark Age of Technology. He is the Carrion Lord of the Imperium for whom a thousand souls are sacrificed every day, so that he may never truly die.

YET EVEN IN his deathless state, the Emperor continues his eternal vigilance. Mighty battlefleets cross the daemon-infested miasma of the warp, the only route between distant stars, their way lit by the Astronomican, the psychic manifestation of the Emperor's will. Vast armies give battle in his name on uncounted worlds. Greatest amongst his soldiers are the Adeptus Astartes, the Space Marines, bio-engineered super-warriors. Their comrades in arms are legion: the Imperial Guard and countless planetary defence forces, the ever-vigilant Inquisition and the tech-priests of the Adeptus Mechanicus to name only a few. But for all their multitudes, they are barely enough to hold off the ever-present threat from aliens, heretics, mutants – and worse.

TO BE A man in such times is to be one amongst untold billions. It is to live in the cruellest and most bloody regime imaginable. These are the tales of those times. Forget the power of technology and science, for so much has been forgotten, never to be re-learned. Forget the promise of progress and understanding, for in the grim dark future there is only war. There is no peace amongst the stars, only an eternity of carnage and slaughter, and the laughter of thirsting gods.

'Only in your deepest self is the truth of what you can be, and, without a doubt, that truth is terrible to bear.'

– Adeptus Astronomica, *The Book of the Astronomican*

CHAPTER ONE

IN THE DARKNESS, the Tower.

It is far out from the star, here. The blaze that brings warm yellow daylight to Hydraphur is too far away for warmth here. An observer could stand at a window in the Tower and eclipse the sun with a single tine of a dining fork, and there is no opticon on the Tower powerful enough to detect the tiny glint around that star that is Hydraphur itself.

However, aboard the Tower there are other ways of seeing.

It coasts through the gloom of its long, far, strange orbit. The Bastion Psykana: a broken child's top pierced through and through by the silver lengths of its spires. At its waist is a tricorn slab of adamantite-laced rockcrete: the Curtain, its outward-bowing edges wrinkled with toothless gun-ports and gaping hardpoints, each blunt corner sprouting clusters of docking towers and grapple-gantries.

Back in its Naval fortress days, the ornate towers above and below the Curtain – the keeps – were mirror images of one another. The upper keep, aligned towards system zenith, is bowed in along one whole quadrant, exposed girders emerging from the distorted wall to shore up the integrity of the sagging topwalls. The lower keep, pointing down towards system nadir, sharpens like a stalagtite. Despite the repairs and the attention of its artisan-engineers the Tower looks malformed, hunched in the dark of its orbit. The texture of its walls in the wan backwash of its own stablights seems soft somehow, waxy and yielding.

The eyrie-spikes punch through the station like skewers through an old fruit. Slender, barbed, shining steel, arranged with a finely calculated lack of symmetry, they rake across the stars, their shafts webbed with access wells and stairports to bind and link them. The housings of their engines are clustered around their bases, cables and vanes crawling up their lengths like creepers.

Those towers and engines might seem to glow, their lines crawling with corposant, or rumble like a great machine, a heartbeat, even out there in the vacuum that carries no sound. Their sides might sometimes appear to heave, or their perspectives seem odd, too flat or too angular. The sensitive mind may see these things.

The sensible mind will ignore them, because this misshapen thing in Hydraphur's secret reaches is the Blind Tower: the Bastion Psykana, the Witchroost. It burns with the invisible psyker-light of its astropaths, rings with the silent warp-music of their choirs. The sensible mind does not dwell on the strange echoes that those choirs' music might sometimes evoke. It does not wonder too deeply what shadows the beacon-light might cast in the corner of the eye, and in the deeps of the soul.

* * *

MUSIC AND ECHOES, *screams and eyes, the snarls of infants and the hymns of beasts, the breath of a prey-killer on the back of his mind: all this is rushing in on Qwahl like a torrent. Burning fingers crush his mind. The fist is his and the will is his. His mind sings with the chords of his own will and the meshing-steel embrace of the choir behind, below and around him. He opens his blind eyes and his dry mouths, and every nerve and muscle reverberates with the great bass note, the roar of the white fire that was ignited in his soul so long ago. The stones, shadows. Hands and voices all around him quail and melt. Then he is leaving his body far behind, mind and soul shouting with exhilaration as he bullets down the tunnel that the great white light has lit for him. He sends a thought ahead, ready and open like a hand, a flower, or an open-mouthed polyp-worm. For a moment, there is fear. There is nothing there to take his hand, and fill the hollow vessel that his mind has made of itself. The whispers start, the growls of the deep warp-winds. Even as the laughing no-colour tries to seep into him, he feels…*

ASTROPATH QWAHL SAT halfway up with a wrench that made the restraints on the couch squeal. His knuckles were white on the shotstone aquila that he always carried in his hands. His sealed eyelids quivered. A momentary stir of power came off him like a shiver of static, before the wards in the eyrie walls trapped it and carried it away. There was a brief answering flurry of activity in the Firewatch Eyrie: two medicae attendants flicked their eyes rapidly over auspexes, and a pair of bondservants stepped forwards with poles, ready to push him back down onto his couch. Threads of red and green light danced through the incense smoke as the servo-skull behind the couch descended through the air to scan the plugs and cables in the astropath's lumpy, depilated skull, looking for damaged connections. The vitifer, head encased in a visored ward-cage, took half a step forwards and drew her pistol. The archive-servitor remained impassive, the nib of its pen poised above the roll of recording scrip.

Concordiast Dernesk leaned over to study Qwahl's face. He had seen the astropath in a trance before, and knew his signs and mannerisms. He shook his head to the others: a spasm, no danger yet.

As Qwahl slowly relaxed, they all felt a shifting sensation, as if the gravity or the air pressure had changed. Below them, the choir was changing note.

BENEATH THE EYRIE, between the thick metal walls of the column that supported it, was situated the stacked honeycomb of cells and compartments, serried in layers around the lift well and the coil of steep metal stairs. The psychic-pulse beat strongly here. Tech-priest Guaphon, his torso uncoupled from his spindly steel legs, sat in the throne-socket in the little Munitorium. He could feel the pulse vibrating through the layers of suppression engines and ranks of warp-attuned sensors, charting the energy pulses from above him in exquisite detail. The machine spirits sent up their own beat, signalling their readiness to him in streams of machine-code.

Qwahl feels…

THE CANTOR'S CHAMBER, where Cantor Angazi knelt, was below the Munitorium in the tower. He leant forwards, his weight on a sling of crisscrossing ropes of soft velvet. The mane of cables linking into his cranium was unlike Qwahl's: the connections were thinner, some thread-fine. A single thick cable from the very top of his head shot straight up into the ceiling, towards the eyrie.

Angazi had felt Qwahl's moment of hesitation, and anticipated it: he was skilled and experienced. He knew the melodies of the astropath trance from his own days in the eyries before he'd been appointed cantor. The white fire that the Soul Binding had hammered deep into him flickered in sympathy, and his mind surrounded and enveloped the thick power-flow of woven harmony welling up from the choir galleries surrounding the column's base. The voices came through the warp, through space, and through the circuits of the column itself, swirling through Angazi's own consciousness, and through the ward-engraved walls of his chamber.

Angazi checked them with a thought, and used his own focus to bind the choristers' voices tighter. He rippled his consciousness across them to soothe and direct them. Their note shifted and the intensity of their power changed. The harmony reached up through Angazi as he marshalled the choristers and directed them to their new parts. He rested his own mind on the psychic voices of those who were too far gone; too burned to understand what was needed, and steered them into their new melody.

He knew his work, was sure about it. As Qwahl's spirit pushed deeper into the warp and further out from the eyrie where his body twitched, Angazi tuned the choir's melody to him, fuelling him, bolstering him, giving him the power-stream to ride on and shelter in, and keeping him safe.

Qwahl feels something…

THE CHANGE IN the choir's note reverberated through the Tower. To most of the non-psykers, it felt like a change in the air pressure, or a change in the timbre of the whispering voices in their heads, or any one of a thousand different stimuli. Other astropaths registered it as a change in the constant background energies around them, powerful, but of no immediate import. But one astropath heard it, as she was hearing every psychic voice in the Bastion at that moment, with greater clarity.

The detector vanes that carried the psychic impulses to Guaphon's Munitorium carried them further, down the column and deep into the keep, to a tall asymmetrical chamber buried off-centre below the astropath cloisters: the Bastion's watch-hall. In that great, angled space, the voices of the choir were birthed into the air as actual sounds: a complex layer of notes and cries from vox-speakers. Harp strings and metal plates engraved with sensitive wards, tuned to translate the intricate psychic harmonics, fed into them. The shift in the choir's song arrived in the ears of the watch-hall attendants as a rapid string of chimes. They heard a wave of trills and clashing notes before the long notes settled into their new melody.

A skilled watchmaster could read the sounds of the Tower as skilfully as they read the psychic signs, and Watchmaster Chevenne was skilled indeed. He picked up the change in the music, and understood it immediately for what it was. He picked out the nuances that showed him Cantor Angazi's touches on the choir and Astropath Qwahl's clear, disciplined voice reaching out into the warp. Satisfied that he knew all the important details of what was going on in the Firewatch Eyrie, Chevenne twitched his psychic attention away from the sounds and let it drift. As he passed to each new zone of the hall, his mind registered which region of the Tower it represented. He made sure that nothing was wrong, nothing was tainted, that no power was being over-used, and no mind overloaded. Unstable psykers who might trigger one another were kept apart by quick orders to their attendants. Minds that were palpably weakening were directed into the cloisters to be meshed to a choir, to cover them with power while they recovered.

The Bastion's watchmaster, hanging in his bronze cage in the centre of the watch-hall, was the constant attendant of the Bastion's pulse. He made sure that the psychic flows never built up here, petered out there, or let a taint spread over there.

Chevenne moved with his hearing and psychic sense over the soft, distinctive tones of Astropath Laris, moving towards the base of the Green Eyrie. He moved over Senior Astropath Thujik's mind as his concordiast helped him through mental exercises to restore tranquillity after his trance in the Eyrie of Bones. Then he found the tightly controlled little psychic sun of Master Otranto himself, walking boldly, unattended but for a vitifer, down the Great Concourse and out beyond the astropath cloisters of the central keep. Chevenne let his mind rest on the Master's for a moment until he heard the old man's querulous psychic voice demanding what he wanted. With the mental equivalent of a shrug and a smile, Chevenne moved on.

QWAHL REACHES OUT *with the net of his mind, sensing the flavour of the message, delicately feeling its contours. He recognises the touch of its sender, Skarant. Astropath Skarant in his colonnaded cell in the high pagoda of Gantia. Skarant whose sendings still carry the scent of conifer-flowers.*

Qwahl tightens the skeins of the net, turns the cobweb filaments to something harder, and starts to reel in the message. The great weight, the message, spiky with ciphering and warding, roils up through Qwahl's thoughts like a deadly mine floating up into the shallows of the ocean. It strains the embrace of his mind, swamps it with pain, but will and more still streams in…

DERNESK LEANED OVER Qwahl's body. The astropath's face was contorting and his throat was working as if he was getting ready to scream, or vomit. Dernesk's training kept his own face and mind impassive, even when green-yellow arcs of energy started playing between the cables on Qwahl's skull.

'It's coming,' he said aloud. 'Something big is coming through. Warn the cantor. This is going to hit hard.'

The attendants nodded, and the word went back down the tower. Guaphon moved his control from one bank of psy-instruments to another, keeping them tuned. Angazi led the choir in a change of song, loosening the mesh of minds so that it was no longer a bullet, a psychic pile-driver pushing Qwahl onward. They wove a net, a cloak, surrounding him and warming him, helping to take the strain of the message that had just been sucked into his consciousness, lighting the way back down out of the warp into his body once again.

THE MESSAGE FINALLY *reeled in and contained, Qwahl releases his grip and lets his mind fly loose, and pull back.*

'HE'S GOT IT,' Dernesk said, but there was no need. The choir was already doing its job, and Guaphon had reported the change in the astropath's life-signs. One of the attendants bent over a particular series of cables, whispering blessings. He was conscious of how the metal was heating, watching the amulet runes dangling from the plugs as they flashed green-ochre-green. The system was ready.

QWAHL IS STRUGGLING, *reeling backwards. Groping frantically with feather-tendrils at the back of his consciousness, he fights down the panic that wells up in the shadows of his mind. He gropes blindly for his choir, for Angazi. Fleeing back towards his own body, he is dropping into the beautiful cold sanity of the materium. He drops like an overloaded lander towards a planet, flaming down towards his own body.*

His mind is bulging, smoking, freighted with strange cargo, red veins of information pulsing in the black of his mind that he keeps safe within his soul-bound glow. He has to get it out. He has to push it out. He can feel his soul starting to bleed.

A THIN FILM of blood appeared over Qwahl's lips. With practiced economy of motion, Dernesk crushed a phial of essence, put a taper to it, and dropped the mess into a shallow porcelain dish. He knew that Qwahl responded to essence of epima-oil. He held the dish under the astropath's face, and rested his other hand on the man's brow. The skin flashed hot and cold to his touch, and he began to massage his forehead, chanting a single low note over and over. The attendant behind the chair made a satisfied noise as all the data-runes flickered into the green. The vitifer stood immobile, ready to kill.

QWAHL IS BEING *dragged by the choir-song. He is close enough to start picking up traces from his own senses: the scent of epima-oil, a touch on his forehead, a voice humming. He lets go, and plummets.*

THE ASTROPATH'S MIND slammed back into his body like a fist into an open palm. The shock of the arrival sent him bucking against the restraints, howling with pain, at the pressure on his distended mind. Dernesk bent over him, shouting out phrases keyed to the deep hypnosis triggers that Qwahl had designed for himself. He tried to help the astropath force his mental defences down on the burning and the strain. Alerted by the sound, the archive-servitor started twitching its pen in readiness. Witchfire was gusting along the eyrie walls in odd patterns that were broken and sucked away by the earths and wards.

Qwahl's mouth was working incessantly now, random syllables starting to spit through the air. The syllables became words, endless strings of words. Dernesk recognised the general form and cadence. It was what they had been expecting – an Imperial message, coded to protect the data. The archive-servitor's pen sprang into life, scribbling and scratching over spooling loops of scrip.

Dernesk bent and listened. He knew Qwahl's voice could slur, the man's facial nerves had been steadily deteriorating since his Binding and his lips didn't move as dextrously as they once had.

Dernesk realised he was sweating. Once they had left the eyrie, it would take hours to get Qwahl's mind relaxed to the point where he'd be able to rest for his next trance. He sighed and mopped his brow.

As the information spewed out, the astropath's struggles eased, and his cries lessened. Something like peace came over his features. His speech was more fluid now, less tortured. Dernesk knew Qwahl, knew how the man thought and associated. He began to whisper trigger-phrases again, fragments of rhyme or scripture or song he knew Qwahl would respond to, his attention dancing between soothing the astropath's mind and manipulating it, gratified when he heard the responding thought-motifs and speech patterns begin to shape Qwahl's talk.

The scrip recordings pouring away from the archive-servitor were being fed down the eyrie's data-sluices, down into the keep, into the maws of the logic mills and data-looms of the tech-shrine where the fortress's cogitators had once turned auspexes out into interstellar space and plotted trajectories and firing grids.

The thick braid of code lit up a bank of chattering cogitators under the watchful eyes of enginseers deputed to the Encryptors' hall. They spooled out under the machine-spirits' precise manipulation, into shipping reports, tithing statistics, demographic data, financial movements, crimes and trials, baptisms, Administratum memoranda. Ream after ream of numbers chronicled the pulse and governance of Gantia for the past month in minute detail. By the end of the month, the Encryptors would have broken down the data to be transmitted to the Administratum at Hydraphur, by bursts small enough to be taken in the astropath's stride. Some of the data would be transmitted on sub-light data frequencies, or coded into data-arks. Some would be transcribed onto printouts in the neighbouring Scriptorium and carried in-system by a dromon. To break that mass of data down into transmittable parts would take a week. To transport it from Gantia to Hydraphur on paper would have needed a library lugged in the belly of a transport cruiser.

Other data-skeins had detached from the mass and come in on their own, pulsing angrily with secure-keys and warning codes. Some were classified Administratum, some Arbites, and some Ministorum. The occasional low-level Battlefleet communiqué was hived off to the Navy offices. There was one strand of note: an Inquisition report bound up in venomous coils of encryption forged to trap and break any unschooled mind that tried to look too closely at them. It was pushed out of Qwahl's mind first, to save his sanity, and carried to the Bastion's autists with hushed respect. The Bastion communed with an Inquisitorial astropath at Hydraphur every twelve hours – now they would have something to give him, and good riddance to it.

High above in the eyrie, Qwahl hovered on the brink of consciousness, dimly aware of the movements and voice of his concordiast, and of the delicious scent of epima-oil. The hypnotic commands had begun the work of gathering up his energies, and his scorched mind was slowly collecting together again. Qwahl was largely beyond coherent thought and would be for hours, but one fragment did bob to the surface of his mind. He vocalised it as slurred words.

'What,' he asked aloud, 'is the Master fighting over?'

No one listened to him. Many astropaths babbled, coming out of their trances. It wasn't usually anything to worry about.

ONCE, THESE CLOISTERS had carried munition-carts from the armoured magazines to the weapon batteries, but they are corridors now. The metal floors and steps have been overlaid with layers of soft hessian and synthetic fleeces, to muffle the distracting clang of boots. The armatures for the lumen arrays are high on the inward-curving walls so that their chilly metal will not startle fingertips that brush along the rockcrete of the walls. The lumens are far-spaced and their light is dim – for most who pass this way, sight is far from the most important sense. The intricate veins and whorls carved into the passage sides are polished to a glow by the brushing of eleven centuries of fingertips.

Astropath Kappema's fingertips followed the wall as he shuffled slowly up the passage. He barely needed to touch the wall any more, and as the strain of his duty sapped his body, and his fingers became sensitive, he was more and more thankful for that. He moved with soft, easy steps, slippered feet guiding him up the slope from memory, without the need for sight. Two hundred and eight paces until the turn-off to the stairs that led to the second choir-galleys. Then the slow bend to the right, and another hundred and eighteen paces before the screw-stair up to the maze of access ways leading to the base of his eyrie.

He was barely conscious of the movement of his feet, and the glow of the lumens that fell on his sunken, sightless eyes. The wall that passed his fingertips was alive in his inner senses: he felt the swoops and angles of its carvings as if the air around him had nerves of its own.

Overlaid with the physical layer were the traces and trails of his brothers and sisters, his fellow blind ones passing this way from the cells and chapels of the Curtain and the lower keep, up to the meditation halls, fasting-beds and choir-galleys. Those traces were always there, permeating every part of the Tower where the psykers went, and Kappema, like all the rest, drew comfort from the presence of his companions.

Today, however, he could feel the unease. Thirty-four paces up the passage, where the lines on the wall danced through a series of tight spirals, he passed a scrap of memory left by Senior Astropath Sacredsteel, a brief sound of the old woman's papery voice in his psyker's non-ear, and a sharp stab of resentment left in the air. Sacredsteel had been brooding on the envoy, the man from what she thought of as the Meatsack Masters, the so-called Polarists. This Master Lohjen was corralled up in his dromon at the Tertiary Dock, not deigning to come aboard the station. Kappema felt Sacredsteel's half-day-old outburst of cursing start to form on his own lips. Then he passed the place where the print was strongest, and a reflexive calming exercise helped the outburst slip out of his mind.

With that gone, Kappema was able to focus on a long stream of thought-trail that had the strange dancing cadence of Mehlio's thoughts. Mehlio's focus was good and her discipline strong, and it was unusual for her to leave such a profound sense of herself where she passed. There was apprehension here – Mehlio was unnerved by the envoy where Sacredsteel was angry – but there were tints of disorientation and an almost excited anticipation. Mehlio had been around for long enough to remember Torma Ylante, and she was glad that Ylante was coming back.

Kappema managed a smile, before he had to compose himself and protect his thoughts. A file of choristers was coming down the passage the other way, too lost in the burnt-out mental stink of their own exhaustion to pay him any attention. He felt the puffs and billows of their minds as their handlers yanked on their restraints to urge the chain gang against the far wall. Even then, the passage was so narrow that their shoulders brushed, and Kappema got a quick taste of the mind that they had helped up into the warp scant hours ago. It was a young mind, male, permeated with oddly patterned traces from an unfamiliar psychic choir – an old posting? A message, unciphered, blazed out into the immaterium towards the waiting minds at Darrod and Enla III, a message so simple that fragments of it were still lodged in the choristers' minds: ...*arrived, all here... ready begin... functional...*

Kappema moved on up the corridor, his nervousness now entirely his own: bad omens, bad omens. The sloppiness of whoever had allowed the choristers to come down from their post with a message still circling their minds was a small thing, but it added to his unease. The envoy, the infatuation with the new dead-minded Polarist drones, Torma Ylante coming back to the Tower and causing who knew what waves, right down to the little things like this: bad omens.

Was there worse to come? Kappema thought there might be. For some reason, there was a new conceptnote coming into his mind, radiating in from somewhere: a tinge of violence? It was a thought-echo of Master Otranto, the image of a judge in black and crimson. It flicked into his mind and was gone. Troubled, Kappema bowed his head and walked on.

Unconsciously, he began counting his paces for the next part of his ascent. Behind him, the soles of his boots padded and muffled so as not to distract the astropath, came his vitifer. His heavy helm and mesh visor hid the scars on his shaven head, mind conditioned out of everything but patience and watchfulness. He shuffled placidly, two paces behind Kappema, a short-barrelled hellpistol in his hand, ready on a moment's warning to take the astropath's life.

THE ENGINARIUM LAY in the heart of the keep, a fortified sanctum in the middle of the fortress. It was a sealed shrine to the Machine God built around the blazing plasma coils of the station's reactors. Magos Channery of the Adeptus Mechanicus was governing the Enginarium as she had for sixty-seven years.

And as she had done for sixty-seven years, the magos was walking, making an endless pilgrimage around the walkway that led around the equator of the spherical reactor housing. She had long ago slaved her augmetic legs to the walk around and around it. And while her body walked, her mind talked.

Sprouting from the magos's back were twin armatures of black iron, fashioned to resemble a seraph's wings and encrusted with auspexes and voxponders, transmitters linking her in permanent communion with every machine-spirit in her Enginarium. She had sensed the sudden cascade of data down the cables from Qwahl's transmission, as she had sensed the waves of power flooding out of the reactor core and the operation of the psyk-engines installed in the eyrie towers. She was as blind as any astropath, and hadn't used her more elementary senses in decades.

This was something odd, something curious: a ripple of energy through the sinks and wards designed to funnel away any build-up of energy. It was subtle, so subtle, and even as it crossed her senses, it seemed to drop away.

Channery didn't pause in her plodding gait around the walkway. She routed the data from her observations through a savant-servitor and into her records, set a sub-routine of her own mind to working to see if it fitted a pattern, and directed her mind elsewhere.

IN THE WATCH-HALL, Chevenne's mind was flickering back and forth through drifts of sound where he hadn't expected to hear any. The notes suggested Master Otranto's mind, but where was it? Ripples were coming through in odd places, thought-notes tinged with fear and rancour, moving into the cloisters, too quick and subtle to get a grip on.

Chevenne was less sanguine about the matter than Channery was. He couldn't locate it, but he didn't dismiss it. He sounded a warning chime of both sounds and mind-waves, and sent a messenger scurrying to Master Warden on post behind his cage.

THE OLD FORTRESS from which the Bastion Psykana had been built had had balconies and panopticon towers and vantage points worked into every level of the design. Command and vantage points should there ever be a mutiny or a boarding, certainly, but even when there was no threat it was still fitting that the high personnel of the fortress, its officers, commissars and preachers, should have strategic high points. They could look out over their command, and could be seen by their subordinates. Like any Imperial building, the structure of the fortress was aimed to make the ideas of authority and hierarchy solid, visual and palpable.

It was wasted on its current inhabitants, whose eyes had looked on the raw glory of Him on Earth and were now darkened forever. So, as the new Bastion was made from the husk of the old fortress, new vantage points were made. Now they were in strange places: in the corners of provision cellars, niches carved out of walls, or platforms swung awkwardly from the walls of the high chambers. They were in places chosen to provide a view for minds, not for eyes.

Teeker Renz stood outside one of those niches, a 'viewing' hole gracelessly chopped into the wall of the Grand Concourse, the high-vaulted walk that ran right through the heart of the keep. He stood and stared. It had been ten minutes since Master Otranto had gone marching down the Concourse. He should have been back by now. This was where he was going to have his meeting with the Ylante woman. Renz knew that, he had ordered the message sent to her himself, although he had protested. He knew the distance Ylante had to walk to get here and knew the route she was coming by. Otranto should have been able to walk there, meet her and come back here. Come back here so that Renz could talk to them both. It would be a terrible meeting, but Renz was determined not to back down.

When they met… Renz stared away down the Concourse again. Why had the old man wheeled and marched off so suddenly?

He started at a movement on the Concourse, but it wasn't the Master. Two uniforms, Battlefleet green and concordiast cream, were walking towards him. His two most trusted associates, Kyto and Dechene.

'Where's Otranto?' he snapped at them. 'He went off in that direction to get this woman of his. Where's he got to?' The tension was getting to him: he was starting to gabble. 'What's she said to him, or done? What's happened?'

Dechene and Kyto looked at one another, and then back at Renz, who began to go pale. Dechene spread his hands and started to say something. Then they heard the warning-bells start to sound in the keep behind them.

ABOARD THE LOCKED dromon, docked under heavy guard at one of the Curtain's corners, Envoy Lohjen heard the sound of the bells issuing from a silver gargoyle mounted over the document desk in his office aboard the ship. Lohjen's vox-thief bugs, the ones he'd had carefully planted throughout the Bastion, were reporting the sounds.

He didn't panic and he didn't rush. He leaned over the lectern he was working on and keyed a sequence into a caller-amulet. After a moment, the panel began to light up again with wordless confirmation signals as his people moved to their stations at the docking tower, the hangar beneath it, and in the Long Dock Road, the tunnel that circled the entire perimeter of the Curtain and joined the docks together.

As the bells continued to ring, and the first reports from his spies joined the vox-thief recordings, Lohjen got up from his writing desk and started checking the weapons hidden under his loose, rich envoy's robe. If those messages meant what he thought they meant, he'd better be ready for things to go bad, fast.

THE RIPPLES SPREAD and grew stronger. They flowed up to the eyries, and many astropaths who were in communication with the Tower at that moment were bombarded with inexplicable images of anger, pain, flight, black and crimson, and waves of panic. They flowed into the watch-hall and surrounded Chevenne with loud discord from his chimes and frantic, unnerving ghosts from his psyk-senses. They swirled and washed around the choirs and the junior astropaths, and frightened them into fits and spasms – four fell to the guns of their vitifers by the end of the day, their precarious minds caught at exactly the wrong time and unable to recover enough to be proof against the warp.

They found their way into the senior astropaths, who fended them off with will and skill, and even into the minds of the blunts. For months afterwards, there would be non-psykers on the station who'd be haunted by dreams of frantic chasing, wild-eyed violence and pain.

Chevenne wrestled with the psychic spasm for over an hour, ordering psykers to move from one compartment to another as thunderheads of nervous energy built up or dissipated, as some minds spun off their rails and others collected themselves. He juggled wards and cullises and seals, and directed concordiasts and wardens from place to place as parts of the Tower flared in his mind's eye, or calmed.

Chevenne's watch was nearly over and his mind was exhausted by the time he was able to piece together a pattern for the ripples, a path they had radiated out from, and find the taste of the psyker who had left them. It took another half an hour to sound the emergency alarms, break the seals on certain secret orders, and bring long-disused protocols into force. It was two more hours of painstaking orders and oaths, seals and counterseals, before the locks on the heavy armoured door of Master Otranto's chamber could be opened.

After that, it took several whole minutes for the astonished onlookers to properly understand the wound on Otranto's corpse, to realise what it was, and to know that this was no death and no possession. This was murder.

CHAPTER TWO

IN THE SUB-EQUATORIAL deserts of Kleizen Onjere (Shira Calpurnia read from the data-slate), the planet's millennia-old soil conditioning has decayed beyond the inhabitants' ability to restore it. The water table has sunk too low and the earth has broken back down to abrasive orange gravel. At the long day's peak, the desert sweats out pockets of subsurface air, loaded with chemical compounds that sting the eyes and bring rashes to the skin, while bacteria inflame any cut or abrasion. The only refuges are the chains of steep-sided mesas that stand high enough to be clear of the sand-vapour until it cools and sinks away again in the dusk.

The Adeptus arbiters, whose polar training compounds and orbital docks make Kleizen Onjere a nexus point for fleet movements across three sectors, also keep watchtowers across the mesa chains. Moving between them are the convicts, disgraced and sentenced officers of the Adeptus, trekking across the sand barefoot and in coarse prisoners' clothes. They each pull behind them a metal frame that supports a banner-pole, from which hang parchment lists of the convicts' crimes, the dates and particulars of their convictions, the seal of the judge who passed sentence, and the stamps of the chasteners who mete out penal labours or floggings as their particular punishment demands.

The crimes that brought this sentence were light ones, all things considered. Calpurnia was aware of this before the scrolling text pointed it out to her. Low-level incompetence in their duties, perhaps, or a speech that a judge had ruled might lead to sedition. It could be impiety, laziness, freethinking, or any of the myriad ways of putting the Emperor behind their personal welfare that the penal codes sum up as 'thoughts of self'.

Whatever the crime, their convictions were judged not to outweigh their ranks, or whatever commendations, ordinations or charters of merit their service might have earned. If there was any question of those weights being equal, the dusty, gasping figure in front of its carriage would be marching into the maw of battle in a Penal Legion uniform, or lying in a red pool in front of an Arbites firing squad. No, the men in the desert were petty criminals.

None of which, Shira Calpurnia decided, was of any real use to her. She rubbed her eyes, and grimaced at the cracking of her jaw when she yawned. As the screen of her slate went black, she slid the data-ark out of its groove, murmured a quick blessing to its anima and returned it to the rack on the cell wall.

Note-sheets lay on the little table in the centre of her cell, neatly stacked and sorted, and covered in annotations and corrections. She had to reposition them every hour or so; the vibration from the dromon's engines was imperfectly damped and whatever she set on the table had a way of wandering imperceptibly if she left it unsecured. Soon after they had left the Incarcery, she had passed a restless evening before sleep prowling about the cell, all three-by-three metres of it, minus the space that the archive-racks, the sleeping pallet and the table took. She had pressed her hand to one wall and then another, trying to work out which way was the dromon's stern by where the vibration was strongest. She hadn't really been able to decide.

She sat down again and looked at the empty paper in front of her without really seeing it, twirling the stylus in her fingers, and wondering whether to write up a summary of the Kleizen Onjere material to look at later. No. It was interesting, certainly, even inspirational in a way: land that had become unusable for anything else becoming, by the Emperor's grace, useful for a just and moral purpose.

She was also struck by the nature of the punishment itself: it resembled one of the heavily symbolic and rit-ualised retributions of the Adeptus Ministorum, rather than the stern and pragmatic punishments handed out by the Arbites. Back on Hydraphur, she might have chased that thought down, traced the development of the desert as a place of punishment, and studied how Ecclesiarchal customs had blended with the rigid Arbites penal laws. She could debate it with Nestor Leandro at one of the formal commanders' banquets, or delegate Culann or Umry to research and declaim on it; the experience would be good for–

That way, bad thoughts lay. She suppressed them. It simply wasn't much use to her now; that was all. It was a curiosity of a penal world almost a whole segmentum away, and nothing more. She had to concentrate.

She had to prepare for her own trial.

* * *

SHE JUMPED AT a booming blow to the cell door. It was not the first time she had heard it, not even the hundredth, but of course it was calculated to startle and unnerve her. Her notes were full of blots and accidental pen-strokes where she had been startled, mid-word.

She had a moment to brace herself between the blow and the bell-toll from behind the vox-grilles in the other walls. The deafening voice of a bell brought its own bad memories. By the time the sound had died away, she was kneeling in what little free space there was in the cell's middle, as law dictated.

The door rumbled open, but she kept her eyes ahead, drill-ground steady, as the two men walked in. The master chastener raised his staff, brought its metal foot down on the deck with a crash, and the door slid shut. There was silence for the mandated count of eight seconds, and then the two took up their second positions and the staff crashed into the deck again.

Calpurnia's rank allowed her to watch this. More junior arbitors would have had to fall to both knees with heads bowed, or prostrate themselves on the cold metal with the foot of the staff hitting the deck beside their ears. As arbitor senioris, Calpurnia was permitted to remain on one knee, head erect and shoulders back, and look her chastener in the eye.

Deferring to that same rule, Dast removed his helmet and set it on the table, staring at her over his broken nose and the thick brown beard he had dyed in vertical bands of black to mimic his master chastener's livery. The fingers that gripped his staff were bright steel augmetics.

Calpurnia kept her eyes on Dast's faded blue ones. Preacher Orovene stood on her right side, four paces away. Calpurnia didn't look at him. The garrison preacher wore a gold-embroidered red sash over his Arbites uniform, and looped around his neck, a narrow strand of parchment with the complete text of the First Lawgiver's Psalm written upon it. As usual, the preacher smelled faintly of lho-smoke.

The staff crashed into the floor again. Calpurnia did not flinch.

'Declare to the Arbites your name.'

'Shira Calpurnia Lucina.' She had been through enough self-denunciation sessions that she no longer had to stop herself from reciting her rank. It had been a close thing, those first few times.

The staff crashed.

'Declare to the Arbites the Emperor's accusations against you.'

'The Immortal Emperor does accuse me, through the vigilance and wisdom of His chosen Adeptus, of the crime of failure in my charged and chartered duties.'

Crash.

'Declare to the Arbites the nature of your failure.'

'By the just and benevolent will of Him on Earth, I bore the office and the duties of arbitor senioris in the service of the *Lex Imperia*. My duty and my orders, given to me in the name of the law by my Emperor-chosen superiors, were to preside and judge on the inheritance of an Imperial Charter. The hearing failed.'

She had been through this many times. Her words no longer caught in her throat when she said them. She liked to tell herself that this was because she had come to terms with what she was saying, and not because she had numbed herself to it. She went on:

'The hearing failed. I was overconfident and I was careless. I failed to plan and I failed to enforce. On Selena Secundus, the very Court of the Arbites broke in bloodshed and mutiny. It succeeded because of my failure. The Battlefleet Pacificus and the Adeptus Ministorum witnessed it, and the law was diminished before them, because of my failure. The Charter was lost

and its Emperor-chosen succession ended, because of
my failure. Loyal and pious Arbites had their lives
ended because of my failure.'

In some of the sessions, she had been required to list
their names and ranks, but Dast did not command that
of her today. She was glad when she didn't have to
name the Arbites who had died at Selena Secundus.

Crash.

'Declare to the Arbites the nature of your weakness.'
Calpurnia took a breath.

'I declare myself weak in vigilance, weak in resolve
and weak in sternness. That I was not vigilant against
the treachery and mutiny of the heirs, blinded by the
mask of mourning and duty that they wore, shows my
weakness in vigilance. That I was dismayed by the dis-
order and violence that overcame the hearing, and
judged rashly and hastily, not allowing the law to speak
through me, shows my weakness of resolve. That the
lawbreakers and mutineers were brought to heel and
stamped out by the Navy, where the fist of the Arbites
should have been seen by all to crush them, shows my
weakness in sternness.'

The careful formality of her words was her own
choice; Dast had not ordered her to adopt any particular structure or phrasing when her imprisonment had
begun. During her career, Calpurnia had attended many
self-denunciation sessions, and had presided over more
than a few. She had watched cold-eyed as many of the
accused had slid into hysterics, into broken weeping at
their own failure and disgrace, or into screamed denials
that they had done wrong at all. 'None can truly know
one's criminality, but for that criminal and Him on
Earth,' Chastener Nkirre had told her once on Don-
Croix. 'And so for criminals, self-denunciation before
the law may be the one service their nature has left them
fit to perform.' Calpurnia was proud of the dignity with

which she performed that service. She liked to tell herself that her pride had nothing to do with not letting Dast see her break down.

'My weakness caused my failure. My failure is my crime before the law of the Imperium, and in the sight of the Immortal Emperor.'

Crash.

'Declare to the Arbites what punishment you will accept for the crime of failure, and for the sin of incompetence.'

'I will accept the verdict and the punishment brought forth from the magisterium of the *Lex Imperia*, and the judgement of the Adeptus Arbites,' Calpurnia replied. 'It is not my appointed place to accept anything else.'

That last line was one that she had not used before, but it had come to her earlier that day while she was reading trial histories from the Clementia Pacification. She was pleased she had thought of it. She liked to tell herself that it had nothing to do with being a step ahead of Dast in the details of her punishments and self-denunciations.

She remained on one knee with her head high, carefully keeping defiance out of her face – this was for her own good, after all. Dast and Orovene stood over her, impassive as statues, for twenty silent breaths. Then Dast lifted his staff, held it across his body and turned to the door. The lock clanked as the junior chastener watching them through the internal opticon array worked his controls, and then both men were gone in a clamour of boots on metal decking and a last lingering whiff of lho-ash. Calpurnia met the black-visored gaze of the arbitrator stationed across from her cell entrance, shotgun at arms, for the few seconds more until the door swung shut and locked.

She remained on one knee for a few more moments: leaping straight up and getting back to work would, she thought, show disrespect for the self-denunciation and its objectives. Sometimes, when the sessions came close together, she was barely starting to get up when Dast and Orovene came marching straight back in. Sometimes, when they sprang a session on her in the middle of the sleep shift, she found she stayed kneeling for many minutes longer, floating back into drowsiness, before she could stir herself to lie back down on her pallet. When she had been surprised with a session in the middle of one of her exercise bouts, she could feel her body shaking with the strain of holding the position so soon after she had worked it close to exhaustion.

There was an art to timing self-denunciations, spacing them out over days or packing many of them into half an hour, never letting the accused know how long they must wait before they were forced to survey their crimes again, nor how long each denunciation would last. The techniques had been developed and honed by hundreds of generations of chasteners, and Calpurnia didn't waste any effort on trying to second-guess Dast's schedule. She stood up, bowed briefly to the aquila on the wall over her pallet, sat down at her table and went back to work.

THERE HAD BEEN many times, in the little spaceborne Incarcery on the Hydraphur's very outer fringes, that Calpurnia had almost forgotten that she was a prisoner at all. She was on her way back into the heart of the system in the dromon system-runner that held her current cell, and it was harder to forget. Her trial was a matter of weeks away, and the thought of it bearing down on her had sharpened her mind and brought a constant tension to her emotions that she was reluctant to admit to herself.

On good days, she could still lose herself in the reams of data-arks and legal codices, the miniature library that

she had been entitled to bring from the Incarcery to prepare herself. Hours would pass when she sat alone over
the table, oblivious to the tiny sounds of her breathing
and her stylus, and to the distant rumble of the ship's
machinery.

Those times helped the memories of Selena Secundus
to slip from her mind, and the shadowy dread of her
own coming trial lifted a little. She might have been
back at the senior inductees' barracks at Machiun,
scratching away at one of the rote-tests that every recruit
had to pass. She might have been back in one of the
great Adeptus libraries on Ephaeda, Ephaeda with its
sober, courtly ordinates and priests, and its city-
spanning archive banks stocked with the finest wisdom
and thoughts in three Segmentae.

Those moods were wonderful when they came, and
that was why she worked to resist them, and felt a sharp
steel pride in her gut when she did so. She might never
be recorded as one of the great Arbites of Hydraphur,
her rulings quoted and her wars of enforcement studied
by other young recruits from here to the segmentum
borders. She might never (and this was a bitter thought
to her, more bitter than the first) enter her family annals
at Ultramar, her likeness put up in the hearth-house on
Iax as an example for future women of the Calpurnii in
how to uphold the proud family name.

She was damned, however, if she was going to consider her duty over, simply because her career might be.
Duty is not a word coined in idleness, she had written
down the margin of her notes, deep in one particularly
sleepless night, *duty being the first grace the Emperor
extends to the newborn, and the last connection with Him to
comfort the dying, and so the forsaking of it is damnation in
evident form*. Her duty had been to be a strong child of
the Calpurnii, and she had upheld it. Then it had been
to be a stern and loyal arbitor of the Adeptus, and she

had upheld that... until she could uphold it no longer and failure caught up with her.

If she must be a prisoner and a convict, then she would do her duty, as it was expected of a prisoner and a convict. She would not allow herself to forget why she was here. She would meet every demand of the chasteners, answer strongly and clearly through every self-denunciation, be it a session of a few minutes or twelve hours. She would not seek favours or forgiveness from the law, and she would bow her head to the justice of Imperial punishment. If it were her fate to be a prisoner, then she would bring every scrap of her determination onto this goal: she would be a lesson, an example to the Arbites.

Arbites scholars would write, and instructors would declaim, that if any arbitor should find themselves wanting and face the charge of failure, that if they must bear the punishment of their order in their own turn, then they should look to Shira Calpurnia Lucina, the former arbitor senioris of the High Precinct of Hydraphur. Calpurnia who saw her duty through, whose service to the law did not flinch even as she saw the judgement of law served upon herself, even as she–

She did not weep. She had promised herself that she would not weep. The ink dried unnoticed on her notes, her breath hissed, the stylus shook in her fist and began to crack between her fingers, but her expression did not change and she did not weep.

SHE HAD NO way of measuring time, but she guessed it would be hours before the next staff-blow sounded against the cell door. She had forced herself through the remainder of the treatise on the punishment of erring Adeptus, forced herself through a set of exercises, and prayed before the aquila; that done, she had finally managed to start drifting towards sleep. Then the noise came. Adrenaline snapped her awake with a physical start that the strike on the door had not produced, and she sprang off her pallet and knelt in the middle of the floor without stumbling.

She tensed herself and narrowed her eyes ready for the bell-toll, secretly pleased that she had beaten it to her position even from being half-asleep, and it took her whole seconds to realise that the bell was not sounding. She blinked, her shoulders, already sore from her exercises, twinged as she tensed them. The same tension boiled her gut: was it concluded? She had not expected a summary execution, but she was an arbitrator, not a judge, there could so easily be a provision she was ignorant of that would allow it, and if Dvorov had decided to try her in absentia then–

Then she would meet her fate properly, she told herself, and willed her body to co-operate.

The door clanked open. As always, it was Dast and Orovene – but this time they were different. Dast still carried his staff, but he wore an austere duty uniform and was helmetless. Orovene was in plain uniform, a preacher's red-trimmed white collar, epaulette and shawl over arbitrator black. He was twirling an unlit lho-stick in his fingers.

'Calpurnia,' Dast said without ceremony. He picked up the chair from behind her little table, clattered it to the deck in front of her, and straddled it, facing her. He gave a tilt of his chin, pointing behind her.

Calpurnia remained on one knee, looking up expressionlessly. They stared at one another for a few moments.

'She's waiting for an order, Dast. You're going to have to face up to talking to her sooner or later.' The garrison preacher's voice was smooth and trained, showing only the faintest of rough edges from the lho-smoke.

'Hm.' Dast let the grunt stand as his reply for a few moments more, and then pointed his staff over Calpurnia's shoulder. 'Sit, Calpurnia. This isn't a denunciation. It's not part of any kind of regular procedure.' The distaste in that last sentence dripped from his voice.

Slowly, carefully, Calpurnia rose, backed up to her pallet, and sat down. Dast was staring over at the neat arrangement of her note-sheets on the table. She had the impression that he was enjoying the effort of reading her writing upside-down more than he was enjoying having to talk to her.

Orovene broke the ice.

'How far are you through preparing a defence, Calpurnia?' Dast liked to glare and scowl, but Orovene's face never betrayed much at all.

'With another ten hours' total time,' she answered with a confidence she wasn't sure she felt, 'I should have integrated all the basic precepts into my case. The overall shape of my argument hasn't changed much from my initial premises, but there are rulings and precedents from courts in this segmentum that I've had to familiarise myself with.' She went over Orovene's words again. 'My case will be a true witness against myself, presenting my failures as seen through the eyes of the law, so that both my strengths and weaknesses can be found wanting. The voice of accusation is the voice of the Emperor made concrete through law. It is not for me to "defend" anything.'

'Good.' Orovene nodded. 'Pious, and sound at law. Thank you.' He glanced at Dast again, but the chastener stayed silent.

'You will not be prevented from completing your studies before your trial,' Orovene went on. 'So don't concern yourself with being denied what you're owed by process. You will be interrupted, however. We have an–' he thought for a moment, 'an *irregularity*. Better you hear it from the master chastener.'

Dast scowled at the table for a moment longer, glanced at Orovene, and finally swung his head around to Calpurnia, lips tight.

'We're not going to Hydraphur,' he said, and caught himself. 'We're not going *directly* to Hydraphur. Your trial has been deferred. We've all got a duty to attend to before we go any further in-system.'

She sat and waited for his next words. The silence was long enough for her to notice, and wonder. Once she would have been impatient to know more, and would have tried to begin a conversation about the news.

Had all the time in the cell rusted her grip on any words apart from self-denunciation? She knew enough about chastener work to know that that was often the point of it.

'This isn't about you, Calpurnia, so don't think it is. You're useful, that's all, and so I'm putting you to use as we all do our duty.' Dast stopped to think then snorted and kicked the table leg. One note-sheet skated off the edge and slid back and forth through the air until it rested on the floor.

'You'll have your rank back, Calpurnia, but don't get too attached to it. It's not permanent. This is a brevet, nothing more. It's not a complete one, either, so don't start giving me orders.'

Something inside her clicked and lit up, and suddenly it was an effort to keep control of her expression.

'We're being diverted,' Dast went on. 'The orders came from the Wall, and the Incarcery pilots have passed on a course correction to us. I've given orders for adjustment and burn. We'll be on our new heading in half a day.'

'I know the basic principles of law at work here, master chastener,' Calpurnia said, 'but I don't yet know the reason. If we're being diverted from a course bound into the system then it means that we're staying out on the fringes, and that means shipboard action or Navy installations.

I'm trying to think of an example of either that would cause trouble enough for an Ar– for an accused to have their trial postponed because only they could properly do an arbitor's duty there. Are we on our way to a mutiny, a xenos quarantine…?' She tailed her voice off deferentially, but a little late. The old command was creeping back into it, and there had been a shift in balance, small, but a shift between the three of them nevertheless.

Dast and Orovene had both picked up on it too. Orovene was eyeing Dast, waiting for his reaction.

Dast's reaction was to stand and kick the chair over. It hit the table and, one of Calpurnia's books thudded to the deck, a slew of note-sheets falling after it like a shower of petals.

'Not Navy,' he told her. 'Adeptus Astra Telepathica. Were being diverted into the path of the Witchroost, and we'll dock with it when we rendezvous in three days' time. There will be more personnel on the way, but we'll be arriving there for the moment with nothing, and no more than the personnel on this craft, including you, Calpurnia. You're there as a figurehead. You've got until rendezvous minus four hours to get yourself ready and prepare your uniform. One of the arbitrators will escort you to the cargo racks. I'm sure you can get yourself cleaned up without assistance.'

'I'm sure I can. Master chastener, why are we docking at the Bastion Psykana?' Mindful of his talk of rank, she carefully avoided belabouring her use of the correct name.

Dast was already banging his staff on the door. Over the noise of the locks and the opening mechanisms, Orovene told her, 'A crime against the Adeptus, Calpurnia. It is a matter of law. Someone has murdered the Master of the Bastion Psykana. We're going to go aboard and find someone who can tell us who it was.'

CHAPTER THREE

'ARM ME, PLEASE, master chastener.'

Dast turned and looked at Calpurnia as the distorted bulk of the Bastion Psykana swallowed more and more of the dromon's bridge windows. At first, it had been little more than a silhouette against the stars, but as the distance had shrunk, the fortress had grown into a mosaic of window-lights and oddly angled shadows. They were already more than close enough to see its strange, slumped stature and the incongruous bright spikes of the eyries.

'Throne, Throne look on us,' Orovene had breathed, and he had spoken for all of them. The pilots standing in the scooped control pits had exchanged uneasy glances. Calpurnia and Dast, standing side by side before the captain's pulpit, were the only ones to remain impassive.

Then the transmission had come, asking them to abort their approach. As she looked out at the Bastion,

Calpurnia's hand closed on empty air at her belt where the pommel of a power-maul would normally have hung.

'You're not fully reinstated,' Dast said. 'If I'd agreed to your going armed, I would have had you armed already.' He put a hand out to steady himself as the dromon adjusted its trajectory, and the internal gee took a moment to compensate.

'With respect, that will undermine my authority,' Calpurnia replied. 'I'm an arbitrator, I should be armed. You made the point that an arbitor senioris will give weight and fear to an investigation. If that's true, you don't want people looking at me wondering where my maul and pistol are.' She turned her head as a burst of tinny vox traffic came from one of the control stations in front of them.

'Same message as before, sir and ma'am,' the vox-operator called over her shoulder. 'They ask us to defer our docking and accelerate away on a provided vector, because the docks are not secure.'

'Defer docking, hell!' Dast snarled, and whacked the doorframe behind him with a fist. 'We got here just in time. This is part of it, you wait and see. The bastard witches are trying to pull something.'

'The astropaths don't have operational command of the docks, master chastener,' Calpurnia corrected him. 'The Navy supplies crews and junior officers to do that. The Telepathica officials may not even know about the order.'

'So it's the Navy that'll be telling us the docks aren't secure?' Dast demanded. 'Why would the Navy do that?'

'I can't tell you until I've found out myself. We don't even know what they mean by not secure. Is it a seal breach? Contamination? Who knows what else there could be?' Calpurnia stepped forwards, peering down at the vox-operator's transmission panel, and then out at the scarred grey flank of the Bastion.

'Send this,' she told the woman. 'We do not accept their deferral of our docking. By the authority of Arbitor Senioris Shira Calpurnia, we *will* dock and we will know the reason why docking is being denied us. If they still try to divert us, they will answer to me. Use those exact words, please.' The vox-woman, back stiffened by her proxy authority, leaned over her mouthpiece again.

'You'll answer for that,' Dast growled. 'You're only to pull rank like that in ways approved by me. You're still an accused, and I'm still your chastener.'

Calpurnia's reply was cut off by another burst of traffic, boosted by the vox-operator so that they could all hear clearly.

'Hailing the Arbites. Please advise your arbitor senioris that we have, uh, we have problems on the docks. Possible…' there was a brief burst of static, a few moments of dead air, and, '…possible physical danger. Possible danger to the person of the arbitor senioris. Possible, uh… hostile confrontation.' The voice sounded wretched. 'We convey from the dock superintendent…'

'Convey to him our thanks for his concern for my safety,' Calpurnia said, 'and inform him that the arbitor senioris will apply herself to this confrontation as soon as docking is complete.' The woman bent over the controls again, and Calpurnia turned and locked eyes with Dast.

'Something's happening on the docks down there, something violent, by the sound of it. I don't think that young man was making anything up, do you?' Her hand hooked around the empty spot on her belt, again.

'*Arm me please*, master chastener.'

HE DIDN'T GIVE her a pistol, but that was fine. The maul was a powerful symbol, an arbitrator trademark, and she was more than happy with the heavy-hilted Agni-pattern weapon from the dromon's little armoury.

Clangs and scrapes sounded from outside the ship, the casual music of the docking grapples drawing them in. As she walked towards the hatch, Calpurnia felt the lurch that meant the ship's gravity had aligned with that of the station.

'This is a bad omen,' Dast said aloud. 'Bad. If these witch nests are supposed to be under such tight control, how could there be an open rising like this? Where are our own agents? This is a foul-starred place, I think.'

Calpurnia didn't reply. She had been briefed on the Bastion Psykana when she had taken up her station at Hydraphur, and although she could remember the briefing perfectly well, this didn't seem like the time to share the station's history with Dast. The history included a hellish plasma breach that had gutted the station back in its days as a Naval fortress, and the accidents and ill luck that had dogged efforts to rebuild and reclaim it. It also included legends and ghost-tales that had built up around its lifeless hulk, and had then taken on fresh life when the Adeptus Astra Telepathica had taken possession of the wreck, sealed it, rebuilt it and brought it back to life. It was more than just piety that had sent Orovene to the shrine to pray for them.

'His will,' was all she said, and the other three Arbites echoed her as the hull began to rumble open, and they heard the gunshots.

BELNOVE WAS AT the forefront of the mob as they came up the ladderwells. Below them were the metal walkways that crisscrossed just under the hangar bay's ceiling and just above him, the compartment that led into the docking-tower. At the top of the tower stood the dromon, and blessed escape.

Belnove gripped a short-range shotcaster in one hand. It was a powerful weapon, monstrous at two metres, and useless at ten. His face was slick with blood and sweat – he'd been creased by a Navy flechette at some point after they'd rushed the hangar locks. His breaths were deep, even and quiet.

He gave no sign that he had heard the scattered shouts of encouragement from behind him. His attention was on the movements that he could see ahead of him, the glimpses of green uniform turned dark by the orange safety lights.

Above him, Second Petty Officer Roos of the dock sub-command looked out over the long compartment. Behind him were the steep stairs that began the ascent to the docking tower, a guard alcove where two of his men had cover, and the short passage to the cargo lift. He didn't want to look at poor Ostelkoor, lying headless by Laddershaft Four, the victim of some horrible improvised explosive-thrower.

Roos tried to concentrate, but the more he tried to force the shipboard tactical drills from the academy back into his brain the more slippery his thoughts became. He adjusted his grip on his long-barrelled slug-pistol, listening to the soft whine of the loading motor. As soon as the first head came over the top of a laddershaft, the motor could spin the cylinders fast enough to put eight hollowpoints through it in less than a second. He thought of that for reassurance, and prayed for the dromon to abort docking so this might be over. What maniac wanted to disembark into this?

From up above him came the solid clank and the fluid hissing of the final dock-seals going in. The flashing of the lights on the cargo lift changed tempo as the mechanism prepared itself for usefulness.

A roar of 'It's docked! Way's clear, lads!' came from somewhere, and the ladders shook with noise as the mutineers came up them. That was all right. It took all those frightening choices away. Suddenly clear-eyed and steady-handed, Roos locked his body easily into a firing position and took aim.

DAST WAS FIRST through the dromon's hatch, and went hammering along the little articulated dock-tunnel with the two arbitrators in tow, breath misting in the chilled air, shotgun unholstered in his hands. Calpurnia, all but shouldered aside, cursed and made to follow before she registered a second set of metallic noises further away. She stepped back and listened: metallic noises. They came from the bottom-most of the three miniature decks, some way back – another tunnel was extending up to kiss the cargo hatch.

She turned to shout after Dast, but the others had already disappeared down the first flight of steps. She grimaced and turned back.

'Intrusion!' she yelled, not sure how many more Arbites were on the dromon to hear her. As far as she knew, she'd been the only prisoner on board – how much of a complement would Dast have brought for just her?

She ran for the screw-stair at the beginning of the dromon's thick midsection. 'Muster at the cargo hatch,' she shouted again. 'Muster for possible intrusion! Orovene, where are you? Arm yourself!'

THE FIRST MAN to pop out of the shaft had thrown a fist-sized chain-link to try and spoil Roos's aim, but he'd just let it clang off the bulkhead, and placed a precise shot a moment later, when the man was too slow ducking. The patch of deck beyond the shaft suddenly glistened red, and the corpse tumbled out of sight to cries and curses from below. Roos worked the speed-loader and flicked the cylinder motor down to two-shot as three more men came up through the holes at him.

'I order you to–' he got out before the shattering noise of a shotcaster filled the compartment and Warden Wheyett, who stepped out to meet the charge with a long-handled neural goad, groaned and spun backwards. Roos got one shot off before he had to duck a swinging length of cable, but he was too slow. It scored off his shoulder and the side of his head.

Roos staggered, bounced off a bulkhead and managed a second two-shot through his enemy's thigh, pitching the man over as the shattered limb gave way. The mutineer behind him was already swinging a long-handled wrench. It connected with Roos's gun-arm and numbed it. The other end came around under his jaw, and suddenly Roos was lying across the steps. Someone got a hand on his throat and started squeezing, and he could dimly feel kicks landing on his ribs and hips. Somewhere in the roar of fighting, he heard the sound of the cargo lift opening, but the shouts were all blurring into one another, and his hearing was dimming.

BELNOVE JAMMED ANOTHER cartridge into his shotcaster and spared a glance for the brawl around the bottom of the stairs. Someone was throttling the young officer on the steps, while a free-for-all surged around them, fists, bludgeons and blades, and from somewhere in the mess, the dry chatter of a flechette gun.

Screw fighting his way through that. As far as Belnove was concerned, there was no more brotherhood. It was every man for himself. He jinked to his left and down the little passage to the cargo lift. He was a foreman; he knew the codes to that hatch.

In the time that it took for the lift to open, four others had joined him: two came inside with them, and then another two before the hatch closed. Someone outside shouted, 'Come back for us!' and Belnove raised a hand as if he would. Then they were on their way up,

packed tight in the little cube, eyeing each other as they
ground up towards the dromon's belly.

'Quick and clean, boys, and we need the crew alive,'
Belnove told them. They nodded and grunted their
agreement, grim-faced. They were past the point of no
return. Whoever had brought this little boat in to dock
had better damn well do as they were told.

Roos BUCKED AND goggled, and took a great, harsh gasp
for air. The pressure on his neck was gone. The red-shot
grey blur in front of his eyes passed a moment later and
he began to sit up. Another moment and he managed a
word:

'What?'

The big-shouldered man in black and brown didn't
reply. He just stepped heavily over Roos and drew his
boot back for a kick. Roos realised that the sound he
had dimly registered a moment ago had been the butt
of the big man's shotgun connecting with the head of
the docker who'd been choking him. The kick connected, something in the man's face crumpled, and he
went over on his back.

The big man – an arbitor, Roos registered fuzzily, in
chastener's black and brown – fired his shotgun from
the hip, catapulting a cleaver-armed docker off his feet
and down a laddershaft. As Roos gaped, the chastener
spun on his heel to confront a burly man who was
wrestling with Warden Schai for control of a knife, and
slammed the stock into the mutineer's head. His target
groaned and staggered, and the chastener finished him
off with another swing, turning the movement into
another pivot that saw him face the room again,
weapon reloaded and ready. The deck lights gleamed off
his visor and steel hand.

'Down!' barked a voice behind Roos, and by reflex he
dropped his shoulders to the stairs as two more men

bounded over him: arbitrators, these, in unbroken black, one with a shotgun, one with a buckler on one arm and a long counterweighted power-maul.

There was barely time for the arbitrators to catch up to their leader before someone shouted, 'We can still take 'em!' and the fighting was on again.

WHATEVER BELNOVE HAD been expecting outside the cargo lift, it hadn't been what he found: the passageway was empty, but for a short woman in black carapace. He had been ready to cut his way through a throng of ships' guards to get at the cockpit, but his mind worked fast enough to change his plan.

'Spin around, girl, and take us to the cockpit. We're not bad men. We only want to keep the lives and souls the Emperor gave us, you understand? So you just–'

That was as far as he got before the upward stroke of a high-charge power-maul blew the shotcaster out of his hands and sent it pinwheeling into the ceiling. Belnove howled and dropped to his knees, looking at the cooked flesh of his stricken hands, and while the enormity of it was still making its way up his nerves, the maul was in motion again. A low shot, and a man tumbled, his knee exploded and unable to hold him. Another shot, and someone made an agonised noise that wasn't quite a scream, because the shock to his sternum had stolen his breath.

'Intrusion!' the woman yelled and swung again. 'Intrusion through the cargo door! Orovene! All hands! I'd better see someone down here damn quick!'

As if in answer, Belnove heard the report of a shotgun behind him. The shot was true, and he was pitched onto his face and wounded hands by the corpse falling full on his back. The impact of his hands on the decking drove the shock of the injuries home, and as it reached his brain Belnove finally began to howl. The shots and power-flares filling the air above him reached a crescendo.

THE SKIRMISH AT the base of the docking-tower stairs didn't last long. The mutineers' morale had dried up in the face of the fresh gunfire: down below the ladder-shafts, the would-be rioters dropped their improvised weapons and vanished into the docking bay. Those mutineers who'd managed to get up the shafts had their blood up at first, but the arbitrators had tipped that balance back the other way.

'Drop your weapons!' the chastener was roaring. 'Drop your weapons and submit, you vermin!'

'Rush him!' cried a voice from the back of the mob, as someone tried to make a break for the cargo hatch and was clubbed down. 'He's not station–' another deafening shotgun-blast '–can't order us, they've got no rank here…'

'I am *so* glad to hear someone mention rank,' said a new voice, a woman's voice. Roos, getting unsteadily to his feet, realised that the speaker was walking out of the cargo lift. He heard several sets of footsteps. He looked groggily at the woman as she came out to join the chastener.

'Rank,' she said, 'and knowing your place. If everyone aboard this station is as conscientious as that on matters of authority and deference, then I shall praise the Emperor for sending me a smooth road to walk. My rank, and pay attention, *my* rank is arbitor senioris of the Adeptus Arbites, arbitor general of the Hydraphur High Precinct. That rank excuses me from having to care why you are trying to fight your way onto an Arbites ship, and cheering each other on to assault an Imperial master chastener.' She held her buzzing maul directly over her head, so that the glowing indicators on its hilt and the power-flares along its length were visible to the back of the compartment. 'Nothing matters to me, except your obedience. Drop your weapons and submit yourselves to judgement. Don't doubt that that's an order.'

There was a moment's silence. Then the sound of a shotgun being cocked as the chastener loaded an Executioner shell. One rioter went down on one knee, another following suit. Calpurnia looked at them and nodded, and that was all it needed for half a dozen more to kneel. One man in a grubby mechanician's coverall tried to use the distraction to vault down a laddershaft. Dast calmly shot him down. That did it. Five more seconds and every mutineer was laying face down on the floor, hands stretched out past their heads.

'THEY WERE TRYING to get… onto your… uh, ship,' said one of the Navy men – a boy, Calpurnia realised, who looked barely old enough to have earned his rank pins. His voice was a tortured grate in his throat: his neck was bruised and puffy where someone had been squeezing it in the fighting. 'Trying to get… off station… tried to stop–'

'You did, did you?' said Dast, rounding on the boy and towering over him. The young man swayed in place, staring up at Dast, what little colour he had left in his face, draining away.

Calpurnia turned, leaving them to it. She was looking out over the prisoners, starting to wonder what her next move was, when her vox-torc gave a signal tap on the standard Arbites band and a man's voice spoke to her.

'Arbites? Bastion Psykana garrison to docked dromon, reply. We're approaching your position. Reports are of armed mutiny. Respond. Respond with your status.'

'Status is comfortable enough, thank you, Bastion Garrison,' she replied. 'We are docked and have met the reception you provided for us. I'm pleased to hear that you see fit to follow it and greet us in person.'

There was a pause, and then the man's voice again.
'Arb… arbitor senioris?'

'So you did know we were coming by. Good. Make
your way up here, please, whoever you are, and you can
identify yourself and explain to me exactly what kind of
station you are running here.'

THEY RODE AWAY from the docks on a glide-truck, a long
electric corridor-crawler of a kind that Calpurnia had
seen in fortresses and space stations across the galaxy. It
was little more than two running boards down either
side of a long central rail, the whole thing tipped with a
sharp-nosed driver's compartment, and rolling forward
on thrumming electric wheels.

The truck was almost empty: the arbitrators who'd
ridden down on it were still in the docking tower, man-
handling the mutineers into shackles and strait-capes.
Aedile Bruinann had told Calpurnia that the Bastion
Precinct had little cell-space to keep them in, so the
prisoners were to be stored in the spare cells on the
dromon they had been trying to fight their way onto. It
had been fitted out as a flying gaol, after all.

Calpurnia gripped the rail and looked across at the
local commander. Joeg Bruinann wore the sparkling
green laurels of an aedile majore on his helmet, and the
red and gold badge and lanyard of a marshal isolate. He
was the officer in charge of a precinct formed under
extraordinary circumstances. Bruinann didn't return her
gaze, although Calpurnia caught the truck's driver looking steadily at her in the rear-view mirror. Dast stood
further back on the truck, with Orovene opposite him.
It was hard to tell under the helmet, armour and shawl,
but the preacher seemed nervous.

The ride was a short one, even though the truck rarely
went above running speed. From the glimpses she got
through the thick armourcrys skylights above them,

Calpurnia was able to piece together their progress under the outer barbicans, and in under the looming cliff face of the keep wall. We're in, she thought to herself. We're in the Witchroost, and she didn't even notice her own use of the term that she reprimanded others for using. She wondered why the simple fact of her arrival struck her as such a terrible portent.

In the keep, the decking changed from metal to rockcrete, and the bright ceiling panels and skylights ceased. They rode through a dimmer, narrower tunnel. The grates in the arched ceiling were encrusted with fluttering paper prayer seals, their downdraft warm and carrying an odd scent that Calpurnia couldn't place. Finally, the twists and angles of the corridors grew too sharp for the truck to negotiate easily, and they continued on foot through the oddly quiet passageways, boots gritting on the rockcrete. The driver followed them, simply leaving the humming, activated truck behind.

The entrance to the precinct chambers stood in a nest of intersecting tunnels and ways, arched halls marching away at the sides, and staircases and ramps leading from above and below, meeting at a circular floor of plain black metal. Calpurnia craned her head back and peered up the high well above them with its spiral of bright lanterns under eagle-shaped reflectors. Then she looked at the precinct doors, a low tunnel-slot in a black obelisk set into the wall, deliberately dimly lit. It was a good design. The march from a bright, airy space into the close gloom of the portal would put any accused prisoner in exactly the right state of mind.

'These chambers used to accommodate the Battlefleet Commissariat,' said the arbitrator who'd been their driver. She was slightly taller than Calpurnia, wiry and genderless but for her voice. 'The symbolism was cut into the architecture for them. It made it ideal for us, of course.'

'Speech discipline!' snapped Dast as Calpurnia blinked at the woman's informality. They stood in silence, listening to the buzz of the vigil-auspex built into the gates as it read their skin-scent and eye-patterns.

It was some time before the auspex was satisfied, but finally the buzzing ratcheted to a halt, and somewhere, the machine-spirit behind the auspex stirred itself to turn the lock for them. The sound of the gates opening was the same clank and rumble as any heavy blast door across the Imperium, and the familiarity of the sound comforted Calpurnia as they trooped through the passageway.

THE PRECINCT STATION was a block of the keep built around an open well like the one outside, a high narrow space ringed by stacked balconies and walkways. A polished marble eagle hung in a suspensor column below the ceiling, over a judgement pulpit and an old executioner's pit. There was activity, too, boot steps and voices, the smell of gun-oil and armour polish, familiar maxims engraved in the walls. As they emerged from the portal, they passed a plinth holding an ancient data-codex, as long as Calpurnia's arm, wrapped in a blue-black velvet shroud and safely sealed under an armourcrys dome. The front of the plinth was polished mirror-smooth and slightly dished inward from wear. As Dast, Calpurnia and their guides passed the plinth each kissed their fingertips and pressed them to the stone.

Calpurnia noticed that the woman walked in front. The other Arbites made way for her and their salutes in her direction. They did not climb all the way up the spiralling ramp: two turns from the top, where the Calpurnia would have expected the marshal's chamber to be, they stopped at a door no different to any of the others they had passed. Even before she had crossed the threshold, the woman had yanked off her helmet and was scratching in the mop of curly black hair that had spilled out from under it.

The long, angular room was not the austere barrack-room of an arbitrator, nor the crammed library and study-room of a judge, although for a moment that was what Calpurnia took it for. Data-arks and reading slates were scattered across every surface, starting with the untidy bed at the far end of the chamber, and continuing up the long desk and onto the little round table right in front of them. The cushioned chair in the near corner, beneath a powerful blue-white illuminator panel, was clearly intended for reading. It was piled with dossier wallets and rolls of transcripts, all decked out with marker ribbons and note-pins. The gun-rack and shelf of legal books to Calpurnia's left were both small, and she thought she could see dust on them even from here.

A long scriptor-tapestry hung on the opposite wall, and that was far more used. The thick woven fabric hung heavy with circuitry, and the touch-reactive surface was alive with images and letters. Some were obviously uploaded from the data-arks that hung from the tasselled docks along the tapestry's edges, while others were added by touch-stylus in two or three different hands. Calpurnia saw pict-images in that display, and data-runes that would play snatches of vox-recordings captured from spy-circuits.

She'd seen enough to guess what was going on, and when the woman whose room this was – olive-skinned and sharp-eyed under the black curls – turned back towards them, Calpurnia saw the flash of crimson at her throat, and knew that she had guessed right.

THE FOUR OF them sat, the little burner between them warming a jug of recaf infusion whose steam turned the air pungent. Shira Calpurnia, Master Chastener Cholyon Dast, Preacher Orovene, Aedile Majore Joeg Bruinann and

Master Detective-Espionist Lazka Rede, in her plain arbitrator uniform and the slender red collar that marked her true rank. Rede was the ranking arbitor aboard the Bastion Psykana. Bruinann, her figurehead, soaked up any outside attention, while Rede presided over her spy-flies, communications taps, webs of informants, and her hypno-conditioned deep agents.

It was a common enough arrangement anywhere that the detectives needed a major presence, but Calpurnia was curious to find it aboard the Bastion.

'It's not the arrangement itself, of course,' she told Rede. 'I understand the need for a high-level detective operation in an environment this complex and this insular.' Bruinann gave a little smile and a heartfelt nod of agreement. 'I'm just interested to know how you maintain the appearances, the Tower being the environment that it is.'

'You're wondering why the witches don't see through us,' Rede said. She was perching in her chair at a crooked angle, one lean leg stretched out straight along the floor. There were circles under her eyes, and she hadn't sounded anything other than tired since they had all sat down. 'I mean, all right, if you want to start with the espionist setup here–'

'No' snapped Dast. Bruinann jumped. 'Let's remember the task that brought us here and not deviate from it, in this conversation or anywhere else. A high officer of the Adeptus has been murdered: the Master of the Bastion Psykana. Perhaps that needs to be further forward in our minds.'

'A crime against the Emperor's Adeptus, His law and His Imperium,' Calpurnia agreed as Bruinann and Rede flicked their eyes from one of them to the other. 'We're not rookies here, chastener. I think we all know our duties. My point was–'

'Misguided,' the chastener finished for her. 'We'll begin with the murder.'

'Pardon me for a minute,' Bruinann put in. 'I'm not as subtle-minded as Lazka, so help me keep up with you. I had been expecting a taskforce to lock down the Tower under the arbitor senioris's control, not just the three of you. Is there some kind of arrangement here that my simple arbitrator's brain isn't getting a grip on?'

'You would have had the communiqués,' said Dast, 'about the botched trial at Selena Secundus?' Calpurnia saw her hands twitch at Dast's words. She reminded herself that she had no right to protest. It was the truth. 'It may not have been general knowledge that Calpurnia is on trial for her failure as a result,' Dast went on. 'Her authority is suspended and she has been confined in my custody until the arbitor majore's verdict is ready.'

'Out in the fringe Incarcery stations?' Bruinann was still addressing Calpurnia, and the warm twinge of gratitude she felt towards him surprised her a little. 'It explains why you were so close at hand. We were wondering how you got here right bang on the heels of the murder.'

'First we were told to hold tight and make no move "Because someone's on the way",' Rede carried on, 'and we'd barely digested that when we got your docking request. Joeg's right, we wouldn't mind knowing what's going on. Is Calpurnia in charge or isn't she?'

'I am assuming command of the investigation into the murder of Master Otranto,' Dast declared with perhaps a little more force than was needed. 'Calpurnia has been restored to her former rank on an honorary basis, temporarily and at the pleasure of the master of the Hydraphur Incarcery. Her reduction in rank isn't generally known among Hydraphur's civilians–'

'Not even among Hydraphur Arbites,' commented Rede, to no one in particular.

'–and has not, pending her judgement and sentencing, been widely spread among the Arbites,' Dast continued stiffly. 'Therefore, she will lend her authority to the investigation. The sentiments of the Hydraphur high command are that the presence of an arbitor senioris will extinguish any urge the Adeptus Astra Telepathica might be feeling to try and cover over the circumstances of the murder and address it themselves.'

More nods of agreement. They were all familiar with the fortress mentality that grew in so many Adeptus.

'For the purposes of anyone outside these precinct chambers,' Dast said, 'Calpurnia is still an arbitor senioris, and we proceed by her grace and her authority. In practice, her authority ends with me until such time as I consider the investigation concluded.'

The feeling in Calpurnia's guts took a new twist, and she realised that it was fear. She had been afraid of glancing up, seeing the other two Arbites looking into her face and having to return their gazes. The disgraced commander, reduced to–

She stamped on that thought before it could get a running start, and to prove a point to herself, she forced her eyes up to meet Rede and Bruinann's.

Neither of them was looking at her. They were looking at each other. It wasn't hard to guess what they were thinking. They were wondering what this meant for them. They were wondering if the investigation would turn to examining mistakes of their own. They were thinking that Calpurnia and Dast might be there at first to investigate the Master Astropath's murder, but that they had no reason not to add a pair of Arbites scalps.

So be it, she thought. *Every one of us who breaches the Emperor's trust must answer for it, whether their name is Rede or Bruinann, or Calpurnia.* That thought stayed with her as they turned to the schematics and names glowing on the tapestry, and Rede began to talk about the Master's death. She said nothing aloud, but the thought was never far from her mind for the rest of that day.

CHAPTER FOUR

THE MYSTERY OF the murder of Master Astropath Otranto of the Bastion Psykana was waiting for them in Rede's briefing and her records. Calpurnia and Dast listened to the briefing, shot questions at her like darts, and went back and forth through paper files. They looked into flickering data-slate displays, and pored over output from Rede's menagerie of pict-thieves and eavescopes. They followed her notes and schematics, and weighed up her work, but no matter how rigorously they tested her logic, they found themselves circling around and around the mystery just as Rede had.

Master Otranto had been walking on the promenades over the Grand Concourse of the Bastion Psykana, a thoroughfare outside the astropath cloisters that nearly anyone on the station could go to. He had been conferring with his major-domo and confidante, a herbalist and concordiast named Teeker Renz, and some of Renz's colleagues. He had left that conversation and

walked away down the promenade, apparently to a
meeting with a new concordiast named Torma Ylante,
who had just come to the Bastion from service with the
League of Black Ships a station-day before.

From there the trail vanished. All anyone knew for
certain was that he had passed into the astropath cloisters – the next sign of him was when the scrying arrays
in the watch-hall had picked up a mental cry, alarm,
anger or fear. The reports that Rede had been collecting
were semi-coherent blends of descriptors that Calpurnia suspected would only make true sense to a psyker.
The trail grew clearer after that, as Otranto had careened
through the cloisters faster and faster, triggering alarms
and defences, until he had been sprinting faster than his
aged body should have allowed, racing as if damnation
itself was after him. Finally, he had sealed the great
psyk-warded door of his rooms behind him.

That, as far as the Bastion Psykana was concerned,
had been the end of the old man's life.

That was the top and bottom of the mystery, the start
and end of it. Dast gave up, stamped out of Rede's office
and left Calpurnia with the records and picts, but even
Calpurnia felt daunted by the opacity of it. She had
been relying on some insight, something Rede had
missed, because she was too closely embedded in the
environment, but there were no loose ends for her to
worry at. It was insane.

'We're in a tower full of psykers!' she finally snapped
at Rede, as the other woman fiddled with the data-
tapestry, and the recaf pot went dry again. 'I'm fed up of
reading reports about echoes and traces. Half the place
seems to know that something was wrong, but whose
attention was on the actual crime?'

'The Famous Invisible Traitor,' said Rede, 'that's what
we called it at my last post. Everyone sees the flames and
the running people, a dozen accounts swear they saw

someone running from the scene of the crime, but did anyone see him pitch the bomb, deface the temple, attack the ordinate? Why, no.'

'These are people,' said Calpurnia 'whose vision, by the Emperor's grace, can look through stone and steel, and tracts of space whose distances we have trouble even understanding. Not *one* of them thought to direct their attention to where these damn ripples were coming from? *Nobody* was watching what went on in there?'

'You'll see when you walk through the cloisters, ma'am,' Rede told her. 'It's how they're built. The old fortress walls have been lined with a psyk-cage that's melded into the wards and earths that run through the whole fortress. They're specifically made to contain psyker emanations. They carry them off, fuzz them, and dilute them so that they're not a threat. My understanding is that they're like cooling fins on a hot machine, or earths to carry away electrical power. Get waves of power coming out of their heads and sloshing back and forth in the tower, it gets… overpowering, volatile. They lose control. I've got records from places like this where they lost control. They can unbalance each other, cook one another off like bullets in a fire, or leave themselves open to, well, to…'

'…things not spoken of lightly,' said Calpurnia. 'I understand. So Otranto ran into the cloisters where the defences acting to contain the, what, the overflow of any psychic power actually served to blur his trail. How certain are we of where he went?'

'We know where he entered the cloisters and his path after that.' Rede was running her fingers over the tapestry. 'Those in the watch-hall know where he passed. The path is laid out on the Bastion schematic on the slate there–'

'Thank you. I have it. The trail ends at the door to his chambers. The scryes couldn't follow it inside?'

'Correct,' said Rede. 'The Master is the only psyker on the Tower allowed the privilege of living alone.'

'And his chamber is psychically sealed, armoured against scrying.'

'Yes,' the detective snorted, returning to the table and picking up the recaf pot. 'Psychically speaking, the Master's chambers are a fortress; the psychic protection is even heavier than the physical protection. Even if the rest of the tower turns into a warp-damned nest of, well, we both know what, the Master's chambers are supposed to be his final sanctuary. Whatever happens, he can retreat to his chambers, scream out a message, and still be alive when rescue comes.' She shook the pot, grunted and put it down again. 'And before you ask, the blurring effect of the wards in the cloisters is a hundred times worse in there. The combination of those and the Master's death-shock apparently makes the room next to unreadable. Two senior astropaths tried. They both had to be helped out of there. The death-shock is so overpowering that any fine details that might have been left are blotted out.' Rede shivered. 'The killing had a lot of the astropaths spooked to begin with.'

'They're not the only ones,' said Calpurnia darkly, pushing back from the table. 'I'm the one who fought her way in here through an ignorant pack of rioters who wanted to hijack her ship and escape off-station.'

Rede didn't answer. She just scowled and stared at her boots.

'Our killer is smart,' Calpurnia said, standing up. 'He attacks Otranto somewhere in the fringes of the cloisters, and gets the man's blood up to the point where the Master's panic blurs his own footprints for us. He hounds him through the cloisters, although how this chase ran with no physical witnesses I can't begin to bloody well guess, and chases him into the one place where his death is guaranteed to be almost opaque to psychic probing. A psyker, are we thinking? Or someone who knows psykers well?'

'On this station,' Rede said, 'that's effectively every-one.'

'Very well, I – we, uh, the chastener and myself – we can't use their senses, so we'll have to use our own. I want to see the cloisters and Otranto's chambers.'

'I thought you might. I've got a detail standing ready. Say the word.'

'I'm saying it now,' Calpurnia growled. She could feel her temper going the way of Dast's. 'We've found a way that doesn't work. Somewhere in this place there's going to be a way that does. Let's go.'

IN DIM LIGHT and with soft sounds, the Arbites made their way through the astropath cloisters. A proctor from the Tower garrison went first, carrying a rod from which the precinct's seal of authority hung on a heavy silver chain. Then came Bruinann, with Rede slightly behind and to his left, once again in her guise as a humble attendant arbitrator. Calpurnia came next with Dast, Orovene and two more arbitrators behind her.

Orovene carried a little reliquary box in cupped hands, a cloisonné cylinder holding scraps of a scroll of decree personally scribed by Grand Provost Marshal Lunkati. Dast had insisted that Orovene bring it from the precinct's chapel, and had been careful to stay within a half-dozen paces of it. Even so, he was ill at ease, twitching his hands and flicking sweat off his brow, even though the air was cool.

The shrouds on their boots had been the first surprise. No trademark hammer of hard Arbites soles here, the traditional warning to the citizenry, *Make way for the law*. Here the astropaths' tight-strung minds needed tranquillity, and they moved with muffling-pads snapped into place over their boots, reducing the proud crash of footsteps to an eerie little soughing sound on the matting.

The astropath cloisters weren't the austere environment of a Navy or Arbites fortress, nor the imposing ceremonial spaces of the Ministorum. Rede had told her that the old walls had been lined with a psyk-cage and then a layer of rockcrete. The lines of walls and ceiling were rounded, blurring into each other with none of the clean straight surfaces, ornate pillars or vaulting that Calpurnia might have expected. At first, she imagined walking down the smooth bore of some giant gun, but when she peered through the gloom, she realised that the walls were anything but smooth.

Every wall was textured, the rockcrete bearing banks, grooves and whorls that might evoke skin, the contours of clouds, or the print of a finger. Calpurnia found herself wanting to slip off a gauntlet and trail her touch along the wall to feel it under her skin. She blinked and ground her teeth to force herself back into some kind of decorum.

Long pennants of cloth, that looked ragged and grubby to Calpurnia's eyes, hung at every corner and intersection of corridors. They had passed half a dozen of the pennants before she realised why they appeared so slovenly: they were there for the touch, not the eye, and the sigils down their hems were sharp and cleanly embroidered, easily read by questing fingers. Not one of them was frayed or ravelled. The pennants were being maintained in the way that counted.

She noticed something else, too. A fresh patch of rockcrete stood out, as if some damage to the wall had been repaired. The patch was pallid and raw-looking, and around its edges, the wall was speckled and stained.

Calpurnia didn't need to ask what it was. She had seen spray-patterns like that against courthouse walls. The bloodstains were old, long-dried, but they were a reminder where she was and what business had brought her here. Calpurnia set her shoulders, and kept step as they moved on.

NOT LONG AFTERWARDS, they came upon the first astropath that Calpurnia had seen aboard a fortress that was full of them. He was a blot of green robes, in a mass of shadows, where a knot of passages and rampshafts met. Even at first sight, it was obvious that he wasn't well, but the Arbites in front of Calpurnia didn't slow or stop. She took care to keep up with them, keenly aware that she was ignorant about how to behave here.

As they passed, she had a quick impression of a scrawny figure, steadying itself against a buttress with one spidery hand. The hairless ball of his head hung listlessly, his face invisible. The veins on his skull were clearly visible, weaving among skull-plugs and dermal wiring. An attendant in a plain cream-coloured tunic crouched in front of him, holding up a cloth. It was speckled with blood, although Calpurnia couldn't tell where the astropath was bleeding from.

The other attendant, taller, robed and masked, loomed behind the astropath like the figure of Justice in a morality play. He held a silver-chased handgun. A length of crimson ribbon was elaborately knotted around the muzzle, and a small ward-charm hung from it. 'Vitifer', Calpurnia remembered from the briefs.

'The witch is dying,' rumbled Dast.

The walk took them up a short switchback of steps and back past the little tableau, now half a floor up. As they turned down a new passageway, a voice, deeper than Dast's, but hoarse, came up from where the astropath still stooped against the wall.

'Tilting!' was all it said, although the tone was that of a razor-edged parting insult. Calpurnia had no idea what it meant, and in a few moments, the Arbites were

gone down the passageway. If the man said anything
more, she didn't hear it, and she never saw him again.

THERE WERE ROWS of holes in the floor matting as they
came closer to the Master's chambers, set after set of
them.

Calpurnia missed the first ones: she had been
watching a procession of astropaths ushered past them
by two attendants, tailed by another vitifer with his red-
ribboned gun. These were junior, less puissant than the
man they had passed earlier, with a retinue to himself.
They were choristers, not full astropaths. Their green
robes were little more than tunics, and their surgery had
been brisk and savage, heads cocooned in containment
circuitry like bronzed birdcages, held fast by armatures
screwed directly into their skulls. They shuffled along,
each with a hand on the shoulder of the one in front,
the leader holding a rope that an attendant trailed
behind him.

For Calpurnia, the sight was almost hypnotically
strange, the dim light adding to its power. She was sure
she could hear echoes, too, a strange syncopated whispering, counterpointing the choristers' soft steps. In that
space, no echo should have been possible. When she
saw each of the choristers stumble at exactly the same
point, their bare feet catching at a row of gouges in the
matting, it was merely one more dreamlike, outlandish
touch.

They crossed the second set of holes under an archway hung with three long pennants that they had to
push aside like a curtain. However, it was only when
they arrived at the third set, on the lip of the little lowered foyer outside the Master's chambers, that she
finally asked what they were.

'Witchcullises,' Bruinann told her, indicating upwards.
A row of elaborate spearheads jutted out of the ceiling,

directly over the punched and torn matting underfoot. Calpurnia winced, wondering how much force the barrier must have come down with, and how many of them she had blithely walked under on the way.

'Part of the defences for when one of them loses control. The cullises stop them from roaming, and hurting too many other people by unbalancing one another. They also cage them if something… taints them.' Bruinann looked edgy. 'The cullises come down around them to contain them.'

'They're blast-doors?' Calpurnia asked.

'No, ma'am. Well, not for that kind of blast. Cage doors, as I say, wards and protections that turn psykcraft back on itself. The same as what lines the walls under that 'crete. Magos Channery and her priests do the forging.'

'Move on,' Dast broke in as she started to speak again. She closed her mouth and followed Bruinann into the Master's chambers.

THE CONVERSATION, EVEN Dast's rebuke, had grounded her a little, broken some of the spell of the cloisters. As they stepped into the anterooms, Calpurnia was looking around her with arbitor's eyes once again.

The outer foyer was a long oval, punctured once at each end and on each side by arched openings, with the black metal spikes of witchcullises poking through the lintels like teeth through gums. Only one of the arches boasted actual doors, although they were barely worthy of the name. A sliding partition blocked the far archway, honey-coloured Hydraphur silk stretched on a frame and lacquered to a brittle stiffness. The frame was broken, and the stiffened silk was ripped and gaping where Otranto had crashed through the partition in his terror.

'How are these fashioned?' Calpurnia asked as they walked down the length of the room.

'As you see them, ma'am,' Bruinann answered. 'Lacquered silk on the wooden frame. You'll see those around the Tower. If you're asking are they like the cullises, they're not. They're purely ornamental. Ma'am?' He had noticed her brief smile.

'It was important. I caught myself looking for designs painted on the doors. How long does it take to get used to living among people whose primary sense you don't share?'

'It's a tough place to get used to, ma'am, in all kinds of ways.' He ended the matter there and walked on, leaving Calpurnia to wonder at the tiredness she had heard in his voice.

She stopped as they made their way past the broken partition and ran her fingers over fabric and frame. The lacquer was rough, the texture of the brush strokes left there deliberately. Patches of screen that must have had especially pleasing textures were polished and stained dark by touch after touch. Calpurnia let her fingers wander over the wood of the frame: lightweight to be sure, but not brittle the way the fabric was. It would have taken quite a turn of speed to break through the frame.

When she stepped through the broken gap into the next room, her first thought was *it's a vineyard*, and for the rest of her time aboard the Bastion that was how she thought of it: Master Otranto's vineyard.

The room was full of ropes and cords. They hung from the ceiling in neat rows, forming aisles like the fruit-vines she remembered on Iax, anchored into the floor by chains and rings that gave each rope a little room to swing. Four lamps shone from mountings in the corners of the room, shaded in silk as golden-brown as that of the door-screens, to give a quality like Hydraphur daylight. Shrouded lanterns hung here and there casting a crazy lattice of rope-shadows across the floor. The shadows fell at all angles beneath Calpurnia's feet, and crisscrossed her legs.

Some of the ropes and cords were woven from rough hemp, some were beautifully brushed silk, or plaited ribbons of velvet. Some were thinner than Calpurnia's little finger, others thicker than her arm. Some had scraps of paper woven into them, holding sayings and devotions that Calpurnia supposed were part of some astropaths' creed, and from others dangled tiny metal chains, chimes, or pendant crystals. There was an elegance about the room that had her smiling again before she realised she was doing it.

The smile flicked off her face when Dast's hand clamped down on her shoulder and he spun her around.

'You broke formation,' he said. His helmet was still on, and she couldn't see his eyes, but there was an ugly, angry twist to his mouth as he spoke. 'We were in formal procession here. You broke the procession and defied my instructions. Remember I have rank here.'

'I fully understand the special nature of my rank, master chastener,' she told him. 'In fact, that was what motivated me. I'm working on the premise that we're under observation whenever we're outside a sanctuary like the precinct chambers or, or here.' She motioned around them. 'Since my nominal rank is providing the authority for us to launch our investigation, it's important for any observer to conclude that I am still a full arbitor senioris, and that I am in command here. I am conducting myself accordingly.'

I scored a point, she thought, as she watched Dast's expression, and then immediately yanked at the choke chain she kept her thoughts on. She made herself remember that Dast was right. Her duty was to comport herself according to her station.

Without my duty, who am I? she thought. The thought had to fight with a tiny flicker of satisfaction that Dast had taken her point and backed off, but it won comfortably.

'Who am I indeed?' she murmured aloud, and walked through the vineyard to where Rede and Orovene were standing over a tangle of ropes at the far end.

'HE GOT MOST of the way through the ropes alright, we think,' said Rede as Calpurnia joined them. 'This room was one of his favourites, he knew it very well. Even if he hadn't been pushing out his senses, he wouldn't have needed to think about where anything was. It wasn't until he got right to the end that he got tangled in these two, and he couldn't get out.'

Calpurnia crouched down over the snapped cords. One had been pulled against its rings with such force that they'd given way and broken open, and the rope lay like a kicked-off bed sheet. The other rope was thicker and heavier, trailing streamers of scripture-paper. It had only come loose at the ceiling, but the Master must have become tangled in it. The little chain that anchored it to its floor-ring was pulled taut, towards the doors, and most of the paper had been stripped out of the weave, leaving little stubs like torn-off insect wings. Calpurnia looked around for signs of the torn-out papers, but couldn't see them.

'The Master's close associates had already spent some time in here before we arrived,' said Bruinann as he joined them. 'One of the things they seem to have done was clear away the prayer-papers from that rope. You can see where they were. As we read it, it got wrapped around him as he struggled through here, and the paper ripped out as he tried to get free.'

'Prayer-papers? Is that what these are?' That had caught Orovene's interest. 'Might there be some specific motive in damaging them?'

'They were written by the Master before last,' Rede answered. 'The third most recent, that is. It's a form of meditation for the astropaths who still have enough function left to perform it. They use dense inks that make it easier for a psyker to perceive the words and track them with their minds. It is very slow work, very precise and hard to do without their eyes to guide them. It focuses them, and calms them down when they need it.'

'Who selects the prayers they use?' Orovene asked, but Rede shrugged. Calpurnia leaned carefully over one of the remaining papers until she could read it aloud. The hand was laborious and over-precise, like a child's, and the ink had a strange, laminated gloss.

> *This Sea does beget Unreason and the Awakening of our Shadows.*
> *Undying Beacon and Protector, to whom we are Bound,*
> *Your Light does ease the Weight of Shackles.*
> *Your Song gladdens our Labours in the Crying Darkness.*

'Not any catechism I recognise,' said Orovene.

Rede shrugged again. 'Speak to one of the attendants,' she said. 'I'm sure they'll track it down for you if you feel it's important.' Her tone rankled Calpurnia – the detective seemed oddly detached from an investigation that could land her in the Incarcery, as Calpurnia's neighbour, if the Hydraphur command decided it had been botched.

'We've spent too much time here,' Dast declared. 'Move on.'

BEYOND THE VINEYARD, the Master's chambers were a cluster of low-ceilinged circular silos joined by simple arched doors, their lintels empty of cullis-teeth. Orovene was the first to remark on that.

'None of the individual chambers are separated,' Rede said. 'That's the final defence, over there.' She tilted her head back past them, and the three off-station Arbites turned to consider the door they had just walked through. 'Door' was a mild term, Calpurnia thought as she took a proper look and remembered Rede's remarks about fortification.

The outer defence was a witchcullis like the ones they had already seen, its spikes hung with prayer slips and ceremonial charms. Inside that was the auspex arch, the walls carved into gargoyle faces with sniffers and sensors for eyes. The nozzles of flechette-spitters and acid-misters jutted from mouths, and were clutched in sculpted claws. The whole arch was so shallow that Calpurnia could have crossed it in one long stride, but there was more than enough lethality in the walls to stop an enemy in their tracks. Calpurnia could see that the fittings were chipped and tarnished: these defences had been triggered by Otranto's mind shout against whomever he'd been fleeing. For all the good it had done him.

The final door was a great armoured shutter on its oiled and noiseless slide and hinge. It was an oval slab of adamant, thicker than a hand could span, its surface worked with blessings and wards, crystalline psyk-earths, silver eagle inscribed with holy texts, mag-locks and sliding bolts.

'Stronger than the witchcullis behind it,' Bruinann told them. 'Stronger than most of the containments in the rest of the walls, so I'm advised. It locks physically, with those bolts, as well as magnetically. The Mechanicus has built an engine into the locking mechanism whose spirit can animate a stasis field: the bolt can't move until the correct codes allow the engine to rest. The moving parts are worked with the same witch-wards as the rest of the door and the cullises. The patterns are machined so that when they turn to the locked position, their wards mesh with those of the door and compound the strength of the defences.'

'Something you can put your faith in,' said Orovene. He caught Bruinann's look. 'I'm not making fun, aedile.

The works of the Machine come to us by Imperial grace, exactly the way my own sacraments do. The engine-spirit obeys His rule just as the human one does. The Emperor protects. You haven't had that conversation with this Channery yet? No?'

'The magos is not the most approachable,' said Rede. 'She helped us open the door when we got in to find Otranto, and she spoke with the auspexes in the arch there. That was how we confirmed that Otranto used a code to trigger them, and it was just the auspex sniffing a hostile. She did it all through proxies, speaking through servitors, or junior priests slaved to her voice.' Rede's own voice was strained. Mechanicus mysteries could be confronting to people outside the Tech-Priesthood.

Dast had been inspecting the entrance with the practiced manner of one used to working with defended doors, tracing the lines of the wards with his hands, and then inspecting the closing mechanism. Calpurnia walked over and joined him, looking at the micro-detail of the wards, and the powerful closing mechanism that could slam this giant slab shut in moments.

'I'm closing it,' said Dast curtly. 'Check and clear the doorway.'

'Shutter closing!' Calpurnia yelled, back-pedalling to look out of the entranceway. There was no need for the alert: the proctor who'd led them here had positioned the other arbitrators in a cordon line across the vine-yard. They did not move from their sentry positions as the door glided along its rails, and swung in and sealed the archway. Calpurnia braced herself for a great clang, but there was only a silky hiss as metal met metal. They came together with the smooth motion that only the meticulous craft of the Mechanicus could perfect. A puff of air, pushed from between door and lintel, brushed their faces, and then they were sealed in at the death-scene.

THE DOOR HAD taken less than four seconds to close, start to finish.

'Whoever was on the Master's tail, as he ran into his chambers, must have been breathing down his neck,' Orovene said. Dast had walked to the door again and was examining the way it sat in the lintel. From what Calpurnia could see, it met the wall so smoothly that there might not have been a join there at all.

'Tripping and tangling on those ropes would have slowed him down. They might have caught him up,' said Calpurnia, but she was frowning as she said it. Rede nodded.

'So it doesn't add up for you either, ma'am. The witchcullises drop in about half the time it takes for that door to close, so whoever Master Otranto was fleeing was right behind him when he came down that passage.'

'Too fast for the archway weapons to catch, too,' Dast put in as he came away from the door. 'The bastard was so hot on Otranto's heels that he sank the knife in as soon as the Master turned around. So what the hell happened when Otranto fell in the ropes outside?'

'That's where our answers dry up,' said Rede. 'Our killer chases Otranto halfway across this fortress. The Master's in a state of mortal terror that sends ripples out across the Bastion even with the containments in place. The killer hounds him so closely that even though the cullises drop and the door slams, he's through without a scratch. Our Verispex tools are crude, but we found no bio-traces anywhere that the pursuer might have been wounded. On the other hand, Otranto tangles himself in rope, falls and lies there struggling, and the killer doesn't strike. He waits until

Otranto's free and running again, and then follows him into the inner chambers as the door seals, and does the deed.'

'And,' said Bruinann, 'he's gone. We open the door and Otranto's corpse is alone. No door has opened for the assassin, no cullis has raised. No auspex has sniffed him and no witness has seen him. No psyker-seance can pin him down, and no Verispex can track him.'

The Arbites stood in silence and considered her words.

'I'm very glad you're here to direct us, arbitor senioris,' Rede said, but there was no warmth in her smile at all.

HER ATTENTION OFF the fortified door, Calpurnia could look around the room and see the scars that the Master had left as he fled through it.

The floor matting was finer than outside, straw-like to the eye, but woollen-soft to the touch. The colour was a uniform grey-green from wall to wall, but she could see the weave forming subtle patterns that would tell a bare-foot, blind psyker where he was in the room. The walls were finished in panels of dark timber, lightly treated to leave the natural grain exposed and raw to the touch. Braziers had stood on each side of the door, but their slender gold columns had been overbalanced. The burners were extinguished, but Calpurnia could still catch the ghost of a scent, a complex layering of perfumes.

The Master's trail came from the doorway. It seemed to change constantly: now the matting was crushed as if a tank had rolled across it, a pace later it was scorched and the weave pushed outward as if from a red-hot furnace-wind. A pace later and it was whole, but bleached, as if it had sat under a fierce sun for a month. Beyond that, the colour came back, but the pattern of it was ravelled and frayed, the fabric apparently corroded. Above the overbalanced brazier stands, the wooden panelling of the walls was scorched and ragged.

In the dying minutes of his life, Otranto's terror had overwhelmed his control and left its wake through the room. The thought of what it must have been like for him made Calpurnia shudder. Looking around the room from there, she realised that none of the Arbites were standing on the path left through the matting. Without word or direction, they had all instinctively shied away from that patch of floor.

Calpurnia winced at a cramp in her hand and realised that the silver aquila at her throat was pinched between her thumb and forefinger, hard enough to hurt. She released it with an effort of will, and walked through the inner doorway into Otranto's bedchamber, the death room.

The single dusty lumen fitting in the crown of the chamber's ceiling had burst at the moment of the Master's death, and had not been replaced. Instead, the room was full of hot, shadowless light from free-standing Arbites lamp arrays. Calpurnia took in her sparse surroundings, by the lamplight.

The trail through the floor matting faded to scuff marks as it entered the room. Marks that anyone's feet could have left. The bedclothes were lightly tousled from the last time that Otranto had slept – would ever sleep – there. The man had collapsed against the foot of the bed and had died without disturbing the sheets. The mark of his blood still stained the floor beneath the bed.

Six small tripods had held incense burners and chime-boxes, set in a careful circuit around the bed. They had all been knocked over, their legs pointing like fingers, like compass needles, back to the spot where the Master had perished.

THAT WAS ALL. Calpurnia, who had seen murder scenes before, felt the anticlimax as a loosening of her shoulders and a quiet exhalation of breath. She wasn't sure what she had been expecting: the old man's ghost? Some creature made of witch-malice, such as the Navigators were supposed to see out between the stars? She didn't know.

There were two doorways before them, one on each side of the bed, at eleven and one o'clock to the main entrance's six o'clock. One stood dark, the other was softly lit. They were the side-rooms that she had seen on Rede's schematics. She wandered towards the left one, and saw Dast go right.

The dark archway in front of her led into the meditation room: even barer than the bedchamber, a small mat on the naked rockcrete floor the only hint at furnishings. The light from the arc array in the main chamber washed into the little room, enough for her to see the bare walls and high ceiling. She leaned in through the door and–

–back-pedalled frantically out of it, grabbing at the maul-hilt at her belt. She collected herself, ignored a curious glance from Orovene and stepped back inside. The glitter of light from above, when she gave her eyes time to adjust to the shadows came, not from eyes in the dark, but from pale gems. An Imperial aquila adorned the domed ceiling, and the gems picked out its pinions and made a halo around the blind left head.

She took a breath and turned back into the room, conscious of Orovene's eyes still on her. She had the feeling that her moment of fright would cost her with her two jailers when they were back in the Arbites chambers.

Then Dast gave a bellow from the other chamber, and straightaway Calpurnia was running, her maul in her hand. She passed Orovene and ran through to where the master chastener was glaring over the sights of his shotgun at the grey-haired woman in the concordiast's gown. She sat amid the greenery and regarded the Arbites with no surprise at all.

CHAPTER FIVE

THEY WERE IN the chambers with Ylante.

The halls from the attendants' decks met the astropath cloisters at a broad polished platform underneath high intersecting arches hung with lamps. The Bastion's bells had rung to signal half a dozen transmission-trances in the coming watch, and the air was alive with quiet bustle. Gaggles of housemen and drudges passed this way and that, bent under their loads. Solemn-faced junior apothecaries, with baskets of instruments and medicines, emerged from the stairwells leading to the eastern side of the Second Barbican, ready to join their masters in the keep and assist them in the eyries. Concordiasts and herbalists were passing through from the barrack-decks crowding the sides of the keep. They bore down into the Curtain, on their way to help soothe strained bodies and wrenched minds. Scribes and savants shuffled to their posts in the Encryptors' vault or the Scriptorium.

Teeker Renz, in formal garb that marked out his ranks and offices, stood in the middle of it all. He was well known for prowling the halls, ostensibly so that he could report to the Master that the pulse of the Bastion was beating as it should. More often, he did it so that he could be seen and found, to hold a strolling sort of court in among a pack of his protégés and friends, and anyone who wanted to petition for his favour. Now, he prowled beneath the arches, eyeing the gates that led to the upper keep's stairs, directing baleful thoughts up those stairs to the inner astropath cloisters and the Master's suite.

They were in there with Ylante, these *Arbites*, who had somehow come aboard and marched straight into the middle of all this trouble without Renz being able to do anything about it.

Renz knew about the Arbites, who didn't? Until now, they'd always been an impersonal threat. When the uniforms and grim helmet-plates of Bruinann and his thugs had come down a hall, Renz had always done his best not to look at them.

Now... now he didn't want to think about it. How could they be in there with Ylante when he wanted to be in there talking to the little bi– talking to the woman. Things had to be worked out, but the Arbites were in there. He needed to talk to Ylante, but he–

Where the hell were Dechene and Kyto? They were supposed to be here. Wasn't this their job? To counsel and assist him? So, where the hell were they?

It wasn't much, but it was something for Renz to aim his anger at, and blaming the other two men let him order his thoughts a little and sidle back towards that terrible, central fact: the Arbites. They had no place here. Whoever decided that the Arbites knew anything about... anything? Kyto had said something about how this Calpurnia woman could take command of the

Tower if she wanted to. Take command! Run the place just as if she had some damn right to!

What would some clumping-booted arbitor from Hydraphur know about keeping the Blind Tower running?

She wouldn't know them the way Renz did. She wouldn't know that Concordiast Ottre had a mental hide like a trooper's carapace, and could work the most punishing shifts with high-strung astropaths like Jaul and Ankyne without cracking. She wouldn't know that Kyto was the man to ask which astropaths knew the Navy's psykers best and should be on duty in the eyries when a warship squadron was due to pass close by.

She wouldn't know that Astropath Sacredsteel shouldn't be allowed to ascend any further in rank, whatever her nominal level of ability might be, until Angel-of-Auriga had been made Deputy Master of the Watch, because Renz had promised him that. She wouldn't know how the apportioning worked, how the provision orders needed to be... modulated the way Renz had always arranged. She would know nothing of the subtleties of directing assignments and rations to reflect who needed to be kept in their place and who had earned consideration: subtleties with which Renz was perfectly familiar, but which he had never written down.

For a moment, the tension got the better of him and his hands flew to his temples, scrunched the edges of his velvet cap and left it sitting askew on his sweating brow.

How could he explain to some jaw-champing arbitor with planet-dust still on their feet how it worked? These arrangements had just, well, *developed* with time, as Renz had started to interpret and correct the Master's instructions. How could he make them see that the privileges he had slowly drawn about him were rightfully his, see that his friends deserved the places he had carved out for them? It would be so obvious if he could just explain, providing that Ylante didn't get in first. He needed a plan.

Dechene was good at this kind of thing. Where *was* the man?

'THE ARBITES,' SAID Gessante Lohjen, in a low voice that barely ruffled the quiet of the astropath cloister. His hood cast his face into shadow in the dim light, 'Shira Calpurnia and her staff. Remember what I said.'

The posture of the two astropaths he was addressing did not change. They continued to stand, like bookends, slightly turned towards one another, each holding one of the tasselled pennons that hung in a cluster from the ceiling of the intersection. Their fingers worked at the embroidered fabric with eerily identical motions. Their faces, with the care-worn features of long-serving astropaths, remained serene, faintly distracted. Their empty eyes – Brom's lids sewn down over the sockets, del'Kateer's simply shrivelled so deep that they were hidden in the wrinkled skin of the sockets – stared impassively past the Lohjen's shoulders. Standing between them, conscious of the two armed vitifers standing behind him, Attendant Acquerin tried to hide his nerves. He stole a glance at the velvet envelope Lohjen held low to his side, and then made an effort to look away and pretend he hadn't been watching it.

'We'll keep you in mind, sir,' Brom said mildly after a moment, his voice papery-dry. 'But do you really not agree that you're misjudging what we can do for you? We've discussed this.'

'We have, and I don't see the need to repeat myself.' Lohjen began to bow before the two blind men, hesitated, completed the gesture uncertainly and turned away. A moment later, his dove-grey captain's coat was fading into the dim light of the sub-eyrie passages. As he turned a corner, a flash of light turned him briefly into a silhouette, startling Acquerin's eyes, before the light and the man were both gone.

'What was that, a moment ago?' asked Brom in the same mild voice.

'He turned on a lumen, sir. To show his way, I think.'

'Thought so,' said del'Kateer. 'I tasted a change in the air. There's a feel to light, when you know the trick of looking for it.' Acquerin wondered if that last had been for his benefit, if his surprise at the blind astropath noticing the light had been that obvious.

The two astropaths were turning towards him as the thought crossed his mind, and the identical small smiles that flickered across their faces showed that he'd allowed the thought to radiate. He laced his hands in front of him and bowed his head. By the time he had run through ten lines of one of his childhood catechisms, and his mind was calm again, the two old men had passed to either side of him and were shuffling down the passageway to the Green Eyrie. Acquerin waited respectfully until they and the vitifers had passed by, and then turned and took up his proper position, between them and a dozen steps behind, where he wouldn't be in the vitifers' sight line.

Senior Astropath del'Kateer registered the boy as a brief, vivid patch of texture at the fringe of sensing. It settled into part of the pattern, in with the thrum of energy through the Tower's power-conduits, Brom's footsteps and his clinking amulet-chain, and the distant sound of his own feet and staff-tip.

'What do you think of the man?' he asked Brom. The words came out as the barest mutter – but that was all they needed to be. He and Brom were old friends, old colleagues. Where the trailing edges of their minds overlapped, they meshed; the white fires in the centres of their skulls burned and danced to a rhythm so closely that they were effectively one.

Brom picked up the question easily. He just didn't reply.

'I know, friend. Bad times, turbulent, and that Lohjen's just a shadow in the middle of it all.'

Del'Kateer did not say 'shadow'. That part of his sentence was an image-flash through the mind-haze. Lohjen was still a mystery, a blank spot in their knowledge, unpredictable, and dangerous to examine too closely.

Brom's answer was to take that image and turn it. In the experience of astropaths, such vortices would unravel as the currents shifted and weakened. The image of that happening would often be sent from mind to mind to show release, an end to hard times, and a relief of tension.

'Shady or not, I wouldn't have put speaking directly with the Arbites as beyond his capability.' That gave some texture to the meaning of the image Brom had sent: the mystery would unravel, or would be unravelled. Brom was counting on the Arbites to pull apart any danger, any conspiracy.

Del'Kateer considered this.

'Odd how directed they've been. Are you thinking that with me?' The mental image of an astropathic choir, a giant one, such as might stretch even the Blind Tower's abilities to assemble, using all its might to push a routine Administratum surveillance code through clear space. The sense of a powerful force left unused or directed to puzzlingly simple ends.

'You know, we're not the only ones to wonder it.' Brom's reply was entirely verbal, his mind preoccupied with ordering his thoughts, 'Sacredsteel and Thujik, and, well…'

The sentence hung in the air. Del'Kateer adjusted his grip on his staff, leaned on it for a moment and let his mind caress the microscrollwork on its heavy, gilded head. He'd had the staff for eight decades, and the patterns were as delightful to his psychic senses as when he had first been given it. That was back when he had taken ship for Hydraphur, with the pain of the Binding still lingering in his dead eyes, and the new white fire burning deep in him.

'Well. Indeed.' He sighed as the two of them began walking again. Brom had begun to work a stick of worry-wood between his fingers. 'How many are lining up now, then? Who's approached you?'

Brom gave a dry laugh.

'Formally? Nobody. Come on, my friend, would you? Otranto's body is barely cool and his echoes have barely died away. Whatever's left of him is still flying home to the fire.' The twitch of Brom's finger looked like a random gesture to Acquerin, walking behind him. Del'Kateer, with senses the young attendant did not possess, knew his friend was pointing Earthward, into the light of the Astronomican. 'There's worse trouble ahead before his death's put to rest, and I think I speak both our minds, no?' He paced onwards in silence. Beside him, Del'Kateer's mind had busied itself so deeply on the engravings on his staff that the mental picture of them was radiating off him, as clear to Brom as if he was touching them himself.

'Thujik,' Del'Kateer said at length. 'Hm. He's not been subtle about his ambition the last few years, has he? Just built his power base in the wrong places is all.'

'And made the wrong enemies,' Brom replied.

'Do you think Otranto ever cared? I don't remember him being very exercised about the succession. Big part of why things are as they are now, with this arbitor sitting in his suite. On his seat, too, I don't doubt. Ha.'

'Ha. No, you're right: The whole nub of the problem, really.'

Although neither of the two venerable astropaths spoke much aloud after that, the problem they were both considering stayed fixed in their minds to the point where it even began to form in the mind of their attendant. For no reason that he could think of, Acquerin found himself thinking of Teeker Renz, the murdered Master's high-strung, foul-tempered major-domo. Acquerin disliked Renz, and savoured being far away from him on errands like these, but somehow the man kept bobbing up in his thoughts. He lengthened his steps a little to get closer to the two astropaths, and kept his hearing sharp, remembering Lohjen's instructions:

Bring me back news of everything you overhear after I've done with them. Whatever they say about this Arbites investigation, especially anything they say that they didn't tell me. Whatever they say about the succession to the Master's seat, and whatever they say about who they suspect of Otranto's murder. Especially that, first and foremost that.

THE FIREWATCH EYRIE was so-called because it was most commonly used to speak with the astropathic stations lying towards the Segmentum Solar. It needed its astropath's attention to be turned in the direction of Holy Earth and the great god-furnace of the Astronomican. The Green Eyrie, sitting closer in towards the keep, was so-called because for a long time it had been devoted purely to Naval transmissions, decked out in green Battlefleet livery (to whose colour the astropaths were indifferent, although they knew of it). The base of the Green Eyrie was ringed with the old guard-cells and reinforced psyk-wards that the Navy staff had used to keep control of the movements up and down the column. Now that the old restriction had fallen away, the eyrie was used for the more erratic psykers who needed more careful guarding and containment.

The raw young or the exhausted old, on the other hand, went to the Eyrie of Echoes for their work. Its column stood rooted in old ordnance workshops that had been refitted to hold the extra-large choirs that a less confident mind, or one with a punishing transmission to endure, needed to give it strength. The Lantern Eyrie, far out by the secondary docks, had some of the best-forged mechanisms, and was the best for freeing its occupant's mind from any static or mental wash from other transmissions. That was the place for astropaths standing the Silent Watch, a constant, open listening for transmissions, unscheduled distress calls or warnings, or the trauma of an overloading connection by another astropath.

Then there was the Eyrie of Bones. At the same time that the Green Eyrie had drifted from Navy use to become a workplace for all the Bastion's astropaths, the Eyrie of Bones had begun to fall from favour as a personal eyrie for the Master of the Tower. The Astra Telepathica law that the Master of a place like this had always to be a fully capable astropath in his own right, and to perform his duty regularly, was a given, always. Gonvall, Otranto's predecessor, had never bothered much with a personal eyrie, and Otranto had cared even less. Therefore, the Eyrie of Bones, so close to the corner of the keep that someone in a vacc suit could have spanned the gap with his arms, was there for any astropath who asked to be rostered to it.

That, of course, was highly unbecoming. The position of Master had been allowed to degrade under Otranto – that was the confirmed opinion of Senior Astropath Thujik. Things would certainly change. They could have changed already, but for the wretched motions that had to be gone through by the Arbites, and Thujik's tenure as Master would be to see to that in good order. He promised himself this as he rode the lift up the column to the Eyrie of Bones, an adjutant on one side of him, and a vitifer on the other, with his red-wrapped pistol.

Thujik had been taken aboard the Black Ships at nineteen, with two years' service to his father, whipping the family outposts into shape. He had come out of the Soul Binding, carrying that white fire deep in him, his vision scorched black, but his mind still clear, and his memory too, by the Emperor's grace. Grace it was, and grace with a purpose. So many astropaths had their memories, even their higher cognition, burned away by the trauma of the Binding, but if the Emperor had left Thujik with his skills, wasn't that a sign? He would be the one to get this blasted outpost running properly, just as he had in his youth.

The lift door opened. The passage leading up into the eyrie was ribbed, literally. Human ribs were set into its walls, skulls and spines, and the long bones of arms and legs, marched along the walls in grim symmetry. They were old bones, carefully preserved. Thujik hobbled past, stopping every so often to stretch his humped back and let his adjutant adjust the augmetic splints propping up his withered legs. The astropathic message with Santo Pevrelyi was expected some time in the next two hundred and fifteen hours. He hobbled on, musing.

There was none of Otranto's sloppiness, delegating half the running of the place to his jumped-up little major-domo and his cronies, and there were none of Sacredsteel's idiot pretensions either. Oh, she was devoted, certainly. He would have no hesitation in naming her first among equals when he laid out his circle of senior astropaths. He remained confident, however. He had always known that he was going to succeed Otranto. 'Master of the Tower' was his. He deserved it.

With a sigh, he lowered himself onto a couch and began to run his mind through its exercises. Somewhere below, the Encryptors would be in the last stages of coding and weaving the data to go out to Santo Pevrelyi. They would be encoding it for him to transmit. Then out across space to the waiting minds, in their mountain fort on Pevrelyi's highlands.

MEANWHILE, SENIOR ASTROPATH Sacredsteel was walking in the Smoke Garden.

The garden had no plants or trees. It was an old back vent raking downwards from what had once been gun batteries around the middle tiers of the keep. They had once sucked away exhaust gases from the gun decks and the ordnance launching cradles. Now, the tunnel was again full of smoke, the smoke of incense and aromatic oils, burning and evaporating in precise mixtures, brewed and prepared by Teeker Renz and deployed by his assistants and apprentices.

The floor of the garden hall had two levels. The two outer paths were covered with soft pebbles, rounded, polished silky-smooth, and designed to be walked on barefoot. The centre path, set lower, sat under a layer of the same pebbles, just submerged under ankle-deep water. The water could be made warm enough to steam and add to the texture of the air, or cold enough to cause a shocking, cleansing chill to the skin.

Sacredsteel had come to the Smoke Garden fresh from a turbulent trance in the Eyrie of Echoes. For over three hours, she'd struggled to reel in a maddeningly faint message from the Telepathica matrices at Caruana-IV. She'd strained to snatch compacted notes of thought in her mental fingers and swallow them into her brain. She pushed them firmly enough down into her mind so that she could be sure they wouldn't dissipate like smoke when the trance finished. They hadn't, of course: she knew it was not vanity to consider herself an astropath of the first order. She had imprisoned the melody firmly, and let it out again as words and codes into the ears of the transcriptors and vox-captures as her mind settled back down into the eyrie walls and the bone vault of her skull.

The effort of the session had left her shuddering with exhaustion and alive with psychic echoes. She saw a strange repeating vision of the Judge card of the Emperor's Tarot, splattered with blood and black paint, and a hot sensation danced around the bones of her face and neck.

She was pleased to hitch up her gown and walk barefoot along the path, the cool water soothing her feet (the sensation had gradually died out of her upper body ever since her Soul Binding: her head and shoulders were almost totally numb, but her feet felt the cool water perfectly well). She was dimly aware of the perfumed smokes and steams she was passing through as she walked, but to sharpen her perception of them she would have had to augment her failing sense of smell with psychic perceptions. Marshalling them was an effort she wasn't prepared to make right now. She simply walked.

On one path-bank, shoes rattling in the pebbles, her attendant walked, with the boxy mechanical vox-ear that Channery had consecrated for her. It sucked in the sounds around them and transmitted them to the augmetics that hung from Sacredsteel's ears like vines. They fed the sounds to her atrophying aural nerves. The astropath's vitifer, or at least the one given to her today, pistol unholstered as always, walked with her. On the other path walked an emissary from Envoy Lohjen.

'Master Lohjen was curious as to whether you had any views on why the Arbites haven't yet approached you about succession,' said the woman, whose name Sacredsteel hadn't bothered to remember.

'It's all one to me,' she replied. 'I've been about my work, no more.'

'With respect, mamzel, I don't believe this hasn't crossed your mind. You're known to be zealous and ambitious. Your calling has marked you, we know as much from your name.'

It wasn't unusual for astropaths to take a new name after their Soul Binding, something reflecting a part of the experience that had moved them. Sacredsteel had rarely seen metal before; she knew that from the murk of half-memories that she had retained from before the white fire had blasted into her.

'No one's spoken to me,' she snapped, breaking the moment's reverie. 'No one's spoken to anyone. They're in the cloisters now. That's all I know. Sniffing around Otranto's rooms, probably.'

'So you are keeping track?' The woman's voice was amused. 'Master Lohjen would like me to–'

There was a spitting crack of feedback from the hearing-box, and the woman broke off, startled. Sacredsteel hid her smile. She had learned the trick of causing those sounds with a tiny wink of mental energy. It was useful for keeping the edge in a conversation.

'Little girl, I don't doubt that you think your errand here is mighty important. I heard you introduce yourself to my assistant as a representative of Envoy Lohjen. Well, if Lohjen is all exercised about the succession here then let him come and talk to me himself. For a formal Astropathica envoy, your master has done an awful lot of lurking on his little boat and not a lot of, well, envoying.'

The woman started to say something, but was silenced by another *zip-crack* from the box.

'Until then, I believe I'll keep my own counsel,' Sacredsteel went on. 'If you know my reputation, then you'll know that pompous oaf Thujik's and you'll know that, oaf he might be, but there's nothing but void between the two of us and any other possible successor.

Your master will have plenty of time to talk to both of us, and this arbitor. He can petition me for some time when he feels able to stir himself.'

'My master has–'

Zzip-crack. Sacredsteel's augmetics picked up the woman cursing under her breath.

'That will do for now. Run along and let me be, please. I've to send a cipher to Avignor in twenty-seven hours, and you're not helping me calm down so that I can rest up for it.'

She pushed her psyk-sense out to perceive the woman bowing and loping off down the garden. She grunted and kept walking. The truth was that she was nonplussed by the Arbites, by their tumultuous arrival and by their current seclusion. Weren't all Arbites thugs and idiots? Bruinann and that detective who fancied herself so secret, certainly were. She hoped the investigation wouldn't make any trouble. Sacredsteel was an astropath of the first order, and it was time she had a rank that reflected it. It was well past time that she was made Mastrex, and her patience was running out.

THE MAN WITH the two-coloured beard, who had come storming so loudly into the Master's garden to confront her, was controlling himself rigidly. The anger was clear in his dark eyes and guttural voice. It didn't take Torma Ylante long, however, to see that his shoulders and hands remained steady, the volume of his voice loud, but precisely pitched. How strong must the urge be, she thought, to step forwards and jam the muzzle into her face, her chest, knocking her backward? He controlled it, as he controlled the rest of himself: interesting.

There was a break in the tirade. She wondered how her voice would come out sounding after all this, but it seemed remarkably level. She was rather pleased about that.

'Of course I will identify myself, sir. I am Mamzel Torma Ylante, formerly of the ship's cohort of Captain Galan Vedrier of the League of Black Ships. Lately, I am the Chief Concordiast-Elect of the Master of Hydraphur's Bastion Psykana. Although who knows what will come of that now?'

She met his boiling gaze with the right degree of steadiness.

'As for my business,' she went on, still looking up into his face like a child, as she heard more Arbites enter the garden behind him, 'I am mourning a Master and an old friend. I am simply praying my farewells and putting my spirit at peace.' A whole moment went by without him shouting at her, so she pushed her luck a little. 'To answer your most pressing points, I acknowledge, and have not tried to dispute, that I am under arrest and in whose divine name I am arrested. I very well understand what I have done in coming here.'

'A Master and an old friend.' The chastener's eyes narrowed and some of the aggression had died out of his voice. 'You were mourning Master Otranto, but who else?' She watched him closely: a slight twitch of the head. 'What other murder are you talking of, woman?'

'Otranto's both of them, Dast. There hasn't been a second death, and I suggest that she no longer needs the gun in her face.' A woman's voice, harder to read than the chastener's. It was a confident voice in a low alto, used to command, but Ylante heard the tiredness in it.

The man looming over her – Dast – kept the gun in place for a second longer before it spun up and away from her with startling speed, snapping into the scabbard on his armoured back. Chastener Dast, displeasure radiating off him like steam, stepped back.

A woman walked past Dast and dropped to one knee to look Ylante in the eye. This, Ylante thought, must be Arbitor Calpurnia. Five years younger than Ylante herself? Ten? She doubted it. She didn't recognise the badges of rank on Calpurnia's shoulders, but they looked like ones that would take until about Ylante's own age to earn. Three scar-lines ran up from her eye into the woman's unruly dark-blonde hair. The scars themselves were old, just neat lines, but the skin around them looked red and sore as if from constant rubbing.

'You're the one from the Black Ship,' said lady arbitor.

'I am.'

'You came on board to act as some kind of adjutant for this Master Otranto. Concordiast, that was the term you used.'

'The Master of the Tower must serve as an active astropath,' Ylante replied, 'and so he requires me. Or someone like me,' she added, thinking of her one bitter meeting with Teeker Renz. 'The Master reserves the services of a concordiast as part of his own retinue.'

'She has eyes,' put in Dast from over both their heads. 'She's no astropath.'

'Thank you, master chastener,' Calpurnia replied as she put her other knee on the path and tried to mimic Ylante's posture. She was having a hard time of it – her heavy boots weren't allowing her lower legs to fold in the right ways. 'I have eyes too. I see it. I don't believe that Mamzel Ylante was referring to psyker work.' Her eyes narrowed in imitation of the chastener's. 'I do need to know what you do. I've seen the rosters of concordiasts in the Bastion precinct files. Here's your chance to educate me, and to convince me, by the way, that whatever a concordiast does, it doesn't involve the murder of their Master.'

CHAPTER SIX

TEEKER RENZ CAME stalking through the downdecks, the stacked compartments around the foundations of the keep. Once the fortress had stored its ratings and indentured stationhands here; now the downdecks were home to the Tower's Naval contingent, officers and midshipmen having to endure the indignity of quarters originally designed for their inferiors.

He found his man striking a louche pose atop a flight of steps, making a show of inspecting the unadorned rockcrete walls, and affecting to ignore the bustle of uniforms around him. Few non-Navy personnel came into the decks without a definite errand, and Dechene, in cream-coloured concordiast's livery of unusually rich cloth and cut, was getting a few curious looks.

Renz got them too, although he was too agitated to notice them. He headed for Dechene, stopped less than a metre away from him, and glared into the man's face.

After a good minute or so, Concordiast Antovin Dechene deigned to notice him.

'See what you think of this,' he said. His voice was low and languid, 'That Navy-girl assembling her shift crew there, outside the archway.' Renz didn't look around, but Dechene went on anyway. Giving the performance was what counted. 'Had her; still do, if you follow me. Against fleet policy, doing anything with me, that is, non-fleet personnel. She's terrified the Navy will find out. No fleet commissar on the Tower, but plenty in the places they'd send her to if it ever got out. Hah.'

Dechene carefully adjusted the angle of his lean. He inspected the fingernails of his left hand, one after another. The sleeve fell away to show a slender silver chain at his wrist. It was a token from Renz himself, after Dechene had taken care of an unpleasant business before Candlemas. Dechene pointed his chin over Renz's shoulder.

'Now her, the one with the – look where I'm pointing, Teek, just pretend you're looking at something else.' With poor grace, Renz patted his sleeve, looked behind him as if for something dropped, and registered the petty officer with the cropped dark hair.

'Another one of mine,' Dechene said, his smirk as lazily unsettling as his voice. 'Convinced she's my special little thing.' He gave a sidelong glance over Renz's shoulder. 'See the way she's trying not to look at me? She's still at the passionate stage: all het up with the secret romance of it all.' He shifted his attention to the nails of his right hand. 'This is what it's all about, isn't it, Teek? I live for this. Look at the two of them, both trying to catch my eye. Neither one has a clue about the other. Only we know the truth, hey?' He gave a slow, lecherous droop of an eyelid.

'Where the hell have you and Kyto been?' Renz kept enough wits to keep his voice low, but the effort was showing in his face. 'I waited for you for half an hour. Do you think we can afford not to care about what's happening? Nothing's over just because–'

'Relax, Teek. You're driving yourself crazy and you've got no reason to. Why so set on talking yourself into trouble?'

'Talking? I see. Well, at this moment, the Master's suites are full of Arbites and Torma Ylante is in there with them and this arbitor senioris from Hydraphur. The Throne alone knows what–' Renz caught himself, moved closer and lowered his voice.

'–what rubbish that woman is stuffing the arbitor's head with. Well? Have you thought about that?'

The pleased expression finally began to slide off Dechene's face. The two of them walked away from the steps, around the circular hall that made a collar between the downdecks and the keep. The crop-haired brunette in the petty officer's uniform was pretty enough, Renz supposed. She gave a shy smile in their direction, which fell away when Dechene ignored her.

Neither man said anything as they made a long clockwise path around the edge of the downdecks and then turned in below one of the great buttresses that ran through the downdecks and then up the side of the keep above them: one of the great pillars that the fortification walls rested on. They turned and made their way through the narrow tunnel through the buttress, under the metal stripe in the ceiling that was the lower edge of a seven-tonne shutter-door. Then they passed the little rat hole guard posts where an armed overseer from the Navy garrison recognised Renz and waved them through.

They were coming into the techmens' quarters, where the lay artisans lived who performed whatever tasks the Mechanicus priests saw fit to delegate outside their own orders. Their workshops surrounded Channery's sealed Enginarium. Renz and Dechene walked through arches

carved with barcoded litanies and watched over by
skeletal Mechanicus gargoyles, between walls that
sloped and swerved. Even through the metal and rockcrete, the sound of machines surrounded them.

A month ago, Renz might have found this exciting.
The games and manoeuvres that being Otranto's ear
and voice had let him play had been fun, because he
knew he was in no danger. Things had changed, dra-
matically: he and Dechene had come to a place where
the rumble and click of machines would make spying
hard because, suddenly, it *mattered* that they be hard to
spy on. Without the threat of the Master's proxy anger
to hold over the heads of anyone who displeased him,
Renz had to consider the concept of consequences if his
plans went wrong.

He didn't like that sensation at *all*.

'So you're telling me,' said Shira Calpurnia, 'that you
have completely free access to the Master's suite? You
can come and go as you please?'

Torma Ylante shook her head.

'I have done since Otranto died, whenever the chambers have been unlocked, but I can't open the suite
myself. I couldn't get through there now.' She tilted her
head towards the massive shutter-door.

They were back in the Master's bedchamber. Calpurnia hadn't wanted to keep Ylante in the garden, where
the woman had seemed far too at ease. In the bedchamber, Ylante would be confronted by the
bloodstain, the violent echoes of the Master's death. As
Ylante had calmly seated herself, Calpurnia had been
shocked by the strength of her desire to rattle the other
woman, to shake that serenity off her face: to make her
eyes widen and get a fear-sweat on that pale forehead.

Be careful, she told herself. *Know the difference between
the law's anger and your own.* Oh yes, *the* Lex Imperialis *is*

the timeless law of the Emperor, not the flickering whim of His servants. Oh, yes, but the maxims she had mastered back at Machiun and recited so recently in her self-denunciation sessions seemed lighter and more shallow here. They wrestled in her head with bright bursts of temper and a silver lode of migrainous pain.

Do your duty, Calpurnia told herself. *Without duty, what are you?*

'You don't want to make me chase the answers out of you, Mamzel Ylante,' she said aloud. 'Pay attention when I tell you that your best choice is to volunteer everything you know that might bear on what we're asking. I don't doubt that you can sense for yourself what kind of temper I'm in.'

'It isn't hard to deduce,' Ylante answered, her eyes deferentially lowered. 'Well, then, my comings and goings. Chief concordiasts do not work with other astropaths unless the Master orders it, or I – the chief concordiast in question – chooses to, and the Master agrees.' She looked down at her fingers lacing and unlacing in her lap, and Calpurnia took in the movement carefully.

'So, the chief concordiast generally has the freedom of the Master's chambers,' Ylante went on once she had collected her thoughts. 'My own investiture in the position wasn't complete – did I remember to introduce myself as chief concordiast-elect? Not finalised, you see. So by rights, I've the freedom to be here as I wish, but Otranto was to grant me the final keys and pass codes when I formally took on the mantle.'

'Which never happened,' Calpurnia said levelly.

'Which never happened.'

'Because Otranto died on the blade of a filth-hearted murderer,' put in Dast.

'It is as you say,' Ylante answered him.

'Before you had even had the chance to speak with him?' Calpurnia pressed.

'You are correct. I came here from Master Vedrier's Black Ship, three shipboard days ago, but Otranto and I... well, I was to rest after my journey. He was on his way to see me when he died. We never spoke again.' Was that the tiniest tremor in her voice?

'And you were in the concordiasts' cells when he died?'

'Yes. You'll have no trouble verifying that.'

'And how hard will it be,' boomed Dast, 'to *verify* that you are not part of the conspiracy that brought the Master low?'

He was carrying it off a little more theatrically than Calpurnia might have, but he got through to her. The knuckles of her laced hands went white, and she shut her eyes for a long moment.

'I was not Master Otranto's enemy,' she said at last, 'and I'm not frightened of whatever questions you ask about that, because they will show me to be right. Whatever it costs me as a concordiast, when you do know who killed my Master, I beg you the indulgence of letting me be there when you rip the skin off the conspiracy's back and show it to the light.'

THERE WAS SILENCE for moments more. Calpurnia tried to think on Ylante's words, to weigh them up and see if they rang true or whether they were camouflage for a crime.

'Master Chastener Dast. Continue.'

He shot her a sullen look. Calpurnia put her back to him and Ylante, and signalled to Bruinann and Rede to join her in the garden.

Calpurnia looked around – she could see why Ylante had come here to clear her mind. The only seat was a block of rough white stone by a miniature pond, its top carved into a slight bow for the comfort of the sitter. The path from the door to the seat had been cut ankle-deep into the floor and then filled with soft, springy moss, perfect for bare, sensitive feet. Outside the path, the ground was soft sand and carefully cultivated patches of lichen. A cluster of vines rose from the round pond, cable-thick and gnarl-barked, trailing bunches of glossy, narrow leaves as they climbed to a trellis high above. A rill of scented water ran down them, darkening the bark and dripping off the leaves like dew, pattering lightly onto the surface of the pool.

'What is it you need, madam arbitor?' asked Bruin-nan.

Calpurnia wondered if his tone was intended to be insolent. He and Rede, she remembered, knew the truth of her position, and Dast's authority over her.

'I've left the chastener in there to continue the questioning,' she said, 'and to preserve the impression to non-Arbites that I still hold my substantive rank.'

Why was she explaining herself to them? She gave herself a mental kick.

'You briefed me on station personnel, but not really on her. A quick rundown now, please: Ylante's background, and this prior relationship with Otranto that she seems to think is so important. My impression was that she came to the Tower aboard that Black Ship.'

'She *returned* aboard it, yes, when it put in here to provision,' Rede answered. 'Torma Ylante was a concordiast at the Tower in her early life. She was young, and a lot of the astropaths she worked with then are dead now, of course. The ones that she worked with who are still here to welcome her back are tough, the best and most powerful of them. Ylante's got old friends all through the senior tier of astropaths here.'

'Including the old Master,' Calpurnia finished.

'Just so.'

'Are we to trust her word? You've briefed me on what's going on among the astropaths about the succession to the Master's seat, with Otranto being so careless about a nominated heir. Is there a chance that she's the puppet of one of them, or could it be the other way around?'

Rede and Bruinann exchanged a look.

'Arbitor senioris,' Rede began carefully, 'may I respectfully ask how familiar you are with the work of the concordiasts? I wonder if perhaps you have misinterpreted some of your conversation with Mamzel Ylante.'

Calpurnia's flare of anger shocked her, as did the suddenness with which it evaporated and left just a queasy nervousness. She was sure that she could feel a crawling sensation on her skin. She took a moment to listen to the sound of water falling into the pond, and let a breath in and out.

'I don't pretend to be above error,' she said. 'Well, I hardly can, given my status, can I? All right, explain to me what I'm misunderstanding.'

Gracious humility had been the right tack. Rede's manner seemed to thaw somewhat.

'I can tell you, so you have an idea, ma'am, but if I can make a better suggestion: ask Ylante about it. I don't believe that she's our enemy, and she can tell you better than I can, so you understand it down to the bone. Better still–'

'Better still,' Calpurnia finished the thought, 'she can show me.'

MOST OF THE space in the Bastion Psykana had been cannibalised from something else entirely, from back before the old catastrophe had reduced the star fort to a hulk. Sometimes, the new function had some kinship with the old, as when the old Fleet Commissariat offices had become the Arbites precinct, although, Calpurnia or Bruinann, or anyone calling the precinct home, would have bristled at being thought of as another kind of commissar. The living quarters in the downdecks were used much as they always had been, and the Enginarium and the docks ran unchanged, albeit for different masters.

There had been changes too. The promenade decks down which the officers had once strolled beneath tall armoured windows, now held tight-packed chorister astropaths, manacled to their benches, their blind eyes indifferent to the view.

The bridge and Strategium at the keep's summit were now full of elaborate workshops for rendering and brewing oils and essences. Teams of junior concordiasts trained by Teeker Renz laboured over salves, tonics and incense for the concordiasts to use. They brought clarity and energy to their astropaths' minds, and soothed the wounds that the turbulence of the warp would leave in their spirits.

Below them were the staterooms that would have held the gate-captain and his household, now little more than lockers full of shelves and crates. Several of the old magazines had been turned into extra apothecaria, so necessary in a place whose basic work took such a toll on its people. It was odd to see stretcher-beds arrayed along walkways or conveyor racks that had once hefted giant shells for the weapon batteries or flak canisters for the point-defence turrets.

Torma Ylante and Shira Calpurnia walked through all of this, an arbitrator following. Ylante sketched out for Calpurnia the pulse and rhythm of the place, how it laboured, what it demanded. They watched Astropath Brom come down from the Eyrie of Echoes, after a rapid and easy trance. They watched Astropath Ankyne, groaning and lurching, come out of the Green Eyrie, after she had sent a tentative connection southward towards Gathalamor, and had been hit hard by an unexpectedly tough, warp turbulence coming the other way. They saw three members of a choir being rushed into

one of the apothecaria, after a momentary spike in an
energy flow caused a witchcullis to slam down on them.

Seeing the Bastion from the inside brought it home to
Calpurnia: this place was more than just another hive of
Imperial functionaries whose noses, as her commander
at Don-Croix liked to say, needed forcing a little further
into their work. This whole place was an engine, a light-
house, a junction box, and the green-shrouded
astropaths were both its operators and its components.
Their minds walked nearly every day in an otherworldly
hell storm whose nature Calpurnia barely pretended to
understand. It was impossible to treat the place as just
another nest of backsliders and suspects, and crash in
among them with maul swinging. She might as well
scatter a clip of shock-grenades among the enginseers
who tended the caged sun at the Bastion's core.

She wondered if Dast understood that. This hunt
would be more complex – how could he not see it? The
shackle of his authority was maddening; having to play-
act at being in charge made it more so. If she had
command of this investigation properly and for real,
she could…

No. She was in her role by judgement of the Adeptus
Arbites, which was the judgement of the *Lex Imperia* and
therefore of Him on Earth. Her duty was not to indulge
her pride and her fantasies of command; her duty was
to serve the law, whatever it required of her. Her duty
would not find her wanting. Without her duty, she
asked herself, echoing the question that generations of
Calpurnii had been taught to ask, what was she?

THEY CAME AT last to the watch-hall and emerged from
the claustrophobic entry tunnel onto steps cut into the
steep slope of the floor. The watch-hall was a cylinder
sweeping up from the long-sealed torpedo magazines at
a forty-three degree angle. The sides of the cylinder

swept out and away to meet thirty metres above their heads. They shone with a deep glow and lustre. Copper and brass plates rode over and under, and interleaved all across the walls. Their patterns seemed to Calpurnia to be a strange mix of careful symmetry and thrown-together jumble. Here and there, clusters of pennants hung in the tilted tunnel, like the ones she had seen in the corridors, and she saw knotted and braided ropes a little like those in Otranto's pseudo-vineyard. Some held oddly shaped pieces of metal or stonework sus-pended at their ends, others simply swayed in the breezes from the ventilator holes in the walls.

Sounds surrounded them, shivering out of the air: strange notes like a rubbed wineglass, the plangent sound of harp strings or tuning-fork thrums. As they went further down the steps, sharing them more and more with scurrying young runners and slump-shouldered servitors carrying messages and order seals, Calpurnia started to see the sounds' source. The pitch of the tunnel let her look straight out from the stairs to a swathe of silo roof, and she could see the nests and platforms cut into the silo all around her. Each one was built next to, or was even part of, a web of shining wire, clusters of glass and metal plates. Some put her in mind of wind chimes, some of chandeliers. At some, an operator hung strapped into the array or perched by it, others were tended by flitting servitor-cherubs.

There was something maddening about it: the way that the gong-like note from a hanging copper plate might be slightly, eye-wateringly out of sync with the way the plate moved. The way the sounds seemed to grow louder or softer in ways that bore no relation to the Arbites' movements, or simply that there was no vis-ible force making any of these things vibrate and sound, was disturbing. Part of Calpurnia was enchanted in a way that she rarely allowed herself to be. Part of her was fighting the urge to clap her hands to her ears and run, howling, for an exit.

As Calpurnia twisted to look around her again, cramps ripped up from her thigh muscles and into her belly. She had to wait for the spots to clear from her eyes before she could focus on the next step down.

IN OTRANTO'S ROOMS, Master Chastener Dast was sweating freely. He loathed the feel of it: the slickness of his brow and neck, his sodden garments. He forced himself to breathe evenly, and stood in front of Orovene for more than a minute with his gauntleted hands resting on the reliquary box. Dast was not one for memorised prayers, so he simply concentrated on the lines of the *Auctorita Imperialis* until he brought his thoughts back under control.

Meanwhile, Orovene was working his mouth as if it had gone dry, and was swallowing with a clicking sound. They made a poor picture, the two of them, and a counterpoint to Rede and Bruinann, who were standing cool and at ease on either side of the Master's bed. That triggered a welling of red temper up Dast's throat that it took him whole seconds to suppress. He turned to them, refusing to allow his hands to make fists.

'You've had far more time and access to this chamber than we have,' he said to them. 'Tell me. Run me through the things I've missed. Both of you have been conspicuous by your silence for a while now.' Neither of them, in point of fact, had said a word to him since Calpurnia and Ylante had left them there. Rede and Bruinann looked at one another.

'Are you asking,' Rede began, 'for a recap of the briefings we gave y–'

'Calpurnia may want to sit and shuffle papers until her fingers shrivel,' Dast said. 'I'll use my own eyes.' He caught himself, but they had already heard the contradiction in his words; he could see it in their eyes. He could bring a dozen accusations against them for that – but there would be time for that later. He needed self-control. He exerted it.

'The assassin struck at a distance, not by hand,' he said. 'Respond.'

'The wound in the corpse is that of a blade, a deep and narrow stabbing,' said Rede. 'We read from that and the bloodstain that the weapon came up at an angle, too steep for a projectile unless the killer lay on the floor at his feet. No scorching or blast residue on Otranto's clothes, no projectile in the wound, no scent of gun smoke or las-burn – the sniffers in the air vents system would have picked that up.'

'There are assassin weapons that can strike just that way,' said Dast.

'True,' Rede answered, 'but I have eighty-seven informants under my thumb on this station, and spy craft besides, and I don't believe that any such weapon could have been fired in here, and then smuggled back with none of my cat's-paws noticing. Believe me when I say that they wouldn't lie about it if they had.'

Dast grunted, unconvinced, and a quick spark of anger marked the woman's eye for just a moment. Rede knew her ring of spies and informants through the Tower was sub-par for what a detective-espionist of her rank could be expected to muster, and she knew it would not be long before Dast and Calpurnia knew it too. She had until the Otranto investigation was over to shore her work up until it would pass muster in the arbitor senioris's eyes. She'd had three years of routine reports and communiqués, three years for her to get comfortable, and now this.

Dast had asked something and she had missed it, but Bruinann had stepped in.

'We don't believe the murderer lay in wait here, no. He was able to enter and exit without leaving a trace, but again, the aerator systems would have registered his presence. Magos Channery has charged their machine-spirit to keep itself alive in all the engines across the Tower. It will notice how much air it needs to circulate into a room to keep it fresh. That means that over time it notices the difference between an empty room and one that someone's breathing in.'

'Will it notice that someone in the room has a nurture-mask, or a rebreather mouthpiece?' demanded Dast. 'There are records of assassins entering trances until they wake themselves up and start their work. How many of this station's people – the subjects of your precinct, Bruinann – have been trained by our own holy Adeptus in how to control their bodies and minds?'

'We accept the possibility,' said Bruinann, 'but we know that, although when he left the Concourse Otranto was in a hurry, in the cloisters, he was running as if six colours of xenos hell were after him. You saw how he broke through the furnishings in those outer rooms. It still seems to us that the best conclusion we can make is that Otranto was chased in here by his killer.'

'Who then exited through *that*, locks and seals and all?' Dast swept an arm at the great door, the contempt for their conclusion obvious in his voice.

Rede answered him with careful respect.

'Master chastener, the man was alive when the door was closed, and dead when it was opened again and he was found. You are left with the fact that the killer escaped from a sealed chamber, no matter how you believe he entered it.'

Dast gave an irritable flap of the hand and went back to inspecting the door. Drops of sweat stood out in his beard. Rede and Bruinann shared a short, sour look.

'Perhaps, sir,' Bruinann said, 'this would be the best time to return to the precinct and review your findings?

The verispex reports will be there, and now that we've got some idea of your thinking, we can pick out the reports from Rede's agents and work out who'll be of most value to you. I don't intend any insolence when I say that perhaps you've got as much out of inspecting these rooms as you're going to get, for the time being.'

Dast's shoulders shook, and for the first time since these new Arbites had arrived on the station, Bruinann felt fear, a stab of pure and direct fear. Then the chastener turned, and startled him by managing a small smile.

'You're correct, of course, aedile, and thank you. I'm a chastener, not, well, you're right, this place has already been,' he paused for a moment, 'uh, better eyes than mine. You're correct. I realise I have a lot to digest.'

Bruinann wondered whether this was a trick or a genuine effort. It seemed too weird to be a tactic. He'd ask Rede later on, she was better at spotting these things than he was.

'Is the font-water in that garden drinkable?' Orovene managed to get out. His voice was badly parched and cracking.

'No ague in it, or witch-taint?' Dast followed up, twisting his mouth at 'witch-taint'.

'Safe to drink, sir,' said Rede. 'Master Otranto would drink it with his guests sometimes. I'll show you where the ladle is.' She led Orovene into the garden, and Dast turned for the door.

'I'll wait for you outside,' he told Bruinann. 'I'm hoping the air will be cooler in the halls. Seal the door when we leave. Have someone find out where Calpurnia went and get her back to the precinct. She can help me go through these documents of yours.'

The break in the clouds had been brief and the chastener's old demeanour was creeping back. Bruinann saluted, and waited until Dast was well out of the room and on his way through the vineyard before he broke the salute and went to pass on the orders. *You're not out of this yet*, he told himself. *Be careful.*

Dast wondered if the air on his skin as he moved was cooling him, or if it was just a fancy – the rime of sweat seemed so thick that it was sealing him in, as stupid an idea as that sounded. Dashing the water off his skin seemed to make things worse, sending flashes of heat and weird electricity through him. His voice was sounding odd and reedy, and something perpetually dogged the edge of his thoughts, as if he was about to remember or understand something, which never came into focus.

Focus, that was it, he had to focus. As he left Otranto's chambers, he could hear Bruinann passing on his instructions, and an echoing slurping from the garden where Orovene was trying to drain the pool, by the sound of it. It was unbecoming; words would be needed. As far as Dast was concerned, the preacher was part of his command crew, pitiful as that crew was: a preacher who couldn't control his bodily needs, and a disgraced convict dressed in a facade of her former rank.

His thoughts revved feverishly as he walked through the vineyard. They all needed to keep control. Bruinann and Rede knew they were going to face scrutiny. If there was trouble, the off-station Arbites needed to show a united front.

The voices he heard coming from the antechamber startled him out of his thoughts.

'Look, I'm not making trouble, I told you, I'm here on orders.' It wasn't the proctor's voice. Someone seemed to be trying to haggle their way in. 'I'm here to speak with Mamzel Ylante and the arbitor senioris. Orders, see?'

'This is your last chance and your last order,' the proctor snapped back. 'One more attempt to order an arbitor around will see you racked for contempt of law. State your petition or return to your post, and be thankful that we've got better business to attend to than giving you what you deserve.'

'Any petition you have to put to Arbitor Calpurnia, you can put to me,' declaimed Dast, striding out into the antechamber. Humility be damned, Calpurnia might be the figurehead, but he didn't have to pretend that he was powerless. 'I am Master Chastener Dast. I am co-ordinating the arbitor senioris's investigation, and you may salute when y–'

He was halfway through the door to the outer foyer when his mind skidded like a boot on smooth mud. It was enough to throw him physically against the threshold, and when the metal Arbites seal came around like a flail, and crashed into the side of his head, it sent him the rest of the way to the floor, limbs limp and mind black.

CHAPTER SEVEN

'TORMA YLANTE. WELCOME to the watch-hall, concordiast-elect. I hadn't expected to meet you here.' The watchmaster's whisper came when they had barely started down the stone causeway that led to his cage. It should never have been audible to them in the first place, but Calpurnia still heard it clearly.

The watchmaster sat in a sling-chair hanging from the bars, his head nodding under a heavy halo of augmetics and leads. The skin of his hands was as soft and smooth as a child's. He stroked and shuffled the engraved cards of an Emperor's Tarot deck. He had already dealt two cards onto a shelf-like table suspended in front of him.

Calpurnia controlled the urge to peer in and see what cards he'd dealt – bad luck, she'd been told once, to do that.

'Come down and sit with me. One to each side, thank you. There's a symmetry to it. It will be very pleasing. My duty is to be so careful of such symmetries. There,

you see?' He seemed to be referring to a quick series of
minor-key notes, a slightly clashing arpeggio from a
rack of wires and chimes high above them. 'It's so rare
to find such a balance. I'd show a card for it, had I one
to spare.' The knuckles of his hands grew white on the
edges of the ivory tarot cards. Calpurnia half-rose,
mouth open, to say something, but on the other side of
the cage, Ylante caught her eye and firmly shook her
head. An attendant in a dusty-blue veil and gown had
come down the walkway, and Ylante curtly beckoned –
him, her? – over.

'A bottle of red graft-balm, please,' she said, 'and a
gauze wand. Mix Tincture of Unzeo into the balm as
you bring it, not more than half a dozen drops.' The
attendant blinked at Ylante from under its hood for a
moment, and then jumped – Calpurnia guessed that
the watchmaster had seconded the command with a
thought. As the shrouded figure hurried away, a wheezing sound floated out of the cage: the watchmaster was
chuckling.

'How long have you been away, Torma? It gets hard
for us to know how time is going, you know, once the
fire gets in us, but it's obviously been a long time. It's
been a couple of generations of attendants since I've
had tincture on my skull. I feel the pressure, Torma, and
the weight, and the work of pushing myself out through
the plugs, but don't trouble yourself about my skin.' He
chuckled again, hard enough to set some of the skull-
cables to clinking. 'Let them bring the tincture if it
pleases you. Change keeps them attentive.'

'You like catching me out, don't you, Chevenne?'
Ylante answered him amiably. 'You always did.'

'These people are not the only ones who have to be
kept attentive,' said Chevenne, some of the joking tone
evaporating from his voice. 'You're a fine concordiast,
Ylante, but your fault was always that you forgot who

was the servant. Otranto has a terrible habit of letting his servants act like his peers. That fop who replaced you hasn't been much better. Proper order has been in too short supply here.' He flicked a third card hard down onto the table, and then a fourth. His fingers stroked the images picked out on their rough bone faces. 'Three ascending cards of the Mandatio, a preoccupation with order. I am wandering, and drawing my reading after me: too far unbalanced, no good now.'

Ylante's face remained expressionless as the watchmaster bent his face to the cards. For a moment, Calpurnia was sure that some kind of silvery haze or tarnish passed over the bright sockets around his skull. Then he made a series of quick motions, moving the cards slightly crooked, breaking up their symmetry. Another moment and he had restored them to his deck with deft, practiced darts of his hands.

Two attendants, a man and a woman, had approached down the causeway, shrouded in the same livery as the first. The man hunkered down at the back of the cage, and carefully unstoppered a ceramic jar. The woman leaned against the cage bars, and began rattling off a schedule in a throaty, musical voice.

'Two hours are left on your watch, sir. I am asked to bring to your attention that Cantor Rhyshko is standing down from the Green Eyrie, and Cantor Mecklin is undergoing preparations to replace him. Astropath Ehlin is required to send a message to Xu Primaris station in fifty minutes. He has been preparing with two concordiasts and will be in the Eyrie of Bones in half an hour.'

Through all this, the gangly man was dipping a gauze-wrapped taper into the jar and reaching a lanky arm through the cage bars, dabbing a spicy-smelling ointment onto the watchmaster's scalp around his skull plugs. His attention to the delicate movements of his hand was total.

'Ehlin has asked for Astropaths Slocha and Weth to support him,' the woman went on, 'but Astropath Golan has come out of the Firewatch Eyrie, and from his reports Ehlin will need a full choir behind him to push through as far as Xu. Cantor Angazi is assembling choirs on the third and fourth seclusion decks. Two small choirs will be in communion with the relay at Bescalion, and will shift their attention to Hydraphur proper at the turn of the hour. Astropath Pharnele will spend the second hour in the Eyrie of Echoes to be ready for ciphers coming in from the Obscuras border.'

'Ehm, is Pharnele up to it?' Chevenne's plangent whisper seemed to owe nothing to his physical voice. 'We'll have put him in the Echoes for a reason.'

'He has Arch-Cantor Aderkin preparing him, and both choir-decks at the Echoes are full. The marshal has diverted three junior concordiasts to work with the ciphers, once he has them, but he does suggest–'

'If Pharnele's still going to be riding the warp when I leave the cage, woman, I won't tolerate any risk.' The watchmaster's hands gripped the edge of the shelf for a moment and the head tilted from side to side. 'Close all the inner cullises around the lower Echo. Who's in the Lantern Eyrie?'

'Astropath Ankyn, sir, with two wardens, and Cantor Nyri and one of his acolytes.'

'Peh, that explains a lot. You're lucky you told me about the extra weight on her, straight up. Clear Ankyn out of the Lantern and have her between cullises at the very least by the time Pharnele begins. There's been a leaden cloud over that whole quarter throughout my watch, and I'll damn well have it unravelled before I sleep, do you understand?'

'Yes, watchmaster.' The bumptious tone was gone from the woman's voice.

'Why is Ankyn in the Lantern and not the Green Eyrie?' The watchmaster asked peevishly.

'The marshal's instructions, watchmaster, shall I ask him to–'

'Ask him why that woman's not under guard in the Green Eyrie, and bring me the answer. Your companion there is done, I think.'

The attendant wittered for a moment, and then bowed. It took three increasingly emphatic jabs into the man's shoulder before he started, looked at her and stood up. A minute after that, the watchmaster, Ylante and Calpurnia were alone once again at the tip of the walkway.

'WHAT WAS THAT?' asked Calpurnia after a moment of silence. 'In fact, what is going on here? That conversation? Is there some emergency coming that I need to know about? Watchmaster Chevenne, you're the one who was on, er, watch when the murder took place?' She felt herself start to gabble. Dignity, she told herself.

'Brittle little creature, aren't you?' the watchmaster twanged in her ears. 'Not a match for Ylante at all, in point of fact. I'll have to station you… thirteen metres away and directly opposite her, or slightly above.'

Calpurnia blinked, hard. Her eyes were aching as if she'd been reading all day. Sheer disorientation made her dizzy for a moment, like a diver in deep water loses track of the direction to the surface. She grabbed her thoughts and forced them back into order.

There was a soft, teeth-on-edge buzz from over her shoulder, and she looked around. A servitor-cherub bobbed in the air behind her on wings inlaid with suspensor vanes. Orange-yellow eyes regarded her through the slits in a scowling gargoyle mask grafted to the thing's face.

'You're more distressed than you're admitting,' Ylante observed calmly as Calpurnia shied away from the thing. It glided forwards as she tried to increase the distance between them, staying less than half a metre away from her head. She found herself wanting to bat it away. 'That's why it's marking you,' Ylante said from the other side of the cage. 'Concentrate on controlling your breathing first, and when you've settled into a relaxing rhythm–'

'I *don't* need breathing exercises, Ylante. Have this thing called off, or be ready to have it replaced.' She brought the maul up and thumbed it into action. The hell with formal reserve.

After a moment, she realised that the strange dead leaves-blowing sound was Chevenne laughing.

'Torma, be the obliging concordiast and go to the Marshal's pulpit. Let's identify the marker she complains about so, and gag it. Leave it in place. We'll just do without the voice. Off you go.'

Her composure finally giving way to a slapped expression, Ylante left them, and the watchmaster shifted. That was Calpurnia's overwhelming impression: that he shifted and turned in his cage, his head questing around to her. The impact of his full attention turning to her was like a physical force, but when she looked into the cage, she saw that the man hadn't moved.

'You're an interesting one,' the watchmaster told her. 'Normally I'm better at first judgements. What does *sizzling* mean?'

She was more on guard for the question this time, and didn't let it trouble her. Dvorov, the arbitor majore who was her supreme commander on Hydraphur, liked lightning changes of subject like this.

'The word was at the front of your mind for a moment,' said Chevenne when she didn't answer. 'You were thinking about balance.'

For a moment, the air between Calpurnia and the cage darkened. Her eyes seemed to pick out washes of colour in the air: black, purple, a pallid white like unpigmented skin. A quick, stinging ache in her eye and head, and it was gone. 'Then your balance shifted and that was an end to it. Your control is actually rather good. It's a–'

There was a burst of sound from below them. The watchmaster stiffened for a moment. A gluey taste swam across Calpurnia's tongue and the barbed queasiness was back in her gut. Behind her, the cherub shrilled loudly for a moment and fell silent.

'It's a different control from Ylante's,' the watchmaster said through the trills of sound around them. 'Different control from Ylante's,' he repeated as two swirls of corposant orbited his head for a moment, and unbraided themselves into worms of light that crawled along the bars of his cage. 'Different control from Ylante's,' he said a third time a moment later, in a normal voice, 'Tougher, in a way. You exert aggression on yourself, not serenity.'

'I don't appreciate you tunnelling into my mind unasked, astropath,' Calpurnia told him coldly, deliberately demoting him with her address. 'You'll learn better than that, or regret it.'

'There now,' the watchmaster said. 'There was no, hah, "tunnelling", asked for, or otherwise. I don't know that I'd have the strength to bore into you nowadays without a chorus to carry me. It radiated off you, madam arbitrator. Are you…' A pale tongue moistened the thin lips as the watchmaster looked for an analogy, '…are you somehow attacking the sun by feeling the warmth it throws on you?'

'Nevertheless, watchmaster, you can consider yourself on notice. However… *affected* by this environment you might think me, I'll have my office given the respect it's due. Believe me, these are not times when this Bastion can afford to backslide and forget the law.'

'Of course,' said Chevenne, his voice, carefully free of snappishness or mockery. 'You are the Arbitor Senioris Shira Calpurnia, here to punish the murderer of my colleague and friend the Master Otranto, and to command the station while you select his successor. I know.'

'The station command has yet to be settled,' said Calpurnia, too truthful to allow that one past. 'The appointment of a new Master will not be my concern.' By the time that issue came up, Calpurnia would be back at Hydraphur, giving account for the Phrax Mutiny. Perhaps they would try her in the same courtroom on Selena Secundus where that bloodbath had begun. She stamped on the thought.

'I do nothing unasked, madam arbitor,' said the watchmaster carefully, 'but I don't need to *see*, to know that you're troubled here today. Perhaps a rest might–'

'Not your concern,' she snapped. 'We'll continue.'

'As you say,' the watchmaster answered, and fell silent again for a moment, as something seemed to occupy his attention. There were no new chimes or tones, not that Calpurnia could hear, but at the upper edge of her vision, she thought she saw a stirring, a pair of cherubs drifting towards one another to meet at a bell-harp that seemed to be shaking slightly.

'All right, then. That. What was that? This is some kind of giant surveillance auspex, is it not? Do you monitor the voices going to and from the Bastion?'

The pale head shook, and the braided cables rustled and clicked against each other.

'From here, mamzel, I watch *us*: the astropaths and the Bastion. My role is patterns and balances. The watchmaster must make sure that the symmetries that build up in the Tower are rare, and controlled, and coaxed away from the destructive. It is subtle work.'

'Explain,' said Calpurnia.

Torma Ylante had made her way back down the platform to join them; she sat back down on the other little seat, but did not interrupt.

'I can best explain by analogies that would match with your own experiences. If you will allow me to look for an image in you that I might base–'

'No.'

There was a pause.

'Very well. You're familiar with the work of the senior enginseers of the Priesthood of Mars? The ones who tend the plasma furnaces that warm ships and stations like this one?'

'I know a little.'

'My understanding has always been that the balance of forces inside those plasma cages is a delicate thing. There is both a craft and an art to running it smoothly. Well, have you met Magos Channery?'

'No.'

Another pause.

'Smoke,' said the watchmaster. 'Black and crimson. Odd, but then I'll use something more human. There's part of your brain that controls your balance.'

'In the ears, I was once told.' The watchmaster made a small dismissive gesture with one hand, but Calpurnia let it pass.

'Think in a broader sense,' he said. 'Those twists in your brain that tell when you've got a sickness, when and where you're injured. Controls that make you sweat when you're hot, or put a thirst on your tongue when your body feels itself drying out. Do you follow me?'

'Yes.'

The watchmaster hung in silence for a few moments, 'Are you the nerve centre that governs this for the station, watchmaster?' Calpurnia asked. 'Was that why

you were talking about a lead weight, something to do
with the station's balance?'

The watchmaster gave a tiny, delicate snort, and when
he spoke some of the snappishness came back to his
voice.

'You're not going to understand the fact of it, judge-
woman, because you were born brain-blunted, without
what you need to see what I do. Truly see it. Therefore,
I'm going to use some ways of talking it out that you
will understand, providing that you also understand
that I'm scrawling in the mud, trying to draw the stars.
Think upon that for a moment.'

'I think I have the idea, watchmaster. Continue.'

'Hm. The watch-hall deals in… movements: energies,
patterns and weight. Have you… can you imagine riding on a raft? Imagine the raft rocking on a heavy sea.
You share the raft with others, many others, holding
torches in their hands, burning. Beautiful white fire…'
The words had started to tumble over one another as
the watchmaster became more sure of his subject, but
for a moment, they tailed off into a sigh. 'If they move
too fast on a part of the raft it will tilt, and if they cluster too thickly together the heat of their torches will
combine and burn them, and if they are not shepherded by someone who can see the whole raft, feel its
tilts and see where the torches are burning dangerously
bright…'

'I am starting to see. You are in this room to look out
over the raft. You keep it trimmed.'

'Trimming, is that two dimensions, or three? And the
forces are mass, gravity, and perhaps a little motion.'
The snap of pride was back in his voice. Calpurnia
found a moment to wonder about the watchmaster's
young days, where he had learned to think of water and
rafts before the Black Ships had carried him away.
'There's so much more for me to see, Calpurnia. The fire

burned away the lid to a keener eye than any that were taken out of my face, and when it was lit with the fire inside me, it gave me the strength to look out and see things...'

Calpurnia was attuned, now, to the way the watchmaster's moods swung from terse and proud, to dreamy and reflective, and back again.

'The watchmaster directs the movements of psykers, and their placement in the eyries and the choir halls,' Ylante took up when the watchmaster had gone for a dozen breaths without speaking. 'He senses the astropaths' minds and moods. He warns where concordiasts may be needed to soothe, and where the physical proximity of too many astropaths needs to be regulated or broken up. He senses where the distribution of psyker-minds through the Tower is inadvertently forming a pattern that will build reverberations, distil destructive humours into minds, or attract... attention. Astropaths must concentrate on controlling their own minds, keeping their footing on the raft, if you like. Their attention is directed inwards. The watchmaster looks the opposite way.'

'And all of this?' Calpurnia swept an arm around to take in the hall, the ringing, chiming arrays, and the hurrying servitors and orderlies.

'My nerves!' The watchmaster's voice was a bark of amusement that made Calpurnia jump. 'A nerve-centre must have nerves to be at the centre of, mustn't it?'

'They're like a display, an alarm array, what?'

'Consider,' the watchmaster said, and began to talk.

Later, Calpurnia had trouble remembering any one detail of what followed, although she tried hard to bring hard facts and words to mind. The sounds and colours, the watchmaster's words and the odd sensations still haunting her body, each one became a hazy brush-stroke in a soft picture that was all shades of light. He talked about how the sounds corresponded to certain places in the Tower, eyries or choir-halls, passages or stairs. He talked about their significance: what an individual scale meant, or a single trill, or what was signified by a shift of keys, or the sudden clashes or harmonies. He spoke of how the shuffling servitors or gliding cherubs might act as mobile markers, gravitating to a certain point to add warning tones or counter-harmonies to modulate a message. He explained how the vibrations in their air sang in his ears and in his mind, tuning his awareness exquisitely fine, and keeping all the bright psyker-voices of the Tower in harmony and balance.

She took no notes, and she could not remember all the places and names that floated through the watch-master's conversation. When he asked her if she had heard enough, and she finally nodded in answer, his time in the watch-hall was not due to end, and they left him there, hanging in his harness and cage, the air alive with sound.

As she walked away, Calpurnia was sure that something had slipped her mind. The thought nagged away at her. She tried to place it, as she and Ylante climbed up out of the watch-hall, but failed. The sensation had been dogging her ever since she had arrived in the keep, and by the time they were back out in the cloisters, it had faded into the general mess of sensations that were sleeting through her head.

WATCHMASTER CHEVENNE LET an idle strand of his mind follow the two women away. Most of his physical senses had been deadened many years ago, driven out of his nerve-endings by the great white fire. However, his psychic touch was subtle enough to pick up a hint of scent from the collar of Ylante's gown, the gleam of Calpurnia's carapace, the texture of her hair, and a faint tracery of ghost-pain from her forehead, arm and hip that was so old that she probably didn't even feel it any more.

Chevenne had long since lost any ambition of his own to the Mastership. Some astropaths' minds only grew stronger through years of wrestling their messages across the stars, but his had been stretched thin over all his years in the eyries, with warp-winds trying to buffet his sanity out through his ears. The Master of the Tower had to be a fully empowered astropath, that law was beyond question, but Chevenne had no stomach for that work any more. Hanging in the watchmaster's cage, using the exquisite psychic control he had learned in the eyries, was a calling that he believed would suit him perfectly well, until the furnace the Soul Binding had lit in him guttered out, and his spirit went before the Emperor for the second, and final, time.

The air in the keep tasted of ambition to him now. There was a burred texture in the mesh of minds that would have set his teeth on edge had those teeth not died and dropped out long ago. There were minds in the Tower who looked forward to Mastery, oh yes.

None of them had murdered Master Otranto, Chevenne was sure of it. The thought was intolerable. His dead eyes crimped in pain as he remembered the afterwash, bouncing along the psyk-conduits and echoing like the thunderclaps that had been the terror of his boyhood on the oceans of Chaoku-Minor. Nowhere in that roil had he made out the shape, sound, scent of anyone he knew. The murderer couldn't have been anyone from the Tower. It couldn't have…

That didn't mean that there would be no strife. Many astropaths didn't care about the Mastership, their minds walking in grander places than this little station. Others might covet it, however, now that damnable rumours about the Polarists coming out of the southern segmentum were rife. Then there were genuine ambitions, Sacredsteel's and Thujik's the worst of them, honed sharp by Otranto's odd behaviours, as the Black Ship drew near amid rumours that he was going to step down. The ambitious minds were brought to a frustrated boil when the old man had announced that Torma Ylante would come aboard from the Black Ship as his new concordiast. A more stinging rebuttal to the rumours of his resignation would have been hard to imagine.

What was happening now? Chevenne had taken for granted that Calpurnia was here to seize the Bastion and rule it until the crisis was over – everyone knew that was part of the remit of the Arbites. Telepathica dictates about the Mastership going to an astropath be damned – the *Lex Imperia* could trump that, and Chevenne's masters could say nothing on the subject. He'd heard the stories of Arbites blowing open ancient Adeptus positions when the law told them that those positions had been incompetently filled.

Instead of marching aboard at the head of a taskforce, however, she was sniffing around Otranto's rooms and asking about the watch-hall, marching out and leaving a trail of black and crimson across his mind's eye. Chevenne had wondered about that two-coloured cloud as she had sat beside him, the coiled tension in her mind such a contrast to the symmetry and stillness of Ylante's. Black and crimson: he didn't normally perceive colours like that.

As his awareness reached out to touch the delicate song of the watch-hall, and out past it to the psychic lifeblood of the Tower, Watchmaster Chevenne's fingers kept brushing the topmost card in his Tarot deck, unconsciously tracing the image of the judge. His other hand, tucked deep in his robes, gripped the token that Master Lohjen had given him when he had ordered

Chevenne to report everything that he heard or sensed from the arbitor's words and mind.

Concordiast Dechene wanted to go hunting for Renz, but didn't want to admit it. Admitting it would have meant admitting that Renz's paranoid stress actually made him feel calmer and more in control himself. That in turn would have meant admitting that he was nervous. He didn't want to admit that he was nervous.

Although, he had a right, everything was so uncertain since the old bastard had been – had died. Who the hell had known that the Arbites would be here so quickly, or that the stakes would rise so high so fast? Hadn't he earned a little nerv–

No! It was fundamental to Dechene's concept of himself: he did not get frightened or uncertain. He caused those feelings in others, but did not accept them in himself. Once his concept of himself started to crack, how could he be sure of anything?

He scowled at Kyto, who had the balls not to flinch. Dechene admired him for that, but it still made him angry.

'So where is he, then?'

'I told you, Dechene, I haven't seen him for two shifts. He was half-gone with neuroses before that Black Ship docked, and he's worse now. You know him better than I do. You tell me where he went. I don't have time to saunter all over the damn tower looking for him.'

The two men kept their voices low as they sauntered, hands behind backs, down the Grand Concourse towards the docks, a servitor trailing them with a lantern held over their heads on a pole. Not many officers of Kyto's rank had the clout to requisition a servitor-adjutant, so it was a useful reminder to anyone who saw them out in public. They were friends and confidants of Teeker Renz, and although the Master who favoured Renz was dead, he and his associates still had influence.

'Well, nor have I,' the concordiast retorted. 'I've been on errands too, you know. Errands of Renz's, and I'd have thought the wittering idiot would have made himself easier to find if it was so important to him.'

'It's a finesse thing,' Kyto said. 'By the accounts I've heard, this woman's a little harder at the edges than that Bruinann fool. Perhaps Renz is making sure that we aren't seen as a group all the time?' He looked at the other man's expression. 'You're young, Dechene. You only really remember Teeker being Otranto's pet, and us being Teeker's mates. That's not always going to be the order of things, unless we all get a bit more careful making it that way. Arbites have a habit of rattling whatever they start stamping around near, this Calpurnia especially. She smashes whatever she touches. Don't you remember how crazy things got after that stupid rogue trader shootout at Galata? And she cost Sambin de Jauncey his gate-captain's commission. His whole family felt that one.'

'I don't care, and you shouldn't talk to me like that.' Dechene's expression had turned petulant.

'It's something you need to hear. It's about time you came up against a problem you couldn't just thug your way past. We need to use our brains, watch what Renz is trying to do and try and learn why he's doing it.'

'The Arbites should be afraid of us, not the other way around,' grumbled Dechene. 'I'm allowed to say it, aren't I?' he added, catching Kyto's reproving look. 'You're not an informant, and neither am I. Anyway, this woman's going to have a bit more to worry about than taking away what's ours.' He managed to grin. 'She deserves it, too. I say they all do.'

CHAPTER EIGHT

MASTER CHASTENER DAST lay on the apothecarion bed like a stone martyr on a tomb-slab. Orovene, reliquary box finally out of his hands, but the smell of lho-smoke back around him, stood at the foot of the bed, humming soft prayers, as an arbitor medicae ran his fingertips softly over the wounds in Dast's skull and face. The chastener didn't twitch as the medicae's deft touch probed the crushed parts of his face. His breathing was laboured and there was a bad grey cast to his skin.

The precinct medicae ward was tiny, and Calpurnia, small as she was, had to stand back to make room. She stood with her hands neatly behind her back, fighting the urge to just sag against the wall.

'Master Orovene tells me that he was alone when the attack came,' murmured the doctor, so low that it took Calpurnia a moment to realise that the man wasn't addressing himself.

'Not alone,' Orovene said, 'alone but for his attacker. The rest of us were in the Master's garden.'

'Madam arbitor senioris?' Orovene's expression darkened at the medicae's dismissive tone, but he said nothing.

'I can't add anything,' Calpurnia said. 'I was elsewhere, with Concordiast Ylante. I only just came away and returned directly here.' She had been walking back through the cloisters when the runner had brought the news; from there, it had been a flat run for the precinct compound. Ylante had kept pace with the scowling, hunched gait of one not used to running.

Still bent over Dast, the medicae looked up at her from under his dark-grey eyebrows. One hand stayed on the chastener's forehead while the other reached out and finger-walked along a rack of tiny drawers.

'May I ask, madam arbitor senioris, if the watch-hall had noted any kind of discord or alarm while you were there? What did Watchmaster Chevenne have to report to you?'

'Nothing.' All that time being lectured about what the watch-hall was for, and she hadn't thought to use it as a detective tool. Well, technically, she'd given a right answer… but no, only cowards hid from their mistakes.

'I didn't ask him. We talked about his work, but the talk went mostly to the nature of his duties.' She thought about it. 'He referred to some of the patterns he was observing in the Tower while I was present, but he didn't volunteer anything about the kind of disturbance a brawl and a death must have created.'

As she spoke, she was trying to replay her surreal visit to the watch-hall in her head: had Chevenne hinted at anything she should have picked up on? Had she heard anything that she should have asked the meaning of?

Orovene was still looking down at Dast and repeating his litany, over and over. Calpurnia recognised it from

medicae halls from Hydraphur to Machiun. The words
wove between Low and High Gothic, poetry and
homily, but the message stayed the same. *The sickbed is
poison to us,* she breathed along with Orovene, *grow
strong in the name of the Emperor's law and rise from it to
your duty. The Emperor's name is your armour; the Emperor's
commandments are your strength. The Emperor's voice
speaks to turn your wounds to scars and your pain to the cold
work of punishment...*

Saying the litany sent memories flitting around her
mind like bats startled out of a cave. Without her knowing it, Calpurnia's hand crept to her head, and her
fingers began massaging the scars over her eye.

'Do we know what killed the proctor, then?' she
asked. 'If that's what he did to Dast with the seal, I have
to think that it wasn't the chastener's response that
killed him.'

'The master chastener didn't respond to the attack at
all,' Orovene said, interrupting his monotone. 'It was
too quick and hurt him too badly. If he'd had the
chance to fight, we'd be sitting in that office upstairs
asking him ourselves. Trust me, Calpurnia, when I tell
you that the proctor and two more of him wouldn't
have bested Dast with his guard up.'

A slightly pained look had crept onto the medicae's
face. The man was studiously examining Dast's head
wound again. He had already attached a coronet of
diagnostor runes to Dast's skull: telltales shone red, and
every so often one would give a tiny chime like the
watch-hall bells.

Calpurnia caught his expression.

'How well did you know the proctor, arbitor?' she
asked him a little more gently. 'Were you friends? And
forgive me, I haven't asked your name.'

'Not close, Mamzel Calpurnia,' he said, although he
didn't look up from his work, 'but it's too small a

garrison for us not to know one another. I knew a little about Proctor Pheissen. He was a good man. I'd give a lot to know what brought him to a death like that.' He paused to secure another diagnostor stud in place, and watched the flicker of its indicator-lights for a moment. 'My name is Scall. Arbitor-Medicae Eschoen Scall, if it please the arbitor general.' His manner was relaxing a little, and Calpurnia allowed herself a flicker of satisfaction. She'd managed to get something right, anyway.

'You know that there have to be questions, Arbitor Scall,' she said, with a soft emphasis on 'arbitor'. 'There are... wrong things about this station, it seems to me, craziness and bad omens ever since I set foot here. A concordiast returns to her old Master's side, and somehow he's dead minutes before they were due to meet again. The Master's murder panics the dock crews into rioting and trying to escape in my ship. A proctor of the Adeptus Arbites attacks the master chastener from whom he'd been taking orders minutes before.'

'And dies in the doing of it,' put in Orovene, 'in a way we can't yet trace.' Calpurnia nodded.

'Let's not forget Otranto, executed by someone who passed through auspexes, locks, armoured and sealed doors, witchcullises and psyk-wards. He was killed in a station full of seers and psykers who can listen to a pot boil half a sector away, but who haven't one word to say about the killing of one of their own–' She stopped herself. *Not to mention how I came here not being allowed to trust my judgement or my competence,* she had been about to say, *and now I'm having trouble even trusting my body, my mind and my senses.* There were things that an arbitor general, even a disgraced one headed for trial, did not say in company like this.

'Bruinann and Rede have worked hard, Mamzel Calpurnia,' Scall said quietly as his fingers worked the diagnostor studs. 'If the witches have given them nothing then it's not because they've been able to keep secrets. Put an aquila in my hand and I'll swear that the way they've been working has been the best way.'

'There are ways of bringing out the truth that we know they haven't tried,' Orovene said, but Scall shook his cropped grey head.

'If you arrested an astropath and dragged him right off the station, maybe. Even the incarceries in the Kuiper belts might be too close. One of the inner stations, or Galata, might work. Even Hydraphur, they say the Inquisition has a place there where–' He grunted and peered at a telltale. 'The details don't matter. Do it far away from here, is all. No matter how sealed you think you are, something will leak out, like a match into a promethium refinery.'

Orovene was scowling and shaking his head, rubbing the *Auctorita Imperialis* badge at his breast.

'You're walking down a dangerous line of thought, Scall. I don't wonder why your investigation was so moribund. You're lost in witch-shadows.' He made a fist around the badge and glared. 'This is moral weakness. Your preachers will have to answer for your straying as much as your commanders.'

There, it had been said. The whole garrison was potentially on trial for their failings, just as Calpurnia would be for hers. That Orovene had finally put it into words would be all over the precinct compound within half a shift, Calpurnia didn't doubt.

'Tell me again, Arbitor Scall,' she said, 'about why it's so difficult to put an astropath to the torture here. If Bruinann came to that conscious decision then I want to know the thinking behind it.'

'I'm not privy to the aedile's decisions,' Scall told her. His guard was up again.

'I don't need you to be. Just tell me about that promethium refinery remark.'

For the first time since she had come in, Scall straightened up from his stoop over the bed. At full height, he was not much taller than Calpurnia, but with a barrel chest and heavy shoulders that he rolled and stretched.

'If you like the promethium analogy then that's what I'll continue with,' he said. 'A psyker creates a haze around himself. The stronger ones can keep it inside their heads, or hearts or wherever the hell it is that the witch gift touches them, but it's always there. Like sweat, or body heat.

'An individual, a few of them together, you won't notice much, especially if they're properly controlled and damped. I've been to our own astropaths' tower in the Wall back on Hydraphur, which I don't know if either of you have… no?' Calpurnia and Orovene shook their heads, 'You'll barely feel anything there, anyhow. Here, we're well over the critical mass. Even with the rebuilding and the wards, and the watchmasters making sure they don't collect too heavily or move the wrong ways, that spirit-haze drenches everything. I won't try to explain it except in terms of the effects I can see and understand as a medicae, but there's a… a *volatility* you get in that haze.'

'Dangerous,' said Calpurnia, almost to herself, and there was something more than physical danger on her mind. A promethium cylinder slung under a flamer was volatile, but it was an understandable danger. A plasma-furnace had to be constantly tended by its tech-priests and enginseers, but at its heart, such a fire was a gift of the Emperor in his guise as the Machine God. If the fire turned on its tenders then that was a clean death, an understandable death. The witch-haze, on the other hand, men and women whose minds stretched reality thin and let things start to seep into it that no-one short of Him on Earth should have to face…

Calpurnia had been in danger of her life many times – the scars on her body and her grim memories were testament to that. To be in danger of her soul, that was a more frightening thing. Faith was what she needed to shore herself up against those fears, but she'd had faith walking into the courtroom on Selena Secundus, and what had happened? Within hours she–

She bit down on her tongue, not hard, but hard enough to make her wince and flinch, and break out of the trapped loop of thought.

'Dangerous,' agreed Scall. 'Most of us on the station are on a knife-edge because of it, even non-psykers. It's like an ague, or pollution-sickness. A good hard shock like a psyker being tortured is going to touch off something you really don't want.'

'Would the reactions frighten any others into informing?' asked Orovene.

'I'm not talking about a *frightening* reaction, brother preacher,' Scall told him evenly. 'The nightmares you might have had when you last embarked on a warp voyage might have frightened you, but they're a shadow of what a psychic shock will do in a place like this. The arbitor general was right to pick up on my talking about matches. Why do you think that the astropaths take every step at gunpoint? Even the strongest of them can succumb if they let down their guard, or if they're caught by something out there that's stronger than they are. The vitifers are there to put an end to any whose energy gets out of control, before half the witches aboard the Tower go off like bombs, or before something…' he took a breath, 'something goes bad inside them. The smaller enclaves don't need vitifers, but a station this size, funnelling this much power? There are people in the eyries, every moment of every day, arbitor, the power might die down but it never stops. Volatile.' He finished with the needle and reached for another.

'So there are the vitifers. Places like this, that don't have them, don't last long. Don't ever– I mean it's against all the laws of the Astropathica to speak with one, or hinder them. I suggest you bear that powerfully in mind, mamzel, if you find yourself in command and needing to make decisions over the Adeptus Astra Telepathica authorities on board.'

'Vitifers?' asked Orovene, as Calpurnia nodded. The preacher hadn't had the benefit of the tour with Ylante.

'The High Gothic for them,' said Scall, 'because they carry the lives of each astropath in their hands. Ugly word, isn't it?' Scall pressed his fingers against a rune-panel for a moment, murmuring some Apothecarion charm. A pair of slender mechanical arms unfolded from the ceiling, little bundles of surgical tools splaying out from their ends like clawed toes. Scall moved the arms expertly into position, fixing them in place with a soft code word that triggered locking mechanisms in the oiled metal joints.

'I'm ready to begin the next stage of my work, arbitor general,' he said without looking up. 'I respectfully request that you withdraw and make room for my servitors and assistants. Arresting the worst of the damage will take some delicate work and substantial time. Brother preacher, a candle burning in the Chapel for Master Dast would warm my hopes a little.'

'The Emperor protects,' replied Orovene, and Calpurnia repeated the words as they turned to leave.

'SOMETHING'S CHANGED,' WAS the first thing Torma Ylante said when Calpurnia had her brought out of the little attending-cell by the precinct compound doors. The woman had tried to follow them right into the precinct compound, and Calpurnia had rudely shoved her back into the arms of a following arbitrator, and ordered her detained.

'Something's changed,' Ylante said again. 'Your bearing is different. What happened?'

Calpurnia nodded to the arbitrator who'd fetched Ylante from the attending-cell, and he took the concordiast by the elbow and started walking her towards the doors.

'Madam arbitor? Wait, please. May I know what's going on?'

'Master Chastener Dast was the target of an attack,' said Calpurnia. 'Our Apothecarion will restore his strength to do his duty, Emperor willing.'

'Thank you. The chastener will be in my prayers.' The arbitrator had picked up his pace, and Ylante was forced to conduct the conversation over one shoulder. 'How can I be of further service? I can provide you with a quick survey of – could you slow down, please? – of some of the astropath eyries if you want to familiarise yourself… er…'

'That won't be necessary. My work here is Arbites business, which does not concern you, concordiast.'

'Arbitor Calpurnia, if I'm to guide you properly, I need to be able to–'

'I think you presume a friendship and a favoured position that does not exist, Ylante. Be careful on that score. I don't know how much more indulgence I'll be able to spare you.'

Those words brought them to the compound doors, and Calpurnia nodded to the arbitrator to leave them. Ylante stepped across the threshold, collected herself and turned around, the two women facing each other through the open gates.

'I intended no offence to you, Arbitor Calpurnia, and I apologise for any that I caused.'

'A knowledge of your place is all I'll require of you, that and your duty to law. Your position on Otranto's staff hadn't been fully ratified, is that so? Then you've no formal place in the Bastion. Have you a sleeping-cell? Good. Return there directly and remain there until I, specifically and personally, authorise otherwise. I'll pay you the respect of assuming that I don't need to have you taken there under guard.'

Ylante bowed, a little stiffly, and made a careful sign to the aquila over the precinct doors before she turned away.

Calpurnia watched her go, then spun to re-enter the compound, and almost walked into Rede.

'Watch and follow?' the detective asked. 'I took the liberty of making some arrangements. She isn't as snaky as some of my informants have painted her, but she's too close to the middle of all this not to be watched.'

Calpurnia nodded agreement as they stepped back over the threshold and let the doors swing shut.

'Can you direct a two-level watch? Ylante has to know we're going to keep an eye on her, so let's let her see us doing it. Let's have an eye on her that she doesn't know about, too. I want reports from both of them: level three delegation.'

'Yes, arbitor. Ma'am?' Rede had stopped in the shadow of the doors, and lowered her voice.

'What is it, detective?'

'Does this mean that you're our sole commander now?'

'Does–'

'What happened to the chastener – You're the arbitor general, ma'am, but we're aware that you came here under a, well, a special situation. With what's happened to Dast, are you our substantive commander now? Your nominal rank came from Dast. Are you still in charge?'

Calpurnia had taken a step back, her hand dropping to the hilt of her maul. A blazing certainty had come out of nowhere: Rede was working herself up to mutiny. She had decided that she couldn't stand the possibility of Calpurnia finding her guilty of incompetence. She was preparing for a murder, just as she'd prepared the murder of–

'I don't intend any disrespect by this, ma'am,' Rede went on, 'but there's not just the murder. There's no successor. Everything that's coming back through my agents is telling me that the whole Tower expects you to annex command and preside over the succession yourself, but no one's seen any signs of it happening.'

'It was the master chastener's decision,' Calpurnia said carefully, 'that with the, ah, *limited* nature of my office we would keep our work here as narrow as possible. The decisions and plans were his, and I was bound by them. The master chastener's work is capture and punishment and we see this reflected in his approach.'

'The master chastener is no longer in command, ma'am. Are we bound to his decisions or to yours? The Emperor's work must be done. I'd know from you, how you want that to happen.'

'Thank you for bringing the matter to my attention, Detective Rede,' Calpurnia answered. The tension had deflated so suddenly that she could swear she had heard it collapse. There had been no mutiny or plot in Rede's words. She had been concerned for the order of things, for the chain of command, and for the rule of law in the Bastion Psykana. Mutiny and murder, what the hell had she been thinking? 'I'll consider my course of action and get whatever advice from the praetory I feel I need. As for you, you have the surveillance instructions. When you're done, I'd like a briefing on exactly why people aboard the Tower are reacting to Ylante the way they are. I know she has a history here, but I need to know what that history is.'

Rede saluted and made to step away, but Calpurnia called her back.

'There is one final matter that I promise I won't keep you on. Medicae Scall made mention that it's the… the *haze* I think he called it. Something about being in a place that's drenched in the energies of so many psykers close together that acts like an ague.'

'Feeling it, are you, ma'am?' Rede stepped back into the gateway recess. Her expression was one of mixed sympathy and a certain professional reserve, a seen-it-before look. 'You're right. Your body plays tricks and your brain does too. Some people can't make peace with it. They have to get shipped out again, and they don't always walk up the boarding ramp, if you get my meaning. The psykers don't care, their minds just float in it like a fish, while we thrash around for air. How bad is it?'

'There's some pain: muscle, joint, head, and some… some oddities in the senses. You're right, I'm having to watch my thoughts, and my temperature perception seems out. Is that unusual for someone new to the station…?'

Rede grunted assent.

'Thank you, detective, I think that's all I needed to know. I won't keep you from your surveillance any longer.'

Rede left her standing at the bottom of the tall well of the precinct compound, head bowed in front of the touch-polished plinth with its ancient, sacred data-ark, deep in thought.

TORMA YLANTE HAD known the watchers were there as she had walked away from the precinct, but they hadn't ruffled her. She had been able to pick two of them out straight away. A houseman overseer plodding behind a whining electric dray, loaded down with soiled bedding. Their laundry run seemed to require an odd, zigzag route that intersected with hers far more often than it should have.

The other one was probably more dangerous: a young woman, an artisan, working her way through the cloisters with a slate and stylus, marking down designs on the pennants. It was a better cover, good enough to work on most. Ylante reckoned she could pick out an armed surveillant when she saw one. If Calpurnia gave the order, that woman was an executioner as well as a watcher.

It was so strange, she thought as she walked. The halls were as she remembered them, but the people had changed. When she had been here so long ago, Chevenne had been in his prime: hawklike, haughty and still fiercely in command of his mind, so different from the files of brain-burned psykers who'd been shepherded alongside him.

Thujik, Thujik had been almost comatose when he arrived, responding to the gentle telepathic questing of the more skilled astropaths, but unable to do anything more sophisticated than add his voice to the very lowest registers of a choir. Now, he was a possible successor to Otranto! She didn't recognise many of the names: Sacredsteel? Ankyne? Del'Kateer? Veterans, apparently, grown old and powerful. So many of the astropaths whose minds she had known almost as well as her own – Tophlio, Light-Of-His-Eyes, Tchangaia – were gone.

Ylante lingered on thoughts of her old colleagues: no matter how strong they had been, how skilled, how faithful or brave in pushing their minds out into that soul-lacerating pandemonium, their calling claimed them eventually. Their brains had burned, their taxed hearts had given out, or their minds had simply worn so thin that they drifted into that grey paralysis that the concordiasts called 'ash-sleep'. Perhaps something darker had happened, Ylante thought with a shiver, and they had pitched forwards into their own blown-out brains, with the hole from a fire-breaker's bullet in their skull.

In a rare melancholy, she drifted through the twisting cloisters. Her followers were out of sight for a moment, and the only signs of life were muffled footsteps around some distant corner. Something about the silence seemed more poignant to Ylante than the racket of a working dock or the constant sounds of misery aboard the Black Ship.

Was she weakening, she wondered? A younger Ylante would not have let a mood like this interrupt her serenity, but a younger Ylante had been able to work on the Black Ship. She had been able to help control the poor lost souls bound for the furnaces of the Golden Throne, and not let it break her. Was the simple fact that she couldn't face the work any more a sign that her own usefulness was coming to an end? Was the time coming, she wondered, when she couldn't even face her old role with the astropaths and their choirs? She had been a servant to psykers since her fourteenth birthday. What would happen to her when she couldn't serve them any longer?

She realised that she missed the Black Ship, the incense-smoke in the prow chapel, the familiar gargoyles at each passage-head, the black-hooded Inquisitorial wardens, the voice of Galan Vedrier saying her name... No. She had turned her back on that, and she would face the consequences.

Ylante heard a footstep behind her. On her guard, she shot a look over her shoulder, and shied a pace backwards when she saw the figure coming at her. It was just a runner, a thickset man in badly fitting messenger's livery, and in his hand an Arbites icon winked for a moment before he palmed it and shook his head at her, for silence. It only took a moment for the paper to pass from his hand to hers, and then he was a receding shadow, a muffled footstep receding into the cloisters.

Ylante, the paper read. *You were dismissed at our gates to maintain a deception, but your knowledge is needed. Otranto's murderer knows the Bastion too well. Come to the Arbites dromon docked at the tower above the hangar at Prime Dock and we will confer. Tell no one. CALPURNIA.*

There was no formal seal, but a gauntlet-and-laurel design that Ylante had seen on Calpurnia's badges of office had been stamped directly into the paper below the writing. The stamp was crooked, and the pen-strokes were hurried.

She didn't destroy the note, but folded it between her fingers where she could shred and pulp it if she needed to. She held it there as she reversed direction, moving quickly, heading for the docks. She had carefully controlled her emotions about Otranto's death, but in life, he had meant much to her, and the thought of his killer being unmasked lent speed to her step.

CHAPTER NINE

'THEY'RE IN PLACE,' said Rede as Calpurnia sat down opposite her. 'She's spotted two of them, and there's a second level hanging back. There's also one remote drone with one of the lay arbitor-techmen from our shrine. Here, eat.' She put a platter of oily bread-balls and heavy grey nutriate strips on the table between them. 'We tend to find that if the station's getting to you, you deal with it better on a full stomach.'

They were in Rede's long, cluttered office, tables and benches littered as ever with papers and slates.

'This drone, it's come to us from the Mechanicus? How long has it been since its spirit was in service to them, not us?' Calpurnia picked at the nutriates. The headache was going, but her stomach still knotted at the idea of eating.

'Fair question,' said Rede, 'but I think it can be trusted. I was at the ceremony when the Tech-priests forswore the thing over to the Arbites.' Calpurnia nodded her approval, and Rede went on. 'The drone will keep her under watch and I've got half a dozen arbitrators on an ostensible snap inspection of the outer galleries. Their paths won't cross Ylante's, but they can be on her at speed if any of the others report something.'

'Operation leader?' Calpurnia picked off a piece of bread between her fingertips. The oil had a crisp scent.

'Proctor Lagny, the drone operator. She's on a level two delegation from me. She's capable.' Rede picked up a strip of bread for herself and bit off half of it. 'While we're discussing our so-respectable quarry, allow me to direct you to…'

With a gesture, Rede brought up streams of script and images across the tapestry-screen.

'So, the concordiasts,' said the detective, 'attendants, keepers, interpreters. Their job is to know the astropaths well enough to be able to calm them down after their trances, interpret the messages, and talk them back into their own bodies after they've been, you know, out there.' Rede made a flippant wave of her hand, but she put the lie to her casualness by carefully making the sign of the aquila at those last two words. 'A good concordiast is sought after. The bonds they develop with any astropath they work with for any length of time can be quite intense.'

'They're allowed relationships?' Calpurnia chewed cautiously on the bread.

'No,' said Rede. 'Not of the sort I think you have in mind. The bond isn't romantic. It's not dutiful, not religious, and certainly not carnal. The astropaths' metabolisms are so unhinged by what happens to them that as far as I can work out, they're effectively sexless. It's hard to confirm. There are some taboos involved in talking about what they actually go through.'

'Probably because, Detective Rede, what they have been through has taken them onto the very soil of Earth where they touch the presence of the God-Emperor. Even though these people you dismiss as "witches" have stood on such holy ground that the respect of poor sinners like you and I can't bother them any more, I'll still thank you to show a little more reverence.'

'My apologies, ma'am. I forgot myself.' To show that she meant it, Rede took her booted foot down off the table and turned to face Calpurnia face-on. 'All right. In the larger astropath enclaves, with a proper concordiast order on hand, the better ones with the calmest minds will develop working relationships with the senior astropaths. The depth of the bonds that can develop is something blunts like us probably just don't have the – what?' She'd caught Calpurnia's look. 'Ah, apologies – "Blunt": pejorative term for one without a psyker gift, as employed by those with.'

'Thank you. My interaction with psykers has been limited until now, so bear in mind that I'm relying on you for some pretty elementary bearings.'

'Understood. Where was I? I was at Torma Ylante.'

They turned to regard the portrait in the tapestry's upper corner.

'Just under forty years ago, Ylante was one of the Bastion's senior concordiasts. According to the dossier from the master espionist at that time, she didn't have the hair-trigger emotional sensitivity that some of them have, but she could attune well to body language and speech, and she remembers *everything* she sees and hears. She also has a calmness of mind that apparently makes direct mental contact, which is something not every concordiast is able to handle at all, easy and soothing.'

'And so she became Otranto's favourite?' Calpurnia turned her attention to the portrait below Ylante's. Knowing so much about Otranto's wretched last moments had given her a curiously intimate sense of him, and it was odd to finally see his face. Master Otranto had been a gaunt man, with a good-humoured cast to his mouth that surprised her. The sockets of his dead eyes had been patched over with skin grafts. A tiny gold stud sat in the centre of each one. After peering at the image for a moment, Calpurnia realised that it was an eyeless eagle's head: the part of the aquila that symbolised the Adeptus Astra Telepathica.

'Otranto was a great one to play favourites,' Rede told her. 'He liked having his personal inner circle: the Master of the Bastion, the Master's personal concordiast, the Master's personal herbalist, the Master's personal Naval attaché, the Master's selected senior astropaths. People known to have Otranto's favour also accumulated influence in other ways.'

'Was there a reason for the Master doing this, apart from gratification?' asked Calpurnia.

Rede shook her head. 'Not that I can make out, it was just the way he operated. I'd have known if it was leading anywhere truly criminal.'

The defensive tone told Calpurnia that the woman wasn't as confident as she was letting on. It probably wouldn't make a difference if things came to a trial: influence peddling from an Adeptus office was a crime on multiple levels, and allowing it at all was something that Rede would have to answer for. There was such a thing as taking pragmatism too far.

'So,' Rede went on, 'the precinct records show that three weeks before Candlemas thirty-nine years ago, Torma Ylante left her position within Master Otranto's circle, and her position as concordiast aboard the station. She departed on a Black Ship commanded by one Master Galan Vedrier.'

'Which is the one that just brought her back. What reason was behind all this? How was she even allowed to do it?'

'We don't know. The espionist cell at the time put a fair bit of effort into finding out – there was a covert society operating in several of the Naval stations, called the Chamber of Optika. They were on record as wanting to get at the Blind Tower's officials for reasons of their own. The fear was that this tied in with them somehow, but nothing was ever established. All the Arbites of the time could find out was that there was some kind of falling-out between Ylante and Otranto. Leaving with the Black Ship seems to have been part of the row, rather than solely the result of it.'

'And so, what, thirty-nine years later – really? Thirty-nine years?'

'The astropaths whose bodies can handle the work tend to age pretty well,' Rede said. 'Bruinann says it cures them, like leather. Somehow, I don't think that's exactly how it works, but the ones who survive do seem to toughen up.'

'And Ylante's been warp-voyaging,' Calpurnia mused. 'I doubt that anything like thirty-nine years have passed for her. So, here she is again, returned on the same ship she left on, ready to pick up where she left off.'

'No sooner has she walked onto the station,' said Rede, 'than Master Otranto is–' She stopped, cocked her head, and put a hand to her vox-torc. Calpurnia couldn't make out the voice, but the easy expression dropped out of Rede's eyes and she half-stood.

'Ylante's changed direction,' she said.

'*Damn!*' Calpurnia was on her feet in an instant. 'Where is she?' She grabbed up her helmet.

'She's dropping onto one of the downward passages to… wait… she's passed through the fourth Manifold Arch.' Rede's brow creased. 'It's one of the ways we came up through, when you arrived. It's on the route to the docks where your dromon's anchored.'

The two women were silent for a moment. Facts and guesses whirled through Calpurnia's head.

'Is there anyone with her?' she asked.

'They... no.' Rede was pacing, scowling at the transmissions she was getting. 'Lagny and Rhiil, that's the agents, both say no. She crossed paths with some message runner a couple of minutes ago, but they're not walking together. She seems in a hurry.'

'Where's the runner now? Can Lagny keep the drone on him?'

'How hidden do you want it to be?' Rede asked by way of a reply. 'It's the size of my fist. It can stay up on the ceilings and not be too obvious in the low light, but the faster it has to move to find him the worse it'll fare.'

'Ideally, this man shouldn't know that we're following him, but following him comes first. Lagny can use her judgement, but it needs to be as quiet as she can make it.' Calpurnia donned her helmet and checked the sit of her maul at her hip.

'Get Bruinann to the gate with a detail to meet us,' she told Rede, 'and with a spare shield for me from the armoury.'

'Ma'am?'

'I gave Ylante a direct order,' Calpurnia growled as she made for the door, 'and what does she do? She turns and wanders off on her own. Keep your surveillance on her, Rede, but I aim to be there when we move in on her. She can explain to my face what brought this on. Who's the arbitrator in charge of that squad you mentioned?'

'Oraxi, ma'am–'

'And is Bruinann on alert? I'm going down there with him and with an escort.' Calpurnia was standing in the doorway, 'the same size again as whatever Oraxi's leading. Send word to the Arbites on my dromon for full lockdown. They stay anchored, but they seal themselves in there.'

Rede nodded and rapid-fired instructions into the vox. Then she looked up at Calpurnia with sharp worry written on her lean brown face.

'What is it?' Calpurnia was gripping the doorframe, ready to propel herself away.

'Order passed on to the dromon crew, but they report in turn. The hangar has just–' she listened to the vox again as Calpurnia fidgeted in the doorway. 'It's shut down. The lights and engines have been put to sleep. They don't know where the command has come from.'

Calpurnia ground her teeth.

'It's either some plot by Ylante or it's an ambush. Either way, I'm in a mood to bust someone's plans wide open. Get whoever you can onto those dock systems; I don't care if we have to drag Channery out of the Enginarium by her collar. Wake those machines up and find out who put them to bed. We're on the move.'

IT HAD BEEN a shock when the lights cut off. Dechene was not used to being in darkness, and he wasn't sure he could remember the last time he had been on the Bastion's docking hangars. Suddenly, the big metal space he'd been skulking through was a black maze, hard metal shapes all around him, cables, steps and ridges, making his footing treacherous. He'd spotted dead Otranto's precious little pet concordiast in the cloisters, and had been curious to see what she had been in such a hurry for. At the worst he had expected that to lead to Renz snarking at him for wasting some time. He hadn't bargained on this.

Still, he was rather pleased with the perch he had found for himself. Once his eyes had adapted a little, Dechene had managed to get his bearings and climb up onto an elevated lifter-tray. From here, by the pallid light coming in from the lit passageways at the rear of the hangar, he could see Ylante in her cream gown.

She'd been as spooked as he was by the darkness, and was looking around her. Dechene hunkered down to make sure she didn't see him and then caught his breath. The movement behind Ylante hadn't been his imagination. He froze, watched and concentrated. Quick, furtive figures, four of them, slipped easily through the darkness.

Dechene was sure that they were people from Lohjen's ship. Hard to keep track of – they seemed to lose definition in the shadows, somehow. He was glad they didn't think to look up. Ylante's pale clothes glimmered in the dark. Dechene, dressed in the same shade, would stand out like a, well, like something he didn't want to be, because it would, most likely, get him shot. Ylante, shivering, had put her back to a lifter-column. He watched and waited, wondering when one of the figures would make a move.

'Mamzel Ylante, to us!'

The shout made Dechene jump, enough to set the lifter tray swinging gently. He gritted his teeth – what if someone heard the chain squeaking? No. He heard two sets of footsteps, no effort at quiet, clattering in from the keep, a wiry dark-haired woman in an artisan's bodyglove and… and a *houseman*? A damn laundry cart pusher with his drudges trotting along behind him! Dechene wanted to laugh out loud. Who the hell had sent these people in for the rescue?

'Mamzel Ylante,' called the woman again. 'You're in danger. Please come and stand by us!' The houseman motioned to his drudges, and one of them directed a heavy hand-lumen into the hangar.

The hot white beam swung back and forth through the shadows underneath Dechene for a moment, and just when he was sure it would fan up and reveal him, the first two shots went by underneath, snuffing out the light and the boy who held it.

The house crew scattered, sprinting sideways and forwards into the shadows, as whispered words of combat-cant came up from behind him. Another shot, stub, not las. Dechene inched himself backwards so that the platform wouldn't sway, and pressed his head down. This would do him fine until the shooting had died down – Dechene could be arrogant, but he wasn't stupid.

THE SPOTLIGHT DROPPED and crashed, and its carrier fell dead on top of it. Suddenly, Torma Ylante was groping through a green-purple haze, a stabbing, pulsing after-image right in the centre of her vision. She squeezed her eyes shut and opened them again, trying to focus on her outstretched hand through the throbbing nova in front of her eyes. Behind her, someone shouted her name again. Ylante gritted her teeth and started towards the sound, sure that, at any moment she'd brain herself on an overhead rail, or break her outstretched fingers on a stanchion. What was going on? She thought she recognised one of the silhouettes as the houseman she had spotted watching her. But that light – had they been looking for her, or deliberately trying to blind her?

She spotted a shadowy shape in front of her in time to sidestep it and get around it – some kind of machinery, too indistinct for her to get a clear idea of what it was. She wondered if she was safe here. No, wherever the shots had come from, it had been somewhere in the dark. She had to keep moving. She closed her eyes for a moment, opened them, and could see a little better. Move on and just perhaps she could get to cover. That or stay where she was, marooned and alone. No.

She took a step and her foot came down askew onto a thick snaking cable that sent her staggering sideways, twisting her knee and ankle. Torma Ylante dropped to

one knee, fighting to keep in the cry that she knew
would bring a bullet out of the darkness.

'TORMA YLANTE! WE'RE here to keep you safe!' shouted
Hasta Rhiil, and then immediately danced three steps
sideways, scanning the hangar through the tiny dark-
light monocular that Rede had issued to her. A
long-barrelled silenced dartcaster jutted from each
sleeve, the spots of light from the black-laser targeters
skittering back and forth over the bay, visible only to
her. Where the hell had the woman gone? And where
were the bastards who'd shot that poor kid with the
lamp? She couldn't see anything moving in the lilac-
tinted image the monocular fed her. Were they cowards,
or they just smart?

She darted forwards between two crates, kicked one
loudly and cursed theatrically, and then doubled back
and around. Nobody seemed to be moving on her.
Moans and shouts came from where she had been
standing: the rest of those boys were trying to drag their
dead companion to cover.

She tried to let the training take over – the combat
training from the arbitrator range, not the endless class-
room exercises of the Espionist schools and let her skills
work for themselves.

Throne alone knew what the houseman made of
what was happening, but he was being stupidly, loudly
brave, helping his crew drag their dead friend behind a
track-loader, bawling for the murderer to come out and
face him man to man. Rhiil pushed deeper into the
hangar, among half-filled containers and abandoned
trucking equipment. Where had the woman gone?

There was a dark human figure against a paler spot of
half-shadow, and Rhiil's arm snapped straight. The
point of violet light dropped neatly to the base of its
neck and her dartcaster made its barely-there

shikshikshik. The figure reeled and clutched at where the shots had hit, but it didn't fall.

Rhiil's eagerness betrayed her. Suddenly, all she could think about was riding her kill and standing over his corpse. She'd save Ylante and hello, full espionist rank, and she could finally wear a proper black carapace again with that wonderful red collar. She ran a few silent paces forwards, but the second assassin had been ready for her and the las-shot exploded in Rhiil's shoulder, spun her around in mid-stride and mid-air, and dumped her hard on the metal deck as her vision went from purple-shaded dark to utter black.

YLANTE HEARD THE crack of the las-round's superheated trail and then the ugly sound of a human body falling. She hobbled three steps to another stanchion, but she was clumsy with panic and fell heavily against it, shoulder-first. She slumped there for a moment and then plunged on through the dimness. Stupid, stupid! How had she trusted the letter, but then how could she have known?

Her chest hit a diagonal support and she grunted, gripped it and lowered herself down, thinking that she could crawl under it and get her breath. Her vision was starting to come back, shapes and distances visible around the livid after-image. If only they could keep fighting each other behind her for just a minute more.

That was the moment that the gun-barrel hit the back of her head and bounced her off the support. Before her knees had even fully buckled, the man behind her had a fistful of her hair, and she was half-stumbling, half-crawling to try to keep up, as he dragged her away.

BELLO WAS DEAD. The poor slack-witted boy hadn't understood why they had come running down to the hangar, but he'd been so proud when he'd been given the lamp to hold, and now he was dead.

Goll Rybicker hammered his great fists on the metal deck. He had chosen Bello to hold the lamp, and now Bello was dead. Goll looked at the hole in the boy's tunic and all he could think was *Emperor, please, how can I make this not happen?*

Goll was not bright. He didn't really understand all the things the Arbites had said to him, that time when he had obeyed his foreman and helped carry some barrels to a storeroom away from the usual commissary compound. He hadn't understood what was wrong with that, but suddenly there had been Arbites there and his foreman hadn't ever been seen again, and then people had talked at him in a dark little cell. It had all meant that he had to do things that the secret Arbites messengers wanted him to do, or he would disappear too. That had been about as much sense as he could make of it.

Goll roared and struck his fists against his face. His voice drowned out the weeping of the other boys. He wanted to get the coward with the gun, but if he ran out, he would be shot, just like Bello. In his rage, dying was something Goll could shrug off, but dying without avenging his boy – a hateful idea!

Maybe, maybe if he was fast and loud? The shooter was a coward, killing boys and hiding in the dark. Surely, the sight of Goll running at him would make him drop the gun and wriggle away like the worm he was, and Goll could run fast. Right now, he knew he could run like the wind.

He began to take great, whooping breaths, building himself up for the rush, but already the other boys were looking up from their dead crewmate, as the racket of arbitrator boots came booming down the steps.

* * *

Lead Arbitor Oraxi spared the little knot of people huddled behind the truck. He had more important things to worry about than a handful of cowed drudges, and the paunchy man baying at the hangar roof. The transmission from Rede had instructed them to catch the concordiast, and the last frantic vox from Rhiil said that there was already shooting. That was fine by Oraxi. For the first time in a mind-numbing twenty-one months at the Tower, he had a real operation to lead.

There were clicks and clanks from above them as the lighting arrays started to warm up. Oraxi and his five arbitrators prowled forwards in three pairs, beams from their shoulder-lumens criss-crossing. The lead arbitor in each pair was ready to volley scattershot, and the man behind him had a body-seeking Executioner round loaded. They advanced through the brightening hangar bay easily and wordlessly, covering open spaces and taking control of sight lines.

Then the lights began to go out.

Oraxi had served longer than Rhiil, and his preservation reflexes were better: his legs had already propelled him into cover behind a stack of rolled freight-slings before he looked up. There was nothing broken that he could see, no shots shattering the floodlight glass. They were simply shutting down. Either they were up against someone who could poison the minds of the machine-spirits against them or... but that thought was bad enough, so Oraxi left it there. He listened for a moment, heard no attacks and moved out again, lumen activated, motioning the others forwards. Arbitrator Arkepp prowled at his side, hunting.

One of her attackers was hurt or dead. Ylante's head was still ringing, and the blow had sent her vision into blurs and spots again, but the fitful on-off patches of light appearing in the hangar let her see what her

captors were doing. Whoever was yanking her along
had had to stop while one of his companions, also
bodygloved and masked, hoisted a third limp form
onto one shoulder.

'Move it, murderess,' her captor ordered, through a
vox-masker that turned the voice into a genderless
rasp. 'You're in our power. Forget that for a moment
and–' it pushed the gun-muzzle against her forehead,
hard enough to make her flinch. 'No sound, just
obey.'

Ylante's thoughts were too jumbled to question the
weapon pointed at her face, and she mutely let them
hustle her on. A fourth figure came ghosting out of
the shadows to join them. It was dark-shrouded, like
the others, but she had enough wit and skill to recognise the man's build, his moves and his walk. It was
the man who'd come to her with the fake letter.

Suddenly the hurt one, the one who was being carried, began to spasm and buck. The others frantically
grabbed at it, but all hope of stealth was gone when it
gave a wet, rattling wail and finally went limp. Its carrier staggered for balance under the now truly dead
weight, and a moment later there was a double-clap of
sound from somewhere behind them. The screams of
the guided shells passing over her were gone almost
before she heard them, but Ylante would remember
the sound of them thudding into the meat of the dead
kidnapper's carcass, for the rest of her life.

The corpse stopped the shells. The body thudded to
the deck as the kidnapper carrying it let it slide off his
shoulders. Something passed between the three sur-
viving shadow-figures, and then two of them were
returning fire with las-shots and curses that their vox-
maskers turned frighteningly flat and metallic. The
third stared expressionlessly down at Ylante for a
moment, and then disappeared into the dark.

A thought forced its way up through the pain-fog and into her brain: *she had a chance – as much of a chance as she was ever going to have*. She managed to get to her hands and knees, as her captor swayed to the side and a whicker of shot shredded the air above and behind her. The racket of the shotguns was infernal, impossible, after the quiet snap of the las-rounds. Ylante looked around, and tested her ankle. She thought she could trust it for a few paces, enough to get her far enough away so that they would have to turn their backs on the Arbites to chase her. If they responded too quickly then she could hit the second one's knees with her shoulder and maybe she could buy herself a couple of seconds before the las-beam came through her shoulders.

She thought of Calpurnia, and of what the grim little woman would say to her if they ever met face to face again. That was a problem to look forward to, she told herself, and began to crawl again.

CHAPTER TEN

'TALK TO ME.'

Calpurnia was first down off the glide-truck, shield in place and maul at the ready. Bruinann came behind her at the head of a pack of Arbites, weapons at the ready. The dim expanse of the hangar spread out in front of her. She could see the lamps clipped to the shoulders and shields of Oraxi's squad, swinging back and forth.

'Three exchanges so far,' came the lead arbitor's reply over the vox. 'Las-fire, maybe some kind of silenced slug thrower, but they've gone quiet. I think we've pushed them out of whatever position they were trying to hold. Instructions?'

'Bear to your three,' ordered Bruinann, after Calpurnia signalled him to speak. 'We're coming in behind you. Advance pattern scale-two, your lead.'

'Affirm,' he replied. Calpurnia fell in beside Bruinann as they jogged forwards.

'Rede?' she voxed, 'Rede, come in. The lights are coming and going on us. Who's got control?'

'We're trying to trace the countermands through the code-channels,' the detective replied, 'but we haven't pinned down the source yet. Someone's working against us, and they're getting the machines' attention better than we are. Their codes are trumping ours. We can fire up the lights, but we can't keep them on.' On cue, the overhead arrays clanked, and the haphazard columns of light died away. Calpurnia, Bruinann and their squad lit their own lanterns and formed a line with Oraxi's squad, spreading out further in the dark.

A shotgun blasted somewhere to Calpurnia's right, and she snapped her head around, breathing softly, leaving the vox open for a report. There was another blast.

'Got a–' came a voice. 'No, there's, damn! Quick contact, hard to see. Maybe masked somehow. Don't think I connected but–' There was the snap of a las-shot and a burst of yelling, followed by two more answering shotgun blasts. 'Forward, it's moving! Bearing right, right of file, 'ware movement!' The enemy was coming past her. Calpurnia set her grip on her maul and got ready to charge.

THEY WERE ALMOST at the edge of the hangar when Ylante finally recognised the broad square entranceway ahead of her and began to fight in earnest. When the shadowy killers had grabbed her again, she had held herself back, certain that at any moment there would be Arbites to rescue her, and determined to be ready when the moment came. As she struggled along in her captor's grip, her injured leg throbbing in time to her hoarse breathing, she realised that they were about to enter the Long Dock Road, the passage that skirted the Curtain and connected the three dock assemblies. They were on their way out of the hangar, and the Arbites were getting no closer. Bitter despair gnawed the back of her mind as they closed on the entranceway without a shot, a shout or a light coming after them.

Then the lights came on. She saw who was holding her, for the first time, and lashed out with bright, wordless terror.

When they were in the dark, their bodies had been the soft black of the shadows. When the lights began to come up, their forms had started to ripple with the same grey as the half-light around them, and now…

They skirted a lifter pillar, and the yellow and black livery of the engine flickered briefly across their bodies. They passed the pulpit, and yanked her over a bundle of power conduits that swarmed up a buttress towards the ceiling. Traces of the conduits' red coating flamed around their feet and shins for a moment before it passed away. Now that they were getting close to the Road, its fat support arches processing away before them, their bodies were picking up the yellowish cast of the Road's lamplight.

Ylante had heard ships' tales of xenos who cloaked themselves in mirror-shard colours and vanished into the air of the strange worlds they called home, but the fragments of those stories didn't stay in her head for long; not when she looked at the faceplates the figures wore, and saw the chameleon colours fading around them. She had seen that design before, in her old days in the Hydraphur system. She did not think any xenos would ever wear one.

She mock-stumbled and let the chameleon-figure drag on the sleeve of her gown. Then she pushed herself quickly straight, trying to twist its arm around so that she could lock it, but she was too clumsy, and the man countered it easily. He simply yanked her towards him while her balance was still compromised. Her forehead met his, but his was shielded by the dull ceramite of his faceplate. There was no contest. He dragged her for another half a dozen paces before the grogginess faded again and she was able to get her feet under her. The other figure, lithe and snake-hipped in its shifting colours, grabbed a handful of her hair and helped to pull her along.

Ylante panicked again as they passed through the archway. Whatever they could do to her in a fight, it couldn't be worse than what they would do to her when they got her somewhere that they controlled. She tried to scream – it came out as a wheezing old woman's groan – and she beat frantically at the hand holding her hair.

'Throne *alone*,' said the voice in front of her. 'Are we really going to be able to get her back down this thing?'

'Voice.'

'Ah, piss on voice-discipline, who's here to hear us? Apart from her, and you're going to have to talk to the damn murderess eventually. Can't we just drug her until then? Let me crease her grey head for her. Dead weight would be easier than this, and I know what I'm talking about.' The slim figure still had the corpse of its companion over its – her? – shoulders.

'Not… murder…' Ylante managed to get out.

'It talks!' The woman had released Ylante's hair to adjust the position of the corpse on its back.

'I'm going to be generous, and put this incessant jabbering down to an adrenaline high from the fight. That had better be all it is, too.'

'Relax, *sir*, I've been ordered off the battle-dope and I will stay off it. Give me a little credit.'

'I'll five you all the credit you want, as long as you full-mask your vox and switch to your silent channel before you utter another misbegotten word.'

'Misb–' and the voice cut off from Ylante's hearing as the speaker obeyed the order.

'Come on, not-murderess, move yourself and I won't give you a kicking. I'll have your face in front of me when we mourn my comrade-in-arms at the next Funeral Lighting, woman, so don't give me any more cause to dislike you.'

'I'm not a murderess,' Ylante gasped again. Please, she thought, just keep talking. Give away something that I can draw you about, or just give away your position to someone. Just talk some more. She stumbled again, a real accident this time, and moaned as her shoulder caught the corner of a high rockcrete support. The man released her arm and gripped her hair, the way the woman had. They proceeded for another twenty paces before the hunched posture she was being pulled along in, cramped Ylante's lungs too much and she sagged onto her knees to pant. He allowed her a moment or two, and just as she was wondering about filling her lungs to yell for help – he gave a curt one-two tug on her hair.

The woman with the corpse had drawn ahead again. She would be the tough one, thought Ylante. The man who was dragging her – she had no option but to take a chance on him.

'The Funeral Lighting,' pitching her voice as low and unthreatening as she could with her control of it reduced to stumbling gasps. 'It's a Hydraphur cere-mony… ceremony for pil-*uhh*, pilgrims. You're not from here.'

He made no reply except a savage wrench at her hair.

'If you're from outside the Tower then you won't know me,' she tried to press on. 'You won't know that I'm not a murderess! Otranto's room was sealed when he was killed, a seal nobody could get through! I was on my way to meet him, but I never *uhh* never did, how can

I be–' She shut up as they came to a set of steps, up and over a switching-circle for the Dock Road's little railcars. It took an effort of concentration to place her feet so that her injured leg didn't misstep and crumple. There was a buzz and tick from the faceplate above her as the man enabled his vox again.

'The Arbites were after you for it,' grunted the flat pseudo-voice. 'They were watching you. Good enough for them, good enough for–' He caught himself, and the vox clicked off again, but it was a crack, a crack that Ylante surveyed and went to work on.

'I've spent hours with the arbitor senioris. She's a troubled woman, but I believe she knows what she's doing.' A part of her wondered about this even as she said it. Even without the psyker-static of the Tower taking its toll, Calpurnia had seemed fogged by self-doubt and a strange, deferential hesitation that Ylante had found hard to interpret. 'If she suspected me, why would she release me?' She wanted to keep him talking. She whipped her thoughts into line as the man's vox ticked.

'She's waiting for you to destroy yourself, waiting for you to kill another one. Astropaths are sacrifices the day they stand for Binding. She decided another astropath was a fair trade for catching you with blood on your hands.'

'*Talk* to her, then, let her stand me up there and accuse me, if that's what she wants to do. Then you can hear it for yourself, not just take guess. What can it cost you to talk to her?' She was shouting. Part of it was panicky despair, part of it was trying to be crafty, sending echoes up and down the Dock Road. She could no longer hear gunfire from behind her. Perhaps someone was following? Or maybe there would be workers somewhere ahead on the Road? *Where was everyone?* Just a single answering voice, she prayed, a

single hand raised for her, a single watching pair of
eyes…

TORMA YLANTE HAD only the smallest part of her wish.
One pair of eyes was watching her stumbling progress
along the Dock Road, but there would be no hand or
voice raised for her.

When the cat-and-mouse firefight in the hangar had
kicked up a gear, Dechene had finally moved, pushing
himself off his platform and scrambling away. He con-
gratulated himself on his escape and headed for the
Long Dock Road as fast as he dared – once those brawl-
ing fools finished what they were doing, they might
start looking through the rest of the hangar. This was a
time to hedge bets. Then the flicker of movement had
caught his eye ahead of him and, entering the Dock
Road and flitting from one arch to the next, he had
started following.

It was starting to dawn on Dechene that he was
painfully exposed, moving down a wide lit passageway
after two targets that were lethally intent on remaining
undisturbed. He stayed back as far as he dared, trying to
make sure that he was safely behind a column when
either blurry figure looked like turning. He had caught
one glimpse of the bland pale faceplate floating at the
top of the indistinct body, and something about the
expressionless pale-yellow eye scopes had chilled him
to his feet.

He had to know. Had the Arbites really arrested
Ylante or were they in league somehow? Was Ylante
steering the seizure of the Mastership? Would she steer
the appointment of the next true Master when the
arbitor considered her work done? Were these her
agents? The dromon that had brought this so-called
Astropathica envoy, Lohjen, had arrived before the
Arbites, but that didn't mean they weren't in league.

If they were her agents, then this would be something that she and Rede had cooked up.

He couldn't hear, however, and he couldn't get close enough. They were coming up on the first Knot, the defensive switchback of fortified passageways. From there they might continue on to the next dock where the envoy's dromon sat, or they might detour into the station – to the Arbites compound?

He peered out from behind an arch, watched the watery outline of Ylante's captor bend over her as they exchanged words, and then ducked forward one-two-three archways instead of one, his heart in his mouth and his heartbeat in his ears. Then he was in cover again, straining to catch what scraps of words he could from them.

'Arbites…' from a flat inhuman voice that seemed to float out of the air over Ylante's head. '…killed? …know everything.' Dechene's eyes narrowed.

'… can't, don't you…' from Ylante. Then something that might have been 'Master' or 'after'. 'Psyker'. He heard that very clearly, and then again, '…cret psyker.'

What was she admitting to? Who was she accusing? Dechene weighed his choices. He had seen the kidnappers in action – they weren't amateurs, caught by surprise, and their defences would be tough. Then Dechene thought about the hangar, which made him remember something else that he had seen there: a weapon, maybe. He didn't have to deal with this on his own.

Dechene wore the badge and livery of a concordiast over the mind of a bully and a thug. He wasn't crafty or patient. Whatever was taking shape, it wasn't something he could easily manipulate or spy out. The answer was easy. Do what comes naturally. Smash it. Renz wouldn't like it, but Renz was a wittering idiot, and Kyto was a purse-lipped coward with sinews like wet paper. Dechene would smash it all up, and trust to his wits and guts to look after the pieces wherever they might land.

CALPURNIA CAME AROUND, and through the gap between a thicket of winch-chains and a generator trunk, running fast and low, she took the first las-shot on her shield. The skulking bastard who'd shot at her hadn't been expecting a rush, and went scrambling backwards, dodging around a stanchion a split-second ahead of her maul-stroke.

'Contact!' she shouted, as a shot cauterised the air by Calpurnia's ear. She ploughed on without breaking step. Masked, half-visible killers shooting at her from shadows – she'd been there before. She lunged and swiped with her maul, and as she followed her target backwards, she stepped straight into the grenade burst.

It was a pellet-bomb, not enough to knock her flat, but the concussion was out of all proportion to the bomb's tiny size, and the shock left her off-balance. As she went down on one knee, retching and dragging her shield in front of her, the lights clanked on above her and shone on empty space.

Bruinann and his squad were by her side a moment later, two Arbites with their own shields closing in on either side of her. Calpurnia managed to stand and make up the centre of a rough shield-wedge, just as a burst of shooting came from back along their left flank. Oraxi's squad had pushed forwards again and made contact. The shadows in the hangar were shrinking to islands and pockets as somewhere the Arbites started to win the battle for the lights. The hunt started to speed up among the parked trucks and loaders, and the marching rows of overhead columns from which the hangar's conveyor cables hung.

There was another grenade-blast and puff of smoke up ahead, but the Arbites were savvy enough to scan around them for a diversion as well as an assault. They quickly spotted the blur of movement by the hangar wall, slipping away from the blast, towards a heavy bank of motivator machines. Three Executioner shells chased it as it dived, but their trajectories swayed in the air, their target-sense blunted. They punched the hangar wall instead, and the snaking blur disappeared in among the mechanisms.

The Arbites came forwards cautiously, bounding pairs of shotgun arbitrators with Calpurnia's shield-wedge at their front, covering the ends of the machine housing and ready for another grenade or shot, at any moment.

The shots didn't come.

The synthetic screech of alarms tore through the vox system, a fast-pulsing siren, code for a shipboard alarm. On its heels, a voice, indistinct through static, shouted the code for the prison dromon docked high above them.

'…igh alert, urgent, we need rein…' The voice swam in and out of vox-noise as if through a damaged transmitter; there was the repeated loud cracking of a power-maul somewhere near the transmitter. '…break, rioters are… all the cells opened, we're overw…'

Calpurnia went cold. That was why the lights had come back on. Whoever had tampered with them had found a better machine to seduce. They had unlocked the cell doors. The mob she had suppressed in this very dock was rampaging through her dromon.

'Keep him penned,' she said into her vox, snarling with frustration. 'Oraxi, you and your squad, keep him penned and flush him. Bruinann and the reinforcements, with me, time you got your own crack at these bastards. Let's rescue that ship.'

THEY SEEMED TO think they were being followed, Ylante's two captors, until they reached the first Knot in the dock road. There, they waited silently around a loop of corridor with weapons ready. At the six-minute mark, the woman flitted back along the passageway, her chameleon clothes wriggling with shades, and was gone for four minutes. From the way they had hesitated and cocked their heads towards one another, it was obvious that they were conferring.

Then they moved again, double time, this time with the man carrying their dead comrade and the woman goading Ylante with a pricking blade in her back. Ylante was looking wildly around. Where were the crews? Even off shift, the Curtain passages were popular for drinking, settling fights, clandestine dice-games or trysts. Why was it empty now?

It was another fifteen minutes of painful stumbling before they exited the passage. Their destination was not like the slender spike that Calpurnia's dromon was anchored to, but a broad little ziggurat, able to provide an open hangar and a ramp up to the dromon's flank. Her welcomers stood at the foot of the ramp: a grizzled man in the white and green of an Astropathica envoy and a Battlefleet officer, the badges and chain of a fore-ensign catching the light against his emerald coat.

'Get the murderess into the ship,' said Envoy Lohjen, 'and notify Hydraphur that we have her. We'll uncouple and be on our way as soon as we're all back and aboard.'

Torma Ylante was starting to realise exactly how badly things had gone for her.

GOLL RYBICKER WAS beyond shouting. His head hurt and his fists throbbed. His legs ached as he hurled himself through the passages that flanked the Long Dock Road. There was little conscious thought left in his head. He was going to kill someone.

That someone was in front of him, their outline shimmering and shifting, a blur that tickled him deep inside his head, but in the edge of his vision, it was clear enough. A man in the bodyglove and tabard of the wardens who'd made Goll's old life on the Bescalion docks a misery for years.

Goll didn't wonder how a Bescalion warden had come onto the Bastion Psykana. Who cared, there he was! This was one of the sneering bastards in his red-bordered tabard, calling his name, mockingly, just like when they baited him for his slow wits. The cur was waving Bello's khaki uniform sash over his head, and Goll could see the pistol in the murderer's hand. He was sure he could hear Bello's voice: 'Goll, he killed me. You gave me the lamp to hold so he killed me! Goll, I forgive you, Goll, but you have to kill him. Goll, my ghost will rest when you've killed them all.'

If Goll could actually feel the pressure on his mind, easing it off its hinges, well, maybe he didn't care; maybe he welcomed it as a mercy. By the time he burst into the docking ziggurat, his conscious thoughts were gone forever. He saw, without really seeing, the figures ahead of him: the odd ones whose colours kept changing, the grey-haired woman slumped between them, the two richly dressed men.

They were all just obstacles to be knocked down. He threw his thick arms wide and screamed his rage at the murderer's friends. His mind a single red loop of revenge with Bello's ghost-voice at its centre, Goll launched himself forwards to begin his work.

HER SHIELD ON her back, Calpurnia drove herself up rattling metal stairs, so steep that she could put her hands on the steps in front of her and climb them like a ladder. Behind her, the compartment that Dast and Roos had defended from the riot was full of the grim clatter of boots and weapons.

'Calpurnia to dromon. Calpurnia to any arbitor alive in the dromon.' She tried to keep the desperation out of her voice as they charged up the articulated pipe to the airlock. It was closed, and she resisted the temptation to grab her maul and beat wildly at the metal. There was no response over the vox.

'Bruinann!' she snapped over her shoulder. 'Where the hell are you? If you don't have the rank to override the hatch-seals, get Rede on the vox.' She was unlimbering her shield as she spoke, and the other two shield-bearing Arbites pushed forwards through the tunnel to join her, walling off the tunnel against whatever might come out of the opening hatch. The walls were already running with the condensation of their breath. Bruinann was muttering into his vox-torc, ordering the transmission of overrides down through the dock, to bring the machine of the hatch-lock to heel. Calpurnia couldn't order those codes: she was still accused, and this ship was still her cell.

There was a hiss and a puff of warm air from the hatch as Calpurnia's vox squawked into life.

'Who goes there! Party at hatch identify yourselves immediately, on pain of armed response!' It was the vox-operator that Calpurnia had stood behind when they docked. Her voice was startled, but not battle-frightened.

'This is Shira Calpurnia,' was her retort, 'coming aboard with reinforcements. Report on the cell-break status.'

There was silence, and Calpurnia feared the worst when the hatch slid up, but instead of a criminal mob ready to reverse their defeat on her, the passageway simply held an arbitrator, hastily pulling his helmet into place, although not in time to hide his surprise.

'Uh, welcome back aboard, mamzel, and aedile majore.' He blinked, looked at the shield wall and the shotgun muzzles, and heard the click of pistol actions and the buzz of mauls. 'Is something wrong?'

IT WAS QUIET in Lohjen's dromon, the hangar and the Long Dock Road still deserted from the spurious stand-down order. Someone would be on his way to the Dockmaster's suite to find out who'd given that order. Oraxi didn't envy whoever was to blame. Bruinann might be sloppy, but Rede was sharper, and Calpurnia was as cold as space-chilled iron. Rumour was, she hadn't even argued her own case in the indictment after the Phrax Mutiny, to set an example that nobody should presume themselves above the law. Oraxi didn't know whether to fear that kind of mind or admire it. From her reputation, Calpurnia would only show mercy if the Emperor Himself called her before the throne and ordered her to, and she wouldn't be happy about it, even then.

'Sir? Master arbitor?' Oraxi was jerked from his thoughts as the twitching man who'd hailed them in the Long Dock Road motioned him across the hangar and towards the ramp. He gave a discreet hand-signal for his team to divide and disperse, and heard two of them take up positions at the ramp, while two more walked up behind him into the dromon. Stay sharp, he reminded himself. Their quarry in the hangar had been flushed out and battered senseless, but they knew he had friends who'd slipped the fighting. His mission wasn't over y–

Ah. Well, maybe it was.

Oraxi was too good an arbitrator to utter the oath that sprang to his lips, but Dolan's balls, what had happened here? He stepped through the miniature slaughterhouse of the dromon's lock and tracked blood into its compartment, gun ready, another arbitrator behind him.

'It was, ah, I can't describe it, it was a terrible spectacle, before the Golden Throne it was!' came the voice of the man who'd come shouting for them, the jittery man in grubby concordiast clothes. 'He was insane, just berserk! What drove him to this, the poor Emperor-fearing man?'

'Quiet,' Oraxi called. He peered forwards. This wasn't a standard dromon. He hadn't seen an interior like this before, instead of the three-levelled passage decks, it was a single high-roofed space, overhung with rich curtains that could drop down to create makeshift rooms. Oraxi smelled scent in the air, could hear music playing when he came up the ramp. He could see racks of books and data-arks, and a table with a reader and a script-book, strapped down for stability in flight. An envoy's ship to be sure, Oraxi thought a little bitterly, not a working one. Well, it shouldn't be hard to clear it out, if there was anyone hiding in here.

'Lead arbitor?' asked Arbitrator Lianch's, over the vox.

'Stand ready. Get Shanizad in here, leave Smey on the ramp to call a second squad and wait for them. We're closing the hatchway, and we'll clear them on a standard three-and-one. On my–'

'Lead arbitor!'

Oraxi bit off the curt reply: the nerves in Lianch's voice had been unmistakable. Keeping his shotgun at his shoulder, he moved back to the bodies in their congealing sheet of blood.

'What is it, arbitrator? Got a live one?'

'No sir. Got *that*.' Lianch was pointing at something that Oraxi had missed. The lead arbitor bent over for a closer look, and then stood up quickly before shock could take his balance away. He tried to swear, as he hadn't let himself do before, but the word came out as nothing more than a soft indistinct breath of air. The two of them stared down at the dead envoy, the velvet envelope that had fallen from his sleeve and the Inquisitorial rosette lying on the deck. With some distant part of his mind, he realised that the concordiast was still on the ramp, looking in, grinning.

'This is just *terrible*,' said Antovin Dechene.

CHAPTER ELEVEN

THEY SAT AROUND Rede's table, the Ordo Hereticus rosette between them, staring at it in silence: Shira Calpurnia, Lazka Rede, Joeg Bruinann and Orovene, who constantly took sips of water from a chilled flask. The preacher couldn't shake the feeling that his clothes were too tight, although he had worn them in perfect comfort at the Incarcery. He also felt that someone in the next chamber was shouting and weeping, although the walls were too strong to carry such sounds.

'I don't understand what he was doing here if not investigating the murder,' Bruinann said. He had been repeating variations on this theme since the gloomy, stop-and-start attempt at a conference had begun an hour ago.

'He couldn't have come here for that. He was here a full day before Otranto was killed.' Rede had answered Bruinann with that, more or less, every time he had brought the subject up. Neither of them looked up from the intricate little thing on the table between them.

Calpurnia felt a little like that herself. Coming back to the precinct compound, she had been trying to work out how long she had been aboard the Bastion Psykana, and how long it had been since she had slept. It was hard to keep a feel for time, here: the shifts were of odd lengths and the lighting levels never varied – the inhabitants for whom the place was run didn't care about them.

'What I don't understand,' she said, 'is why he didn't reveal himself. It's impossible that he didn't know about the murder. It's doubtful that he was unaware of what's been happening since the murder. We know he had a damn fine informers' network for only a few days' work.'

'An Inquisitorial rosette will do that, ma'am.' Rede's tone was defensive, sensing the criticism of her system. Her efforts to roll up the dead 'envoy' Lohjen's network had borne some fruit: they knew about the Navy moles who'd stood down the hangar crews and tampered with the hangar lights, but the wilier agents had dived down deep, and the Arbites themselves were stymied by the question of authority. If the man who'd posed as an inter-sectoral Astropathica envoy had done so under the aegis of the Inquisition, then did they even have the right to root out his spies?

'It's naive to expect that he would,' said Bruinann. 'Reveal himself, that is. We all know the stories, the inquisitor marching out with his polished armour blazing, declaring his condemnations.' Calpurnia thought of Stefanos Zhow, the inquisitor who'd appointed himself to hunt the psyker assassin sent after her when she'd arrived on Hydraphur: Zhow, with his bright green armour, his retainers and guards, and his silent Inquisitorial troopers. 'I think we know better, and I think we know better than to think that Lohjen's presence was anything to do with Otranto.'

Calpurnia found herself nodding with the rest of them. The Inquisition used the fear that their name created exactly as the Arbites did. That treacherous, so-useful bit of doubt – would you leave after you had done what you said you'd come for, or were they your quarry too? Plant the seed and watch what grew; nervous consciences gave a lot away.

Orovene croaked, took a gulp of water and tried again. 'Where's the seal, then? We see his rosette, but where's the Inquisitorial seal? That's the true mark.'

The other Arbites looked at one another. All three of them had boarded Lohjen's ship. 'It would be well hidden if he had to hide it, but I'd be surprised if it was too far away from him. He carried the rosette hidden, I'm betting in case he needed to produce it in an emergency. I think that's what he was trying to do when that maniac attacked them. So if he was that careful about having his rosette to hand, why not the seal?'

'I don't understand,' said Bruinann. Frustration made his voice brittle. 'What you're saying makes sense, but we found no seal on the man, nothing. Two concealed blades, a needle pistol and that.' He pointed to the rosette, diffidently, as if it could order him shot simply for the gesture.

'I do,' said Rede. 'There is a difference between a seal and a rosette. A rosette can be carried by Inquisitorial agents as a badge of authority from their master, but you'll never see a seal on any finger but an inquisitor's. Arbitor senioris, do you agree?' Calpurnia nodded.

'I think you're right,' she said. 'I think Lohjen wasn't a full inquisitor. He was sent here in disguise on behalf of one, on what business I don't know. He didn't have an inquisitor's authority to simply commandeer us–'

'I wouldn't have argued with the rosette,' Bruinann observed, 'but I see what you're saying.'

'–and so he just watched and waited,' Calpurnia finished. 'I think if we dig a little, we'll find at least one message back to Hydraphur from that dromon, astropathic or machine-call, if he's got a broadcaster strong enough and a cogitator-spirit cunning enough to wrap it up in a good cipher. I don't think Lohjen was prepared for the Master's death, and he didn't know what to do when it happened.' She said it with a certain pleasure. The Arbites had gone about their work while an agent of the Inquisition had sat on his hands, unsure. Only an agent, certainly, but Calpurnia was prepared to take her reassurances where she found them.

'So what was he doing here?' asked Orovene, looking around at the others. 'If he wasn't here for the Master's death, then what was he doing? I think we need to know, if we're to do our duty.'

There was another moment of silence. Calpurnia found the rosette on the table, holding her gaze like an eye.

'We can't know it,' she said finally, 'and that's the sticking point. We can't know he wasn't here for Otranto's death. Not to investigate it, but…' She let the words hang in the air. Otranto had been killed by an assailant who'd slipped out of the room like a ghost, through a locked and sealed door, and Lohjen had brought agents with him with chameleon suits. They knew about of locks and warding, and ways to overpower systems and make false messages and alarms. If the murder-trail led back to the Inquisition…

'Was he here to do something to the Master?' Bruinann wondered, backtracking along Calpurnia's train of thought. 'Or was it about Ylante all along, something to do with the Black Ship? Or did, no, that's stupid… I was going to ask, did his dromon simply need a refit as it passed? Hah.'

'The idea's a sound one, though' Rede said. 'Inquisitors have strange, quiet ways, and so do their servants. We may be presuming too much by just thinking he had an errand that we can make sense.'

'We haven't tied Ylante in with anything, either,' Bruinann took up again. 'Otranto was on his way to meet her for the first time when he died. I can't let go of that. If Lohjen had these spies and tools, and he went after her, shouldn't we pay attention?'

'I'll tell you what I can't let go of,' said Calpurnia. 'The way that an admittedly big man managed to sprint through all that empty corridor, home in unerringly on the point where Lohjen's doors were open to let his own people back in, and then massacre the agent, that fore-ensign and two of the warriors who gave us such a bastard of a time in the hangar.' Her gorge rose slightly at the memory. 'Think what he did to those people, with his bare hands, and with those injuries in him. What got him to that state?'

'Scall told us that the verispex tests found no combat juice in the corpse,' said Rede, 'no frenzon or any of its variants.' She looked at the slate again. 'He was a pretty mediocre mole. He never asked questions, but he wasn't violent, either.'

'The Tower didn't get to him, you don't think?' Calpurnia thought about what the place had done to her own mind, and shot a look over at Orovene.

'There are some who turn violent under it, ma'am, but to cook off like that? No. I don't know what pushed him.'

Silence. The rosette glimmered at them from the table in mute accusation. Calpurnia closed her eyes and listened to the churn of her thoughts. She was sure that she could feel them in her head. The sensation wasn't of fireworks any more, but of some kind of red, feverish jelly in her skull, stirring and slowly bubbling. The more she listened, the more the sound actually seemed to be out there beyond her ears, hypnotic.

She snapped her eyes open.

'Rede,' she said, 'do you have a nexus of reports and alarms coming in? Do informants provide those?'

'No need for informants,' Rede said, plucking a dataslate off the table. 'Any alert or station action is reported to us formally, and, well,' she added, 'I verify them through my own sources, of course.'

Of course, Calpurnia thought. For a moment, the rhythm of the flickering slate-light on Rede's face exactly matched the rhythm of the throb in Calpurnia's head, and she had to squeeze a hand over her eyes for a moment.

'Survey the docks and the surrounding passages, please. We've had tunnel vision from that bastardry with the hangar controls and the fake alarm from the dromon. We should have been looking wider. Any other incidents of violence, unauthorised access, hell, I don't know, pollutant leaks, anything that might have got a hook into Rybicker?'

'There's... no. The systems in the–' Rede's narrow forehead knitted in a frown. 'Wait.' *Flick-flick* from the slate display, before Rede walked over and hooked it to her tapestry, respectfully touched the Mechanicus scripture across the top, and brought the display to life.

'Watch this. This is the projected path that Rybicker took from the first hangar, around the edge of the Curtain to Lohjen's hangar.' A schematic flared, and a crude red line began to follow Rede's fingers. She murmured to the slate and made a gesture. 'Look at these.' Along the base of the keep came a series of tiny white glows, flaring like match-heads. 'You can't see the detail, and this map collapses it into two dimensions, but it's... strange.'

'What are we looking at, Rede?' Calpurnia asked.

'Cullises. Each of those flashes marks a closure, ordered from the watch-hall. As Rybicker was racing along those corridors, the watch-hall was sensing him.'

Calpurnia shook her head. 'I don't understand. Slamming down cullises is a hell of a reaction. Look how far the edge of the keep is from those passages. Let's grant that Rybicker was unhinged enough to sing out to the astropaths in the cloisters – not hard to believe, if he managed to tear four people apart while they were shooting and stabbing him. Why didn't the watchmaster try and contain him further out?'

'The psyk-wards, at least those damn great cages and sinks they have all through the keep, they end at the cloisters, ma'am,' said Rede. 'Rybicker was going off in the senses of a lot of the astropaths, it seems, but the only psyk-scryers that would have seen him were over on that side of the keep. Likewise, the only doors that Watchmaster Voices-In-The-Fire could have closed by direct order.'

'Ah. *Ah*. Stupid.' Calpurnia's tone was dry and matter-of-fact. Thoughts were bursting in her brain in brisk succession. She smiled. 'Don't panic, Rede, not you, me. Stupid: I should never have needed this pointed out to me.'

'I don't follow, ma'am.'

'Why were the psyker-scryes in the cloisters unsuccessful in reading Otranto's death exactly?'

'The way that the wards and sinks blurred the traces, they drain away the prints that the witches leave, and – *Ah*.'

'You're going to do another scry,' said Bruinann.

'I am. Out in the docks, where the wards won't break up the trail. Let's find out exactly what pumped up our late houseman into such a killing machine, and I have another idea besides.'

'I'll prepare a representation,' said Bruinann. 'The three watchmasters have been improvising the allocation of astropaths without a new Master to direct them, so they're the ones who can help us find someone who'll do the – ma'am?' Calpurnia was shaking her head.

'No representations, Bruinann, no polite requests. I've had enough. There are too many loose ends, too many shadowy half-answers. It's time to do what I should have done right from the start.'

'IT'S HAPPENED!' SAID Teeker Renz, his voice almost a wail. Dechene ignored the sound, and kept admiring himself in the mirror.

'I said it's happened, Dechene, and I blame your stupid idiotic stunts. Going down into the hangar, like that! Stamping about with the Arbites! And Kyto… Kyto…'

'He might always be alive, Teek,' Dechene said through a sneer. He'd washed and scented himself, and changed the filthy jacket he'd been crawling about in for a fresh one. Considering himself entitled to a little insolence was Dechene's default state of mind, but never more so than after a busy day like today.

'Anyway,' he went on, leaning this way and that, and studying the hang of the coat, 'I don't see the problem. Whatever Ylante thinks she's been up to, I think we can see to it that her reputation's blighted. Look at how everything's gone to crap since she got here. Everyone was ready to believe the worst of her before she ever stepped off that tub of Vedrier's, not just you.' He turned away from the mirror and stared directly into Renz's eyes.

Renz wasn't used to that, certainly not from a man he'd personally promoted up from an indentured serf ship. He tried to return Dechene's gaze, but couldn't.

'I just think it's more than just Ylante now, Dechene,' said Renz without looking up. 'You don't think about this kind of thing. That's fine, it's not, well, you know, I, uh, I'm not criticising you for it, but I need to think about how we're placed. She's done it. That little arbitor woman has done what everyone was saying she was going to do right from the start. She's seized the office of Master. It's what the Arbites do when there's been a crime like this. We can't just rely on Ylante shouldering the trouble for Otranto's death. Someone's in charge who we haven't even met. We need to decide what to do! Do you… does this make sense? Am I making sense?'

Only a grunt, and it hit Renz then with appalling force: he was waiting on Dechene for an answer. He was waiting like a retainer, just as he'd waited on Otranto, asking, with a disgusting pleading tone in his voice, for Dechene to deign to answer him.

A new insight followed, a second horrified shock: *There was nothing he could do.* He had been conning himself. He had been powerful, yes, but he had been powerful as the personal attendant of a man too keen to delegate. It was not because he could outwit someone as crafty as Thujik, not because he had the unimaginable knowledge and experience of someone like Chevenne. He didn't have the strength of will of Sacredsteel, and he didn't even have the stubborn thuggery of Dechene. He had been lucky. He had charmed his way into Otranto's good books through a superficial wit and a talent for his chosen craft, and he had benefited from it. However, everything he thought he had built for himself aboard the Tower, the power base, the network of dependents all greedy for his patronage, the position of influence from behind the Master's seat, the centre of gravity for the Bastion Psykana's power politics…

It was all show: painted paper with the presence of Master Otranto over his shoulder to give it solidity. Renz twisted and spun the thought in his mind, trying to find an upside, some way he could profit. No, he realised with another wave of breathless sickness, the time for thinking like that was over. It was time to look for some way that he could simply hold on to a fraction of what he had. As he spun the realisation ever faster, every turn of it seemed to whip around and crack across the back of his head like a flail. He tried to tell himself that he was being stupid, that he was just gripped by useless fever-ghosts. It took more strength of mind than he had, and he slumped back down into shocked despair. This was how it felt, he thought, to stand hooded and manacled on the scaffold and hear the sound of the executioner's flamer igniting behind you.

'We don't need to care,' Dechene said, running a hand through his hair and grinning at his reflection. 'We just don't, Teek. Even if Kyto's dead, what does it matter? We're important people. There'll be somebody else like Kyto along. You said so yourself. What was it you said?'

'But if we're going to make the best–'

'No, no, come on, Teek. Tell me what it was you said, remember, when we thought Kyto might be ready to spill something about some of our arrangements?'

So Dechene knew as well. Renz's spirits slumped down further. He should have expected it. The man was a thug, but he was a crafty thug.

'I said that Kyto was an ambitious young hot-burning rocket of an officer with plans for himself and his family in the Battlefleet.'

'What was the next bit? The next bit was important.'

'I said that hot-burning rockets of officers weren't hard to come by in Hydraphur,' Renz said, defeated. 'I said that the Daradny academies churn them out by the thousands every generation, and that the day we

couldn't replace Kyto was the day we might as well walk
down to the docks and pick up a scrubbing-ram for our
trouble.'

'There you are, then. You know what? I don't care who
the new Master is. I just don't. We're going to do fine,
Teek, even without the Navy stooge. Too many people
depend on us to look after their little perks and rackets.
We're strong.' Dechene thought about that and said
something that chilled Renz to the core. '*I'm* strong. It'll
be nice not to have to piss about and hide it. Whoever
thinks they're going to supplant us has got another
think coming.'

He turned from the mirror and gave Renz a sunny
smile.

'Who tonight, then?' he asked. 'The tall redhead from
the food depots? That little one from the Encryptors'
chambers with the hips? Or the brunette from the auspex silos? She might be fun.' He clapped Renz on the
shoulder and pretended not to notice the herbalist
cringe. 'If you like, I'll let you watch.'

WATCHMASTER CHEVENNE WAS tired, but not unpleasantly
so. He was sitting on the side of a gently rocking sling-
bed in his quarters. A delicate spiced scent floated
through the room. The mild soporific was aiding the
mantras that were taking the restless edge off his mind.
The embroidered silk and paper hangings around the
walls had been hung a precise distance from the rockcrete, the relationship of soft fabric to hard, dense wall
and the space between them finely calculated to be
pleasing to a psyker's awareness. The only jarring ele-
ment was the masked vitifer standing by the door, bare
hand gripping his gun.

Chevenne let his senses roam around the room for a
moment more, and then focused on a series of beads
hanging over the door. Fixing on two, he pushed a tiny

thought-echo into them and set them resonating in a particular way. A moment or two later a tray-table, like the one in the watch-hall cage, lowered itself down in front of him with a soft ratcheting click of its chains. His tarot cards were already in his hands, and his mind was on the pleasant down slope towards rest where tiredness was relaxing, not burdensome.

In his days as an active astropath, Chevenne had endured fatigue in his body and soul that would have simply wrung the life out of the proud young Chevenne who'd gone into the furnace of the Soul Binding. The bloom of white fire that the Binding had planted was what had sustained him, body and soul. Even so, as the years had gone on, the nightmare of the warp had begun to eat away at his strength. The messages and ciphers he jammed into his mind and pushed out of it again had begun to strain and deform his mind. They had torn at his mind, worn him thin until he had sometimes felt that his whole consciousness was nothing more than a threadbare grey cobweb stretched across that furnace-fire. With every load of information that the cobweb groaned under, somewhere in his mind, another strand or two would part.

Chevenne sometimes thought that he had yearned for that to happen. From the beginning, back aboard the Black Ship itself, the Adeptus had started schooling them in acceptance of death. *An astropath walks from the Throne Room on a circular road*, they had said. *You walk out of here touched by Him, but that touch marks you. It will bring your soul back here to Him before long.* For so many of Chevenne's companions that had been true. Over a dozen had died as the furnace-light had come over them like a storm-front. As the fire had filled every corner of his skull with his own screams, and his eyesight had guttered and died, the senses inside him, which had been wrenched into glaring wakefulness, had felt lives around him buckle and flutter, and end from the strain. His had not. Like Thujik and Otranto, and a handful of others among the thousands of astropaths who lived and died around them, the work had cured him like leather, and tempered him like metal.

It had taken a long time for the wear to start to show, a long time for the control that he had learned in the eyries to lead him to semi-retirement in the safer seat of the watch-hall. Was he luckier than the ones who'd burned out under the strain in their first years? Was this better than being battered into idiocy and left as an empty pool of energy in a lifeless meat shell? Would it have been worse if he were able only to blast out a single note into a choir, in response to the crudest stimuli of the cantors' goads? When the white fire in the centre of his mind flew free, how much of his soul would be left for it to carry back to the Throne?

Almost unconsciously, his hands shuffled the cards, cut the deck, and turned them in his hands. Idly, he laid the two halves of the deck down. He had brought no focus onto them, made no attempt to push his energy into the cards, but the images he turned up gave him pause when he let his fingertips and psychic-sense settle onto them.

The Mountain, inverted. Next to it, the card that had appeared in every reading he had done since Otranto had died: the Judge. Chevenne's fingers traced the outlines of the wires and the delicate glass inlays that made up the picture he had never truly seen. Something was building.

That was why, when his chief attendant's voice came through the grille in the door that he must rouse himself, there were Arbites at the door of his rooms ordering his attendance upon Arbitor Calpurnia, Chevenne failed to feel any real surprise at all.

CHAPTER TWELVE

'She's overstepped her authority,' said Preacher Orovene, looking up at frantic Scriptorium stacks. He had an unlit lho-stick in his fingers, turning it over and over. 'She's acted without even the stamp of the Praetory,' he went on. 'An astropath should have been deputed to transmit the facts and postulations of the case back to Hydraphur.'

Orovene rubbed his jaw. He wondered if he would ever get his voice back properly. He remembered being very proud of his voice, but since he'd been here he'd had trouble calling to mind exactly how it had sounded. He was having trouble remembering his rooms at the Incarcery, for that matter, or the face of the Praetor Primaris. He didn't like to dwell on the way his memories were feathering and greying out.

'What's your point?' asked Rede. She hadn't much taken to Orovene. She knew as well as any non-psyker what the soaked atmosphere of the Tower could do, but she had trouble respecting the way Orovene seemed to be at the mercy of the witch-fog. At least Calpurnia had the guts to fight it. Rede was so used to the marks that the Bastion had left on her that she sometimes wondered how life would feel without them.

'Just that I trust you to pay attention, detective-espionist. You may need to testify to it at Hydraphur.'

'I don't–' Rede snapped, and caught herself and pitched her voice below the background droning of the autists, and the buzzing and rattling of their machines. 'I don't object to doing my duty, preacher, and thank you for pointing it out, but I wonder, did you mention my rank and title loudly enough? I know your voice isn't what it should be, but try harder. Perhaps with an effort, you can even communicate to the autists that I'm not what I seem to be.'

Orovene flushed, but stayed next to Rede, rocking on his heels, his grip constantly shifting on the tall staff he had carried.

The Scriptorium had once been a hangar for the Fury interceptors housed in the station. The fighters had roosted on adamantium shelves around the walls, lifted to the launch bay by crane. Now, those shelves, each the width of an Arbites drill-square, were crowded with narrow lectern-desks. An autist-scriptor was bent over each, the overhead lights glinting off their shaved scalps and optical augmetics. Data-sluices hung in clusters and tangles from the ceiling, and trailed out to each lectern, spewing readout onto green-glowing screens, or up cables and straight into the autist's brain.

This was the antithesis of the hushed, solitary work of the astropaths. Every deck bustled as scribes frantically fielded the information pouring down the sluices. The information chattered into transcription slates or ribbons of printout, before being grabbed up by stooping, scurrying drudges, who milled between the desks, and bore off transcript like harvester ants carting away their leaf-cuttings.

Some data came from attendants in the eyries, frantically scrawling on slate-screens or tapping keys. All astropaths transmitted and received messages differently. For many, the information came across as symbols, images, sensations – while others would relay strings of words or numbers. It was meaningless to them, but recorded by the nimble pen-fingers of an archive servitor and fed into a cogitator, real information would emerge.

The most demanding and dangerous transmissions came through the Encryptors' Chamber, vital messages wrenched out of the immaterium by the most skilled and powerful astropaths working in choir, carried down through minds groaning with the strain.

Part of the Scriptorium had found a different use, now. Seven arbitrators prowled the lowest of the deck-shelves, shouldering gaps in the press of messengers and drudges. They nudged the runners to run faster, and stepped up to random lectern-desks for spot-checks on the autists' speed and focus. Rede found herself wondering, with all due respect for her fellows, how useful they were actually being to the scriptor crews.

They were useful, she conceded, in a larger sense. Since Calpurnia had finally issued her decree, the free-floating malaise that had settled into the whole Tower had evaporated. Few liked it – Rede was well briefed on the complaints – but Emperor's teeth, they knew someone was in charge, now.

Rede carefully policed her thoughts, as a detective must always do. No lying: she resented Calpurnia. She had been carefully priming the investigation of Otranto's murder – ready to start any day – and then someone had noticed an arbitor senioris in transit near the Bastion and had decided that an arbitor general's presence would be the perfect thing to keep delicate

Astropathica sensibilities in line; tainted as that arbitor general might be.

That was what really rankled: Rede's chance of a commendation, and the chance to haggle herself a post back on Hydraphur, stamped out by someone who didn't have any damn right to be in uniform, if what she'd heard was true. A ten thousand-year-old ceremonial tradition was in ruins, a bloodbath had occurred right inside an Arbites court. Rede knew her work here had shortcomings, but all she needed was the chance to put her case, and not to some woman on her way to her own trial, who shouldn't even be–

She kept control, and when Orovene glanced over at her, it was hard for him to tell that she was thinking anything at all.

THE RUNNERS LUGGED their panniers out through the arched doors, through the maze of sorting-rooms and archivists' cells and out into the keep. They toiled along its passages, skirting the astropath cloisters and the outer walls of the Enginarium, to the Arbites' doorstep. The bright chamber outside the precinct doors was alive with voices as praetores and Rede's analyser teams directed the runners to-and-fro, rifled through their panniers, and passed printout and data-slates from hand to hand.

Praetor Secundus DeMoq had taken up post in the doorway. His head was bowed under the low ceiling, surveying the documents that the analysers brought to him, making the occasional careful note of his own. Only a handful of pages or slates made it past him. Looking at the latest slate to be pushed into his hands, he pursed his lips, murmured a few orders and carried the little green-lit tile back through the doors.

* * *

CALPURNIA HADN'T STAYED in the Scriptorium. Unlike Rede, she hadn't found much to watch there. Once the staff whose labour she'd commandeered understood her needs, their minds had utterly bent to their work, and beyond that moment, she had become scenery to them. Anyway, she had somewhere else to be. Chevenne and his assistant would be ready before long.

'Arbitor senioris!' Bruinann's voice, hailing her for the third time. 'DeMoq thinks he might have found something.'

'It took a while for the breakthrough, mamzel,' said DeMoq. 'These ones have wonderful nimble minds, Emperor's grace, but they, well, they're delicate. I think being here doesn't do them any good.'

'Being here hasn't done me any good either, praetor,' Calpurnia replied. 'My patience, for example, well, that's just about been eaten away to nothing.'

The praetor blinked.

'Well,' he said, 'the autists began by using Detective-Espionist Rede's formulae…'

Calpurnia's eyes narrowed. The more she was finding out about the limits of Rede's knowledge of Bastion affairs, the lower her opinion of the detective got.

'…but now we're moving them onto broader datasets and allowing them to draw their own connections.'

'And? You'll have come up from the doors to tell me something, praetor.'

'And there are correlations. Large spikes of correlations. Once we abandoned our sifting formulae with this "Polarist" term, and simply used Lohjen's informants as determinants, the recovery patterns changed completely.'

'How much of the Scriptorium is working on this now?' Bruinann asked. Calpurnia wondered what he meant. Was he questioning her diversion of the Tower's resources?

'One tier,' DeMoq told him, 'about five dozen autists,' and as Bruinann grunted a reply, she could hear them starting to shut her out, starting to turn on her, starting to undermine her.

Calpurnia grabbed a jug of water off the chill plate by the wall and dumped a glassful down her throat. It tasted bitter and recycled, but the cold was what she wanted, driving the cobwebs out of her head. Was she getting that paranoid? Was this blasted fug getting that far into her brain?

'The cold helps clear the head, doesn't it?' Bruinann said to her with no trace of anything but sympathy. Calpurnia allowed herself a small smile back at him and then looked at DeMoq.

'Pardon my being distracted, praetor. Continue, please.'

'As you ordered, ma'am, we haven't attempted to open any of Lohjen's records, just sealed them back in the dromon once the dead and injured were out. If I may be permitted, ma'am, using the records Lohjen was keeping for himself would have given us a real flying start.'

'And a flying finish, too, DeMoq, straight out of the airlock when the rest of the Inquisition found out. Trust me, we're better off not touching those until someone with a rosette picks them up and hands them to us. I'm unpopular with the Inquisition on Hydraphur as it is.' She was exaggerating, but the bravado worked. DeMoq did an impressed double take and got back onto the subject.

'The people that Lohjen went to the most effort to cultivate are one Sanxier Acquerin, an aide and minor-domo to three of the senior astropaths, Vald Kyto, that senior Battlefleet ensign – he also seems to have been some kind of attaché to the Master's staff, and one ordained lay tech-preacher Jagill.'

Two familiar names: Jagill had been the man who'd misdirected the lights in the hangar, and Kyto had been with Lohjen when the berserk Goll Rybicker had taken the whole gang of them off-guard. His corpse was in a vault in the Navy bunker waiting for a Battlefleet funeral detail.

'I know Acquerin,' said Bruinann. 'The boy's so inoffensive that it's almost comical, Lohjen probably just monstered him for a few minutes until he gave in. He hasn't got the stomach for rackets or powerplay. That cut him off from anyone who mattered.'

'As opposed to the astropaths, Bruinann, who apparently don't matter here at all?'

'I'll clarify.' Bruinann's tone had stiffened a little. 'A place like this, well, you've seen some of the briefs, ma'am: politics over the pissiest things. Who can get the Naval procurators to slant their inventories so that one section gets an extra ration of seasoning sticks? Who controls privileges to walk on the upper galleries where the viewing ports are clearest? It's that kind of thing. The astropaths mostly don't give a damn, but there's a lot of people who do. I'm sure you know what I'm trying to say.'

'I know what you're talking about, Bruinann. All games, isn't it? No one seems to care about simple pleasures, Bruinann. Duty and service. No, they play games instead, and people die of them.' For a moment, her thoughts seemed to be elsewhere, and then she locked eyes on DeMoq again.

'Get Acquerin in a cell, anyway. If he's that harmless, he'll be easy to crack for whatever we can get. We'll add anything useful to whatever Rede's dossiers manage to actually tell us.'

Her tone was more acidic than she'd intended, and from Bruinann's pained expression, Calpurnia was suddenly sure of something that she had previously only

suspected: Bruinann and Rede were more than just fellow Arbites. Now, or some time in the past, they had
struck up something more. She made a note to double-
check the pair's judgement in any matter she had to
raise with one about the other.

It wasn't until later that she realised how changed she
was from the accused Calpurnia in the cell on the
dromon, the doubt-gnawed Calpurnia who'd have
denounced herself as unfit to check anyone's judgement.

'Kyto, then,' she said. 'The Navy man, the one with
friends in high places.'

'Kyto was a regular associate of, well, not Master
Otranto, but of Otranto's staff, the ones who had a lot
of that day-to-day power,' answered DeMoq. 'Perks and
privileges, the sort we were talking about? A great many
came indirectly from the Master, directed by this clique
according to their own systems of favourites. Kyto was
one of the inner circle. He used his Navy position to
tweak supply and crew allocations, in exchange for var-
ious little luxuries that the Navy didn't provide for him.'

'Games, games and self-indulgence.' Calpurnia
scowled and rubbed her forehead again. 'What about
his associates?'

'Renz, Teeker Renz, Otranto's old major-domo and
personal herbalist, he's not well liked, but he has genuine skill at his job and he performs genuine work. A lot
of his associates and designated favourites, well, the sifting of the station records is–'

'Long overdue,' said Calpurnia. 'Rede has been lax.'
She noted that expression from Bruinann again.

'So,' said DeMoq, looking uncomfortably from one of
them to the other. 'We've got a couple of other Navy
types whom Kyto was helping to feather nests, and several attendants and wardens owing all sorts of perks to
favour-trades with Renz. No concordiasts, thank the

Emperor, and the Wardens and the vitifers are oath-bound. They wouldn't be touchable.'

'No concordiasts?' Bruinann asked. 'Not one?'

'Actually, one, you're right.' Green light flickered off it as DeMoq scrolled. 'One of Renz's clique, Antovin Dechene, brought up a couple of flags in the records. A lot of movement through the station, fraternising with all sorts of personnel, although he hasn't done any actual concordiast work for a very long time. There doesn't seem to be much indication of what he does do.'

'But he had close access to Otranto?' Calpurnia put in.

'Through Renz, yes.'

'I see.' She drummed her fingers on Rede's table for a moment. 'But his good life came from Otranto. Ditto this herbalist. They have to have wanted Otranto alive for his patronage to continue. That might sharpen their minds on how the murder might have come about, don't you think? Put Renz and that other one, the concordiast, on notice that I'll want to see them soon.'

'Soon?' Bruinann asked.

'Soon, not now. Now, you and I are both going to keep another appointment that's just as overdue.'

'Arbitor senioris,' put in DeMoq, 'there's a final point, a direct message I was given for you. Watchmaster Chevenne is on his way out of the cloisters, I'm told, with his staff and an astropath accompanying them'

'And there it is. DeMoq, the job of bringing in Renz and Dechene is yours. Bruinann, you're in charge here. I went out on a limb taking command so I could order Chevenne to do this. I want to be there when he does.'

BURSTING OUT OF *his skull as if his thoughts were stretched across the front of a rocket launched from a Titan's fist, riding the towering white fire in the heart of his consciousness, riding it up and out as reality falls away and shows the clamouring black tide of power behind everything...*

'Is he under control? Get him under control.'

'Calm yourself, Arbitor Calpurnia.' What seemed to be random jitters in Concordiast Angazi's eyes were anything but. He took in everything: the runes and colours in the glass armature surrounding Astropath Anschuk, the threadlike connectors coming out of Anschuk's and Chevenne's heads, the way the tics and jerks in their bodies were gradually synchronising, as was their breathing; and even the breeze that seemed to come from nowhere to stir the air around them.

...and the lights swimming around like the lanternbugs of the wetlands of home, just like the old days before the masked men took him away, and for a moment the living hammer beat surrounding his thoughts tries to trick him, carving their likeness from the frothing blackness and could this be them, here with him now? But...

The two psykers sat on chairs anchored to the back of a flatbed glide-truck, parked in the Long Dock Road with a vitifer each side. Calpurnia had wanted to set them up in the hangar where Rybicker had killed and died, but Chevenne and Angazi had talked her out of it. Being right in the hot swamp of the man's rage would drown any evidence beyond even Chevenne's rarefied senses. This was as close as they could get to begin the trance.

...but their beloved faces begin to leer and snap with teeth in their eyes, in their tongues, on the hands that grow from the sounds of their voices, as the force of their approach presses like a water-current. Then his mind finds the white fire inside it and the delicate touch of its companion, anchoring the sense-blizzard in the metal chamber that part of him has been left in. He has his footing now, in harmony with the other mind that's looking through him as if he was a lens...

'They're in concert,' said Angazi, nodding to a flicker of colour through the glass and a shifting pair of runes that Calpurnia couldn't interpret.

'Thank you, concordiast. Can they hear us?'

'We can.' As before, Chevenne's answer came partly through Calpurnia's ears and partly through her hind-brain, bringing layers and textures that seemed wrong for a human voice. She felt a soft, feather light crawling across her skin.

...a lens focusing, tightening its vision at the same time as it spins deliriously, feeling the sounds of voices, seeing the hard texture of metal walls, scenting the arbitor's troubled thoughts and the ward-armoured minds of the vitifers. Spinning, spinning, the centre cannot hold until a hot surge from nerve-endings breaks the spell...

'What just happened?' asked Calpurnia. Angazi didn't look up from the rune-bank, either at her or at where Anschuk had jolted with some kind of shock.

'It's a small phrenological manipulation. Anschuk isn't used to this work. Even with Chevenne guiding him, he needs help. Stimulus to certain cerebral nerves can divert high-beating strands and aid with the dive.' Calpurnia was about to ask what the hell that meant, but thought better of it. Angazi seemed unworried: time to show a little trust.

...breaks the spell and the faces melt away, no more the promise of the delicious pain of the bites they promised him. The two minds focus the lens and are penned between their own interleaved wills, like water slamming down a sluice-way...

'What are they seeing?'

'A moment more, arbiter, be patient. I won't have a mind pop its seams on my watch.'

...a sluiceway that carries their sight through all the layers, the ghosts, the ages mixed, brewed, grown together like vines: a hard shape, a slab of metal and stone in space with the towers above and below it. A proud fortress full of warriors attended by ships of war: a black and twisted wreck against the black sky, where only vacuum walks in the halls,

a nest of witches and seers alive with thoughts singing through the great boiling black. A white-hot fireball crumpling in on itself as the little sun inside reaches out through the bars of its cell, blue-hot majesty drowning out the cries...

Calpurnia saw the runes change, and couldn't stop herself glancing nervously at the vitifers. Neither one had moved. She could see black glass glinting from under their hoods, visors or augmetics. She realised that her hand was sticky on the butt of the pistol that she had finally started carrying again.

...the cries that fill this metal space as the lens of two minds flies down the passages, weaving through space (metal walls no barrier, gossamer, shadow, a laughable abstraction), weaving through time, as a bright trail of pain lights up and sings back to their mind, eye, voice, and leads them down to it, leads them on...

'We have it,' said Chevenne, his voice papery with its deep soul-echo. 'We have the dead man's trail, Eagle's cry, but there's pain here, soul stoked 'til it burned. What could do this?'

'Read it and tell me, watchmaster,' Calpurnia replied. 'I need to know.'

...leading them on down into the wake of the pain's passing, where the thoughts still swim in the air. Raw memories and howling guilt spin around one another like the Brownian dance of particles, the footsteps glowing cherry-red with the heat of anger, grief...

'Wait.' The word came from two throats at once, each voice flavoured with the sound of the other. Chevenne's chair edged a millimetre forwards.

...the footprints float, disconnected. The path flows, focuses, narrows as the hate is always fixed ahead. The hate, rage, grief flowing with a Mobius twist, back on itself, a circle shrinking like a contracting pupil. In, not out, closing in on the figure dancing like a mirage, a slim mocking figure flaunting a scrap of khaki cloth. A figure with no wake, no

weight, no print: a phantom mirage that breaks in the grip
of the lens-vision like a reflection that won't allow itself to be
clawed off the surface of a pond…

'He was ghost-chasing.' The words came from
Chevenne, utterly clear and confident, and free of the
wrapping of psyk-shadows. 'Something seeded him. He
was… he… was spider-netted and pulled.'

'I don't understand,' said Calpurnia.

'Something was used to draw the man's thoughts
onwards,' Angazi said, his face still turned to the flickering glass rack behind Anschuk. 'It was a light touch on
his mind, but one that stuck, like a cobweb.'

'You can pick that up from his trail?'

'We see in his wake the shape of what made it,' said
Anschuk in Chevenne's voice. 'We see the trail he was
following. We… dance behind… the shadow… man…
in red and… grey… battlements break when the star
dies… his tabard…'

'Red and grey tabard, they're not Bastion colours.
That's one of the in-system dock wardens. Battlements?'

'Star coming down,' said Chevenne, his lips moving
soundlessly, and the words arriving in her brain in
Anschuk's voice a second later. 'Coming down!'

'Star coming… Bescalion. That's it: their badge is a
battlement split by a comet.' Calpurnia blinked and
concentrated. 'Why would he be seeing that?'

'Not real,' said Chevenne. 'Old, but not real. Caught
in the cobweb, star coming down, caught and netted…'

'Old but not real,' Angazi said. 'In the past, then, but
it hasn't left any substantial imprint in reality that they
can see now: someone's memory.'

The response from the two psykers was a headshake,
a deep rumble of negation, a chilly shock to the skin.
Neither said 'no', but neither needed to.

'No weight to it. No…' Angazi concentrated for a
moment.

'The image I'm getting is an umbilicus to a baby in the womb, arbitor. Whatever ghost he was chasing, it wasn't something firmly grounded in his mind. Drawn from it, but that's all, just a phantom.'

'What else?' Calpurnia asked. Her question was to Angazi, but Chevenne answered.

'Nothing else. Not here. Too slick to the touch. Too deep.'

Angazi already had a vial in his hands, reaching for a drip-tube that snaked into Angazi's scalp.

'I'll begin rousing them, ma'am. We shouldn't move them for a while. They got a hard sting off those emotions they read, and their life-signs are both...'

'We're not done,' said Calpurnia. Angazi frowned at her. Anschuk's mouth hung wetly open. The wooden plugs sitting in his empty sockets made his stare blank, disturbing. Chevenne's mouth twitched with amusement as if he'd expected this. The vitifers stood like statues.

'Turn around,' Calpurnia told them, 'and send your minds up to the Grand Concourse. The test has worked. Let's play the main game. Otranto was last seen on the Concourse before he entered the astropath cloisters. There are no wards or psyker-cages there to blur his trail. Bring the scent of that trail to me.'

AND SO, THEY *swoop up into the heart of the Tower. A white shimmer of delight, this place so rarely seen with an unfettered spirit-eye, and here truly is a fortress made for a mind. Here the runnels on the walls dance in their thoughts, veins of glass and crystal bearing intoxicating rapids of energy; a beautiful mist of mind and energy...*

'We're taking a risk,' said Angazi. 'Chevenne's skilful, but weak, and Anschuk lends the seance power, but he's not experienced. Their harmony will strengthen them, but pushing them will strain them and leave them vulnerable.'

'Then we release them from life and mourn their souls. We all owe the Emperor a death, Angazi. If their debt falls due today then the will of Him on Earth be done. The burden is to see that their lives are spent wisely, and that's mine, not yours. Carry out my orders.'

...mind and energy melded into one the lens, duet, eye wheels and dives through the keep, past the edge of the chamber at the Tower's centre where the power-shocks radiate off the blue-hot fire; through the sluices, pouring data changed from warp-patterns to electron-patterns; down to the Great Concourse. Straight into a shocking tangle of violence and pain, not the simple red hurt of the docks, but a wiry catscradle of shining nerve-pain and deep-flowing soul-pain. Mind sparks bound together by arcing bands of aggression, greenish-black and crack stinging like sandpaper lashes as images spin, green and cream, and steel, and harsh laughter. A voice rises and wails in their consciousness...

'Guilliman's blood, what was that?' Calpurnia had drawn her pistol when the terrified scream had boiled out of the air.

'Something from the reading, something they're getting out of the air of the Concourse.' Angazi's voice was tight with fear. 'We have to stop this. I've got drugs that will break the trance–'

'No! We're too close.' Calpurnia's eyes were alight. 'I was right, perish it, I was right! Make them follow. What can they read?' Ice was forming on the bed of the truck. The air between the psykers was filling with rainbows as if there was water in the air, but those rainbows were of shifting colours, too bright or too dull, sickening the eye.

...wailing in their consciousness, ghosts rising out of the air, the deck, and the past. Shuddering bundles of thoughts held in formation with rough willpower, or the steel bolts of faith: not the cool symmetries of psyker-discipline or the painless white throne-fire of Soul Binding. A bank of razor

*blades heated to cherry-red, clicking open and shut like teeth
–fearful jealousy wanting to spend itself in violence. There
are air-movements of braggadocio, savage arrogance kept in
check, and there is, there is, there is a bound-up thought-trail
that is so hard to pick apart. A man? A woman? A master
and his woman? Thin keening, like an angry ghost, the
memory-flash of a blade – how does it look, how does it look?
All so cobweb-fine, all lost in a moment, tossed away by the
violence of its own wake as the psyk-scent wavers…*

'Arbitor…' said Chevenne, and the rainbows rippled.
His next words were slurred, but something danced in
the images: the rainbows knitted for a moment to make
a flash of blade-metal.

'Yes. *Yes*. We're onto it.' Calpurnia was breathing hard.
Exhilaration was a drug.

*…scent wavers maddening, whisper-faint, twisting
through the corridors like wind, now scraping against the
wards and the cages whose hexagrammatic bars glitter like
imprisoning ice under the insubstantial rockcrete of the
walls. The scent is here like a last scrap of moonlight, the soft
sound of running footsteps, the after-image of a strange mind
flow, snapping out to see the walls and cullises ahead of it.
Turned in somehow, perceptions trapped in recursive folds,
and there's familiarity here, a song they know. The other
images radiate off it like flares off a dying sun, a corkscrew-
ing bitter vacuum around it, which he is only starting to
guess is the oncoming of death. A flash of a grey-haired head
surrounded with doomed regret, the stained-glass image of a
judge in black and crimson. Then they are fighting to release
it as the fear grows and hungers, and starts to fray their
minds at the edges. Their guard starts to fray and the frothing blackness outside chills them with brass and rot and pink
and blue flames. They have to escape, they break, they
break…*

'Saints and primarchs, arbitor, we've got to put a stop
to this, now. Their minds have hit some kind of synergy

that I can barely measure. They're running too hot and too fast!'

'Do we have everything we need?'

'Pity's sake, ma'am, trust me, break the trance now!'

…they CAN'T break, because now something has them, a soft tripping strand across their way that takes their balance, so they tumble and spin, and their harmony breaks. A sharp taste, predatory, acidic, a growing stain, darkening, and…

'Break it. Bring them out. Fast as you can.'

…and shocks begin, blearing hazes begin. The grey weight of suppressors begin as Angazi starts to work his machines and the senses drift up from their crude meat-bodies so far away. The harmony is gone. The harmony is broken and Chevenne's mind goes sleeting away as he withdraws into his barrier of will-shield, and prayers. Anschuk is left alone, unable to hear Angazi's voice as he tries to begin a focusing litany; unable to find his path home, and it is what he had always feared. His terror, the terror that one day, the last of his senses would snuff out, leaving his mind drifting and anchorless, fraying, trapped between witchcullises that were like hot jagged glass on his thoughts. There, or at the mercy of the boiling dark…

Chevenne had sat up, his face working, his voice joining Angazi's in incantation. Anschuk bucked in his chair, blood seeping past the plugs in his eyes and from under his brittle fingernails.

Calpurnia recoiled at the stink, the acrid smell: Anschuk's gown had started to char and burn. He bucked again, jumped half off the chair, and then remained there, floating in a position that his body could never have supported…

(As Angazi yelled in outright fear, Calpurnia was knocked dizzy by a vicious psyk-surge, and Chevenne scrabbled at the leads in his head).

(As ugly clashes of warning-bells sounded in the watch-hall and Watchmaster Voices-In-The-Fire twitched in her harness and shot out a frantic burst of orders, the knot of force gathering in her mind-vision).

(As the cantors and concordiasts of the astropath choirs beneath the eyries saw the runes light on the warning panels and urged their choirs to redouble their song, sending waves of power up the eyrie, and steeling themselves and their psykers for whatever was about to happen).

(As a quick hail of images ghosted out through the geography of the Tower, some gone faster than they could be sensed, others flicking into the minds of astropaths for a nonsensical moment. Kappema saw acid raindrops condensing in a sky that he'd never seen. Thujik saw an acrid smoke-trail through clear air, and felt a terrifying tip in his balance. Astropath Ankyn howled as the shape of a witchcullis branded itself across her raw consciousness. In the Firewatch Eyre, Astropath Ehlin found the word-thought *Judge in black and crimson* caught up in his mind, and blasted out and away towards a star whose light could barely reach the Tower at all).

…and then the gunshot.

It ended. Anschuk made a tangle of limbs and green robes in his chair. The vitifer whose name the psyker had never known calmly lowered his pistol, and took up his vigil again.

CHAPTER THIRTEEN

THE WARDENS AND apothecaries had drawn back when the seance began, withdrawing until they were far enough away not to disturb the delicate interweaving of the psykers' minds. When the spidery metal charms etched onto their phylacteries began to warm to the touch, and when the warning augurs started to hum like tuning forks, they began to shift and fuss. They double-checked protective seals and kit, and when the frantic messages came from the watch-hall that the seance had bolted out of control, they were in motion in a moment.

They burst out onto the Long Dock Road as Calpurnia held Chevenne's shoulders down and Angazi desperately worked the drug-pumps and neuro-electrical sleep-rams. They surrounded the truck with a punchy, economical precision bred over hundreds of hours of drill, and bitter practical experience.

Three long staves were driven against Chevenne's chest, hypodermal spears jabbing out of their ends and dosing the thrashing little man with a flood of psyk-suppressants and anti-cognitive serums. A warden dodged around the vitifer, who had his pistol levelled at Chevenne's head, leaned in and clicked a wand home into one of the watchmaster's skull-plugs. The twisting patterns up the wand's length began to glow as it drained off the saturating warp-energy whirling around Chevenne's brain, and after a moment, the palpable haze around the watchmaster began to dissipate.

Then the warden who'd planted the wand in Chevenne's skull danced forwards again, a skein of wire looped up one arm. He flicked his hand out and let his net uncurl in mid-air. It was memory-wire, coded to its shape at molecular level and imbued with nano-particles of psyk-resonant crystals. As it snapped into position, the particles assumed their proper symmetries. Chevenne collapsed like a rag doll, breathing hoarsely, tendrils of corposant still drifting from his ears and skull-sockets. At the opposite chair, the warden was already kneeling beside Anschuk's corpse. He and Angazi were lashing ribbons woven from more of the imbued wire around the dead limbs in careful crisscrossing patterns.

'Move him,' said a woman's voice.

Calpurnia, down off the truck to give them space to work, couldn't tell who'd spoken: the wardens were near identical under their dark coats and armour. Their visors, like the vitifers', were made of layers of filigree, breathtakingly fine, that made up hexagrammic sym-metries in three dimensions. Their faces were invisible behind them. As the wardens and vitifers made a ring around the truck, one of them at the tiller started it rolling.

On the bed of the truck, the apothecaries went to work, cutting Chevenne's clothes free and jabbing diag-nostor pins into his skin. Runes and chimes began to sound. Chevenne had fallen silent, but his limbs were still twitching. Each lumen they passed under flickered in an odd, syncopated rhythm, and crackling frost was forming in sharp-edged patches on the rough plastic truck-bed.

One vitifer was still up on the truck, his pistol drawn. The other had dropped down to the deck, and was part of the ring of jogging wardens. Calpurnia kept pace behind them, keeping her distance and letting them work. After a moment, she noticed that she was running alongside a trail of red spots on the deck where the blood from Anschuk's burst head was dripping off the truck's edge.

She had barely had time to register it when she dodged something in her path by reflex, a torn piece of bloody cloth the same green as Chevenne's garments.

'Speed up!' The truck began to accelerate, the wardens picking up their pace to a run. Calpurnia gritted her teeth and stretched her stride, racing to catch up and see what had happened. She was on the outside as they rounded into the hangar and swung around to the passageway up into the keep. For a moment, she had to pour on even more pace to keep up, as a second blood-sodden length of cloth was cast off the truck and splatted onto the deck in front of her.

She drew level with it, jinked inwards and slid between two wardens so that she was running inside the circle. Anschuk's corpse was a barely-recognisable tangle in one seat, and in the other the apothecaries had sliced Chevenne's tunic open up its front so that they could work.

After a moment more, what she was seeing sank in, and the shock took all the speed out of her legs. She dropped to half-pace as the wardens dodged, cursed and passed her, leaving her behind as they spirited Chevenne up the passage towards the medicae halls.

Her helmet off, breathing hard, Calpurnia walked back down the corridor alone, to where that second piece of cloth lay in its red stain. She stood over it for a long time, her face solemn, eyes opaque, her mind whirling.

TORMA YLANTE HAD to lie on her side on the bed that the Arbites doctor had given her. The screaming giant who'd torn into her captors had grabbed her by one arm as she had gone to flee, and wrenched her around in a circle that had sent her through the air and into the side of the dromon, barely conscious. She believed that falling down past the ramp where the giant couldn't see her had saved her life. The next people his eye had fallen on had been Lohjen and the Navy man, and her last memory from that hangar had been of wet, cracking, ripping sounds as the man had got his hands on them.

She lay on her side in a futile attempt to keep her shoulder comfortable, throbbing as it was after the arbitor medicae's quick and brutal repairs to the joint. Moving sent bursts of pain scrubbing up and down her arm like razor wire. She tried to keep her eyes closed, concentrating on breathing exercises and stillness.

She jumped at Calpurnia's voice, and moaned aloud as her patched-up shoulder twitched and flashed with agony.

'Lie down, Ylante. Wait a moment and let it die down.'

'Thank you, arbitor.' Ylante's voice was as strained as her face. Sweat had started up on her forehead.

'No need for the tone. I've been through worse than what ails you and I know what I'm saying.'

'Well, thank you. I suppose I'm just having a little trouble resting.'

'I had Scall dose you with stimulants,' said Calpurnia, 'and some fairly specific pain suppressors. I need you alert and able to talk.'

'I… see. May I ask what happened to me? Who was the screaming man? Who were the people–'

'No.'

The two women stared at each other for a moment.

'Tell you what, Ylante,' said Calpurnia. 'I'll start by making an admission to you. We're running low on time. The succession issue is making the senior astropaths fractious, and the operation of the eyries is starting to suffer. This Bastion has too important a place for me to allow that. Whoever else Lohjen was, he was Inquisition, and I need to know how he was involved in this before one of his friends or masters shows up. My own time on the Tower may not be long, and I *will* have Otranto's murderer by the time I leave.'

She caught herself, the next moment and shut her mouth. She had been about to say why, to tell Ylante what had happened at Selena Secundus, and confess that another failure flapped in her wake, another burden of duty had slipped through her fingers onto the floor, and that really would be more than she could bear.

'And so now I need your advice,' she said. 'I need your explanations. I can feel the door of this thing almost open, and I need your hand on the pry bar.'

AFTER A MOMENT, Ylante made a small motion of her eyes that was close enough to assent. Calpurnia forced her hand away from her forehead, and forced her thoughts into an orderly queue.

'When we were walking in the medicae chambers,' she said, 'we saw several astropaths come in, three of them I think, with injuries, similar injuries.'

'I remember them. The choristers: they were walking too fast and the lead one ran into a witchcullis. Their attendant should have been more careful.'

'They didn't have separate attendants?'

'Choristers are the small cogs, arbitor,' said Ylante with the hint of a smile. 'On their own, their powers are limited. It's en masse with their song poured into another psyker's trance that they're powerful.'

'Too weak to deserve individual staff, you're saying.'

'Too weak, or too exhausted, or their mind or sanity has been too damaged by their Binding. An astropath's spirit has felt the tread of the Emperor, ma'am, and the Emperor does not tread lightly.' Ylante shifted a little and grimaced. 'Was that your question?'

'No. Tell me why contact with a cullis is going to have that effect. They're wards. They contain a psyker, do they not? If containment causes injury, why aren't I struck permanently deaf if I put shooters' plugs in my ears when I'm at the range?'

'It's commonplace to believe one's body and mind are separate,' said Ylante, 'linked almost by coincidence. Whether or not you believe it, it's not true of psykers. For them, the energy washing out of their minds, it fills them, like blood.' Ylante shuddered at the words.

'So if there's a bond between their bodies and minds–' Calpurnia began, frowning.

'So there is,' said Ylante, 'but not an equal one. Their bodies can become an afterthought to their minds. The old ones can be almost hollowed out by it. They need powerful wills and containing, and constant attention from their concordiast, to stay anchored in their bodies at all.'

'The older they are the worse it gets?'

'Once in the Adeptus, yes, but also the young ones whose gifts have started to eat into them before they can be trained to contain it. We saw it aboard the Black Ship.' Her eyes were haunted, 'Constantly.'

'So the young man we saw was burned,' Calpurnia said, feeling haunted and wanting the conversation on a new track. 'He hit the wards of the cullis, which are made to cage and repel energies like the ones that flow all through him...'

'...and the wards threw him back and burned his mind,' Ylante finished. 'That's what makes the cloisters so dark and narrow: they're completely enclosed in psyk-cages, sealed in with rockcrete so the astropaths can find their way by touch and not hurt themselves.'

'So the wards burned his mind, but they also burned his body, because his body is so powerfully slaved to his mind,' said Calpurnia. 'His body burned where it touched the cullis, and... All right then. There were three of them: the two who'd been walking along with him. I remember this: lighter burns, just welts and lesions.'

'They'd have been walking behind him,' said Ylante, fidgeting on the bed and grunting with discomfort. 'The cullis would have broken up the forwards wash of his pain, but they would have had less protection.'

Calpurnia closed her eyes and ran her fingertips over her forehead. She could feel it coming, that final click of the lock opening, that grinding that meant the door was finally leaving its hinges.

'They felt the pain in their minds,' she said. 'The pain manifested in their minds, and their minds made that pain burst out onto their bodies.'

'You have it.'

'I have it,' Calpurnia repeated. 'All right, then. The scrying I've just come from had a concordiast helping it. You've done that?'

'Once or twice,' Ylante said cautiously, 'in my time.'

'Can you describe the process? How might we get detailed pictures of something, something I can use the Scriptorium's systems to put in a form I can see for myself?'

'It would be hard, ma'am. Bear in mind, I'm no psyker myself. We're talking about this like two blind pilgrims trying to discuss the colours of a temple fresco. Seance images are rarely like your detectives' pict-captures. You can't make a clear portrait out of them. If you know in advance the man or woman you're scrying, you can bring them into focus, because your own knowledge of them, your memories of them, provides a kind of lens.'

'So, a mind scrying a thing that mind knows…'

'…will do so more powerfully and more dangerously, too. Vedrier once described a seer becoming a still pool: something attuned to event-echoes – the finer the seers' control, the narrower the set of events they can attune themselves to. They also have to let those echoes imprint on their consciousness. Do you understand? Let some of that echo into them. It takes an excellent mind to withstand that for scry after scry. Most psykers who attempt seeings do it in choirs, or through a focus like the Imperial Tarot, and with the most puissant prayers and blessings, they can surround themselves with. Scrying can hurt. Even a soul-bound astropath isn't immune.'

I won't have a mind pop its seams on my watch, Calpurnia thought, and felt a stab of guilt. Chevenne had seemed confident when she had asked it of him. The strength of a single powerful astropath in choir with Chevenne's own fine control, but something had happened nevertheless.

'I'll put it another way,' said Ylante, mistaking Calpurnia's thoughtful look for puzzlement. 'Scrying isn't passive, arbitor. It's not like an eye taking in light that's fallen on an inanimate book. Astropaths exert power in scrying, and what they look at isn't lifeless. It must have been explained to you why the structure of the Bastion's been engineered to break up psyk-traces? It's so that sensitive psykers don't travel across a point where something terrible happened and look into it accidentally, experience it all over again in their minds. Why are you smiling, madam arbitor?'

Experience it again in their minds. I'm right, I know I am. I have to be.

'No reason, Ylante. Tell me why the scryes of Otranto's path report a man and a woman.'

Ylante blinked and gasped, first in astonishment and then in pain.

'A man and a woman,' Calpurnia said, looking at her, 'a *master* and his woman. When the psykers who did try to scry Otranto's path came out of it, they reported seeing a man and a woman, and sensations of fear. Why would they all talk about a master and his woman, Ylante? It's hard to avoid thinking that they were talking about Master Otranto and his new Concordiast Torma Ylante. It's hard to avoid thinking that the fear and his death were because she came off her Black Ship unhinged. She was angry about her parting from this Master Vedrier whom she apparently cared about, and stabbed the master through the heart. Why would they talk about a master and his woman if they couldn't see your faces, Ylante? Is that why you were trying to talk me out of working to find out who the images were of?'

Ylante had rallied magnificently, but then, thought Calpurnia, she had been trained to control her emotions.

'I submit, arbitor, that you're misunderstanding scrying,' said Ylante with great care. 'Things become apparent in it that would not be so for the rest of us: emotions, power, patterns, relationships, symbols, change, all in intersecting layers. One of my old astropaths once tried to explain it to me. He said, "Take the incident you're scrying, interpret it in as many poetic, allegorical, symbolic ways as you can, put each of those into a stained-glass window, put all those windows in front of each other and shine a stablight through them. Now, stand in front of that array and look at all the pictures at

once, try to untangle them and arrive at a meaning."
That's the closest he could come. Except for a psyker,
often the meanings arrive far more tangled than that, and
with the force of a bullet between the eyes. So much of
their training is about calming and controlling their
minds, because what comes into them will knock their
minds off their hinges if they don't tease out the meanings and move to–'

'Shit the information out of their brains,' Calpurnia
finished, and Ylante blinked at the crudity. 'Hm. Who's
this other astropath you referred to? He sounded good
at putting these concepts into words.'

'Five years dead, madam,' Ylante told her with a touch
of coldness. 'Suffice to say that something got into his
head that had no right to be there.'

'I see. I'm… sorry for an untimely death.'

'Thank you.' There was a pause. 'Arbitor? Those people in the dromon I was… taken to. They were
Inquisition, weren't they? I recognised the faceplate
design from other agents of theirs we've met.'

'Yes.' Calpurnia took a breath. 'Yes, Inquisition, you're
correct.'

'Were they Polarists?' Calpurnia felt a chill at Ylante's
question. The concordiast's face wore a look of naked
disdain.

'How do you know that term, Ylante? Your chances
just took a turn for the worse, unless you can come up
with a damned good explanation.'

'The Polarists,' Ylante said, 'are spreading everywhere.
There are some in the Astropathica, not many, but there
are many in the Navy, and the Ecclesiarchy around Chi-
ros is rotten with them. It's said that it's a growing blight
in the Inquisition too, with Tonnabi's monograph
spreading like a brushfire. Vedrier even said he'd met
the master of another Black Ship at Coellow Quintus
who'd fallen in with them.'

'Back up, Ylante. The Polarists: start at the beginning.'

'Polarists: believers in the polarity between human and psyker. The monograph by Eparch Kvander Tonnabi is being spread by some in the Missionaria Galaxia, if you care to read it, but promise me you won't swallow his ravings.' Ylante was breathing hard, clearly in pain. 'The Emperor, so they say, is divine, transcendent. The only place where human and psyker can meet is in the Godhead, and He holds humanity and witchery in his hands as proof of His godhood. In any mortal, the combination of human and psyker is a mockery. The polarity must be enforced: either a human is a human, and walks and talks, and prays; or it's a psyker and it can't be allowed to have any humanity at all. Astropaths that Polarists get their hands on are trepanned, lobotomised, reduced to no more than servitors. They say that the poor ones who're brain-burned by their Soul Binding are the right ones, that that's what the Emperor means to do. The ones who come out still proud and strong are the aberrations, and we must serve the Emperor by completing His plan and reducing them to…'

A tear leaked out of the corner of Ylante's eye. 'They can barely make a choir. Ciphers are pumped into their heads and some idiot blunt plays them like an organ. Orders them around like a servitor. All that holiness and knowledge gone: just a lump of meat on an eyrie couch. They can't handle a millionth of the work someone like Chevenne could, but the Polarists say it's the Emperor's will. How could the Emperor will this? I am dutiful before Him, but how could He will that? It can't be right.'

'I don't believe Lohjen was a Polarist,' Calpurnia said. 'The word appears in what we know about some of his conversations here, but whether he was a full inquisitor or an agent, he spent a lot of time talking with astropaths, and there's no trace in our reports of... of what you describe.'

Calpurnia wondered why it seemed so important to comfort Ylante all of a sudden. 'He may have been warning them, or he may have been part of a backlash, who knows? But no, I don't think he was one of them.'

Ylante lay still, staring past Calpurnia in silence.

'Do you still suspect me?' she asked after a moment.

'No,' said Calpurnia. 'By rights I shouldn't reassure you, but no, I don't. I do think that the master-servant pairing in the scryes was you and Otranto, but you didn't kill him.'

'I don't understand.'

'That's all right,' said Calpurnia, 'I do. You'll excuse me. I've got work to do.'

THE STATUES OVER the stairs up the Grand Concourse had once been heroic. This had been the ceremonial entrance to the station, when it had been a military fortress: the glorious entryway to the keep where important arrivals would process up from the docks. Passing through the outer arch, carved with intricate patterns representing every system in which Battlefleet Pacificus had fought as seen from Hydraphur, the new arrivals would look up and see a three-sided frieze, a mass of statues, staring down at them. Heroes of the Navy, representations of real commanders and of romanticised lower crewmen with clean augmetics and chiselled chins, vanquishing hideous leering heretics.

The statues had been devastated by time: once clean lines roughened and corroded, smooth stone, chipped and soiled.

Like me, Teeker Renz thought, looking up at the statues through a mist of self-pity, just like me.

He watched Thujik's back disappearing down the Grand Concourse. The man's little procession passed through the shadows of the processional arches, light and dark and light, the fixtures on his head gleaming like the gun the vitifer next to him carried. The pompous bastard, all that show. Thujik wouldn't have dared behave like this if Renz was still… If Renz still had… If Otranto…

Renz gave a little moan as anger fought with self-pity, and dropped his eyes to the strange patterns on the Concourse floor. Renz could see his dim reflection in it, see how gaunt he was getting, how ratty his hair and clothes. He shouldn't have to put up with this.

'Don't even bother trying it, Renz,' Thujik had told him with every sign of enjoyment. 'Too little, too late. Were you so coddled by Otranto that you've lost all grip on diplomacy? Once you wouldn't have been stupid enough to ever try this. Perhaps if the Polarists suck out my ability to think through a straw, I'll be as stupid as you one day, but no. You're wasting your time.'

'You're going to recruit Ylante?' Renz had asked, horrified, and Thujik had cackled aloud.

'So you admit it, then? This pestering me for a meeting, all your extravagant compliments: you admit the whole thing was about slipping into a position by my side? Too little, too late, and it would never have been enough anyway. I don't approve of you, Renz, and I don't approve of how Otranto let you get your hooks into this place. When I'm Master of the Tower, you're finished. Stand there in that cloud of sickly fear I can feel radiating off you, and think on that. Since you've been so careless as to allow Sacredsteel to float to the front of your mind, I'll advise you, gratis, that she may not like me, but she loathes you even more than I do.'

Renz had tried to plead, then to lecture, and then to at least manage a civil goodbye, but Thujik had not even allowed him that, having his servitor spin his chair and wheel him away.

Just like me, he thought, looking up at the broken and defeated statues.

It took him a moment even to register the sound of boot soles on the stairs behind him, but when he did and turned around, the fresh weight of fear fell on him as if one of those broken carvings had dropped onto his head.

'Teeker Renz?' said Lead Arbitor Oraxi at the head of his squad. 'By order of the Arbitor Senioris, Renz, you're coming with us.'

SECOND PETTY OFFICER ROOS was frightened of Antovin Dechene, and fighting not to show it. This was his home turf, after all: the sneering concordiast was standing in one of the officers' staterooms in the keep's Naval quarters, well away from the attendant's chambers where he was supposed to remain. The warden still found it hard to look him in the eye, however.

Many of the Navy crews and lower-echelon attendants aboard the Bastion found Dechene unnerving, but few could have said why. Perhaps it the unthinking arrogance of his demeanour. Or, it could have been as simple as the well-known way in which people aboard the Bastion Psykana, both within the Naval contingent and out of it, found their careers withering after they crossed the little power-clique of which he was a part. The station had its share of dead-enders with little ambition to stir them. The ambitious officers usually gravitated to the war fleets, constantly sailing the warp into and out of the system. However, it also played host to a few young lions of Battlefleet Pacificus: young officers with the favour of their superiors for whom a posting to an exotic setting like this was intended to round out their early careers and experiences. They were the sort of people who learned that Antovin Dechene was someone to try to stay on the right side of.

'I'm not sure I understand why you think I *care* where Renz is,' Dechene snapped. 'I don't like being interrupted when I'm sure I intended to be private for a couple of hours.'

Roos, looking past his shoulder through the partly open partition-door, caught sight of the shivering naked woman in the bed behind Dechene. Something about Dechene's eyes reminded him of the reptiles he had once seen in Commodore Vlassion's menagerie at the High Septacian station.

'Master Dechene, he instructed me to tell you the Arbites were taking him to the Master's suite. They were marching with him, sir. He said to tell, uh, he said that you would know what he meant.'

'He sent you to tell me that, did he?'

'He, uh, said it to me when I asked him if I sh–'

'Shut up.' Dechene spared a quick backwards glance for the woman on the bed and gave a dismissive grunt. 'All right. Get your gibbering face out of mine.' He pushed through the door and let it slide shut behind him. 'Master Renz hasn't been himself, you know. He's probably desperate for me to go looking out for him... again. He'll be his usual self when I've pulled him out of trouble, I'm sure, the ungrateful worm.' Dechene ran a final hand through his hair and threw his jacket over his shoulders. 'You never know,' he said, to himself as much as to anyone else. 'This might even be fun.'

STANDING NEXT TO Orovene at the foot of Dast's bed, Shira Calpurnia could feel her nerves stretching. Nothing to do with the psychic fog of the Bastion, this was simple fear. Fear at the slender limb she had gone out on, fear that this might be another monstrous mistake, fear that simply became colder and deeper, because fearing her own decisions was something she had never had cause to do.

Her orders had gone out and her orders had been obeyed. Things were in motion and it was simply too late for second thoughts. That was a thought that was more frightening to her than it ought to have been. To stop it from crawling too far forwards into her mind, Calpurnia concentrated on her prayers. Her hand was up over her heart, fingers stiff and thumb curled into her palm: an eagle's wing, a pious gesture that she hadn't used since childhood. She held it over her Arbitor Senioris rank badge.

Cerebrally, rationally, Calpurnia knew where the fear had come from. It was the memory of the hearing at Selena Secundus, the ugly shrapnel-bomb of a disaster that she had so cheerfully walked into, so full of her own prowess – Shira Calpurnia, the fierce new arbitor general, the woman who'd broken the conspiracy dogging the Mass of Balronas, and foiled the escape of Ghammo Stroon, what could go wrong?

She'd had all the time she could want in the Incarcery, enough time and chasteners and self-denunciations to drive home what had gone wrong, but the self-loathing she had felt wasn't the surprise. Neither was that constant yawning emptiness she felt over her shoulder all the time, the gap in herself: if she couldn't trust herself to succeed in her duty, what could she believe about herself any more? What was left of the Shira Calpurnia she had thought she was for nearly forty years?

What really took her by surprise was the terrible anger she felt: a part of herself that she had never expected would get so bold. She had been in peril of her life from a dozen different kinds of enemy over and over again since she had left Machiun, but the anger she felt had always been a tight, cold thing: anger with a razor-edge of bright Ultramar steel, not this thrashing red animal.

'What are you praying for?' Orovene asked next to her, his breath coming out as a puff of lho-smell.

'Shall I tell you the truth, preacher?'

'We've come too deep into this for anything else. We're both too wretched for lies.' The weariness in Orovene's voice startled her.

'The truth, then: I was praying to the Emperor for strength for our brother. Dast is my chastener and I owe him my prayers. Except that, I was also praying for the Emperor to grant something to me. I was praying that he let Dast lie for just a few more hours. I was praying that the chastener stay asleep and not retake my command, so that I can see this matter through. I need to do this, Orovene. I need to stand before my conscience and my Emperor, and declare that I did this one thing well, for Him.' The preacher nodded silently. 'You?' she asked him.

'In truth, Calpurnia? For the same: for one chance to show strength. I've failed too. I came on that dromon as your preacher, confessor and spiritual guide. Then, when He tested us with this, you were my guide. I haven't walked before you to lead. I haven't walked beside you to inspire. I've trailed you and been mute. I've learned from you, Calpurnia. I wandered in the witch-fog that I didn't have the strength to fight, while you did the Emperor's work. Punished I may be, but I want the chance to restore my faith too.'

'Well then, Preacher Orovene,' said Calpurnia, 'walk with me. The Emperor knows us by our deeds. Let us, by our deeds, show that we deserve what we've asked of Him.'

CHAPTER FOURTEEN

'THE SUCCESSION?' RENZ asked, 'The succession for Master?' He was staring ahead, through the archway into the oval antechamber outside the Master's suite, towards the broken silk partition at the far end that still hadn't been repaired.

'The succession, Master Renz, or should I say Master Concordiast Renz? Master Herbalist Renz? You have had a number of titles. You'll have to take pity on my poor attempts to understand all the protocols of your Blind Tower.' Calpurnia wondered for a moment if she was playing the baffle-witted act a little too heavy. She was painfully aware that deception fitted her about as well as a suit of Astartes armour. Back in the heart of the cloisters, her senses were playing up again and it was difficult to concentrate.

'I had to take over command here, you see, as a matter of duty. Now, I have to establish a succession to poor Master Otranto, and of course, I will depend on your guidance. I know you were the Master's major-domo and chief of staff. You've made yourself central to the running of the Bastion.'

'You flatter me, mamzel arbitor. I saw to it that the mundane life of the Tower ran smoothly, to free up my Master's attention. That was all.' Renz was frightened and wary, but fear hadn't made him stupid. If Calpurnia knew he was at the centre of so much of the Bastion's activities, what else might she have found out?

Time to make sure he didn't dwell on that. She ushered him down out of the passageway and into the room, and sat him on a hassock that she'd brought out of Otranto's bedchamber. He didn't remark on Bruinann and Orovene standing in one of the side arches, or the pistol and maul Calpurnia wore.

'You're ready... to look to the succession?' he asked finally. 'To take full command?'

'I aim to have the matter settled by the time my colleagues arrive from Hydraphur,' Calpurnia told him. 'I will have to leave the station once Otranto's murderers have been neutralised, and it would be poor indeed of me to leave a mess to be cleaned up after me.'

'Who's coming? What?' Renz's eyes flicked to the other two arbitrators, watching him impassively from the passage. 'How long has this been known?'

'The Bastion is no easy destination,' Calpurnia told him smoothly. 'Have you forgotten how far out from Hydraphur you orbit? The Bastion's own orbit has been threaded through the gravity wells of planets in both ecliptics. It's hard to intercept, that's the whole point. It's taking time for the follow-up taskforce to reach here, but I'm sure, with your help, I'll be able to organise their visit so it's not disruptive. Their task won't be complex, after all. Just collect the corpses of Kyto and that inquisitor and the Ylante woman, and cart them off for destruction, and the investiture of the new Master. I imagine you're looking forward to your days returning to normal.'

Renz jerked forwards, and then stood up in a clumsy attempt to hide the reaction.

'Kyto and the inq–'

'Don't fear, Master Renz, please don't trouble yourself. It can't have been easy for you, finding that someone so close by has it in them to commit such terrible crimes, but there's not a place under the Emperor's sun that's free of human folly, aren't we taught that? It was a stroke of justice, that madman catching all three conspirators together. We've got some work ahead of us, piecing together the details of their plot, but if you feel up to– well, no, I won't trouble you with such disturbing work, sir.'

'Oh, no,' exclaimed Renz. He had almost started to smile. 'No, I will do what I must! Torma Ylante, well, she, she obviously was a superb concordiast in her day, of course.'

'Of course.'

'She lacked some of my own skills, though I tell you it myself, she hadn't the, er, the far more onerous range of tasks that I do.'

Throne, he was a smug bastard, but talking about himself was getting him gabbling. Calpurnia shook off the buzz in her head and concentrated on his words. 'But to leave the station addled by this Master Vedrier, as she did! Who knows why, really, why she left, but the Black Ships have a dark reputation, mamzel, and perhaps, well, you yourself won't need telling about the vermin that can slip through the cracks of the Imperium. You said so yourself. Perhaps the inquisitor was attempting to unmask her when her assassin killed him? Ylante, well, name the service I can render to condemn the woman, and I'll do my duty, arbitor.'

'Without duty, what are we?' Calpurnia asked.

'What indeed, madam arbitor senioris, and it is only proper of you to say so.'

'To think Ylante was on her way back here to replace you.'

'Replace?' Renz made a nervous flapping gesture of his hand. 'Ylante was no threat to my position, I assure you, mamzel. My wide range of duties for Master Otranto has required me to become skilled in–'

'I've been misinformed then,' said Calpurnia a little curtly. 'There was no tension between you and the Master over Ylante's return to the staff?'

'Oh, well, mamzel, I did try to point out to the dear Master that the woman couldn't be trusted. I'd seen through her, you see.'

'Ah, well,' Calpurnia said with a bow. 'I'll double-check your reports to Arbitor Bruinann on the matter. I have no doubt you were thorough in setting out your suspicions before the law.'

There were footsteps in one of the other passages, movements. More Arbites: Rede, this time, with a second arbitrator and a concordiast in tow. He was quiet, saturnine, his dark hair heavy over his forehead.

'Reports. Well. My suspicions. I–'

'Or did you discuss them with the inquisitor directly? I commend your intelligence in doing so, Master Renz. You weren't to know that he was in league with Ylante. Was Kyto aboard his ship as your representative?'

Renz was actually almost panting with the effort of steering his thoughts through the swerves she was throwing him. Too much agreement and he might be trapped in a lie, too little and he might look guilty: time to let out the leash a little.

'I apologise, Master Renz,' she said. 'I shouldn't press you so at a time like this. Shall I talk to your assistant while you clear your head for us to talk about the succession? With Kyto dead, the only testimonies I have of the Master's last sightings will be from the two of you.'

'And whoever killed him,' drawled the other concordiast from the passageway. He made to walk forwards and Rede blocked him.

'Of course,' said Calpurnia. Renz was twitching again. *Come on*, she thought. *Come on and lie. Show me you know better*.

'Thanks to you, that is all over,' Renz burst out. 'We now know it was Ylante who struck him down in his room. What a foul act!'

A flash of satisfaction helped clear Calpurnia's head. He had looked towards Dechene as he said it. He wasn't agreeing with her, he was bringing Dechene up to speed on the lie.

'And cunning, too,' Calpurnia replied. 'Think of it, Otranto perishing inside his own sanctuary, whose seals and guards were made to keep him safe.'

'Yes,' said Renz uncertainly.

'And then escaping! Look through there at that door! As Otranto's assistant, you must have known how formidably secure his chambers were. We couldn't understand how an assassin had got in, but it's almost as hard to understand how Ylante escaped it!'

'She's a cunning woman,' Renz said, his eyes sliding back and forth, 'and savage. Such an attack! I had heard reports of how deep the knife went.'

Calpurnia took a couple of idle steps towards the passage they'd entered by.

'It was a fierce attack, you're not wrong,' she said. 'Watchmaster Chevenne read a trace of it in his scry, and even the memory of it hurt him grievously.'

'I am sorry for it,' Renz said with a bowed head. He took a pace to keep level with her. 'The memory must have been very painful.'

'It was. It was vivid, almost alive. So vivid that it printed itself on his mind, and because a psyker's mind suffuses his body so powerfully, it printed itself on his body, too. You're a concordiast, Renz, you must know about image stigmata. A psyker can be made to relive something, or imagine it, so powerfully that they experience it. Come and let me show you what we found.'

The smell of Renz's sweat was rank and piercing. His eyes rolled, but he walked with her, hesitantly, like a child, to the empty archway.

'A psyker can form lesions on their skin when their companion burns themselves on a witchcullis. A psyker can experience an injury that comes to life in a memory they read.' She had Renz's arm and was walking him. There was no time to lose.

'A psyker can be made to feel an imaginary wound if the thought of it is driven into his mind,' she said, and Renz groaned aloud. Her hand on his arm grabbed hard at his sleeve and she slipped her hip under his, rocked him off balance and sent him pitching forwards into the passageway. As he screeched and tried to scramble up, tangling himself in his robes and stinking of panic, Calpurnia jumped back and slapped an amulet on her vox-torc. Witchcullises at each end of the passage slammed down. Calpurnia, in the antechamber, looked in at Renz, trapped and alone between sets of hexagrammic filigree and ward-etched bars.

'Someone did exactly that, didn't they Renz?' she asked him coldly. From behind her, she could hear boot steps as Rede and Bruinann came into the antechamber.

'Rybicker, the madman, he was driven mad,' she said to the quivering Renz. 'He was driven mad by an illusion, something someone spun in his head to fuel what he felt for his dead drudge. They snared him with that and made him chase a phantom. Chevenne was able to tell me that.'

Renz sat on the passage floor staring up at her, wide-eyed.

'I'll guess that's what we'll find killed Anschuk and Proctor Pheissen, isn't it, Renz? Something got into them, toppled them off balance and turned their minds in on themselves. Isn't that right?'

He stared at her, dumbly.

'I don't need to guess about Otranto, Renz. He died in the cloisters, but he left a psyk-trail through the Concourse where there are no wards to break it up. Chevenne read that trail, Renz, and he found exactly the same inward-twisted images that he found in poor Rybicker's trail. The same thing: the same imaginary ghosts.'

She stepped right up to the bars and stared at him.

'Otranto was killed because someone caught him off-guard, someone with a psyker-gift they'd Emperor-knows-how managed to hide.'

Renz had raised a hand, pointing or beseeching, she couldn't tell.

'Was it just a quarrel, Renz? Was it just that he wouldn't turn Ylante away and leave you with all your influence? You lashed out, didn't you? Why not confess?'

He was shaking his head.

'Ylante didn't stab Otranto in his chamber, or out of it. Not a living soul took a knife and stabbed him through the heart. Otranto was stabbed in the soul.'

'No…' Renz whispered.

'Yes, Renz. In the soul,' said Calpurnia. 'You know it. You know how to drive your enemies mad by bringing nightmares to life inside their skulls. You brought a nightmare to life for Otranto. You hammered the illusion into his head that what you wished for was true. Ylante had come back from the Black Ship meaning him harm, with a knife ready for him. That's what he was fleeing, a murderess he couldn't escape, because she was in his thoughts with him. Fleeing and bringing down the defences against someone who didn't care about defences, because she wasn't there, until he was locked away and alone, and the fantasy completed itself. The stigmata: the death-wound he was convinced he'd been dealt. Otranto was a powerful psyker, his mind and his body: no contest. His mind knew it had been dealt a death blow and his body manifested the wound.'

'Someone put that phantom in his head before he went running into the cloisters. Someone he trusted and let get close to him with no wards or psyk-suppressors nearby. You argued over Ylante's return and you were standing in the Concourse at the spot where Otranto started his last run.'

'Where do you actually think there's a chink in the case against you, Renz? Where? Why not confess?'

Renz sat and gawped, tears in his eyes, and breath heaving. His hand was still out. It wasn't a beseeching gesture, or a fending off, or a symbol of defiance. His thumb was curled in and his fingers out, the eagle-wing charm.

He wasn't pointing it at Calpurnia. He was pointing it past her, into the antechamber where Dechene was standing.

'DID YOU SERIOUSLY think he did it?' chuckled Dechene. 'Look at him, the worm. How could he ever stand up to Otranto? I'll tell you, he didn't.'

Bruinann stepped in and whipped the butt of his shotgun around in a curt, ferocious movement, ready to leave Dechene sprawled on the floor with a fractured skull. Things went slick under his mind and *every time Bruinann had shared Lazka Rede's bed, he knew it was a mistake. The detectives were snakes with ice in their hearts,*

*every arbitor knew that. The tenderest of emotions were fod-
der for their dossiers, levers and nothing more. He'd been a
fool to think that he was anything more than that to Rede.
He had known she wanted to return to Hydraphur and leave
the Tower, but he had never expected this. Never expected her
to open her dossiers to show Calpurnia all his mistakes, all
his little laxnesses, all the things he had whispered to her in
the night that she thought were secret. Now here they were
on parchment banners, fluttering from scaffolding on which
he was to hang, stripped and beaten, and branded with symbols of condemnation. Rede was laughing at him, Calpurnia
and Oraxi and every arbitor he had ever known was laughing at him, here atop the Wall under the warm Hydraphur
sun, handing him the shackles that he was to use, to fix himself to the beam that would lift him high in the air to hang
until he died…*

Bruinann's face was waxy and vacant. His swing
missed and tipped him off balance, and he skidded to
one knee. A low moan trickled from his mouth.

'He whimpered and begged,' said Dechene. His face
was flushed, his pupils so dilated that even the low light
of the antechamber should have been dazzling. 'Renz
almost got down and grabbed the old man's skirts.
Pathetic.'

A point of scarlet light flicked into existence on Dechene's temple. Rede's sight had come on as soon as she'd
drawn her own gun, and she held it unerring. She did
not pull the trigger. Her finger didn't move, because *even
with him dead there were too many more out there, the
witches the psykers the shivering twitching forms that
anchored the minds whirling outside in the warp. Rede was
trapped here, sealed in this tomb, so far out that she could
barely see the sun she missed so. Locked in here with these
people whose minds were eating them from the inside. She
couldn't kill them; they were already dead. She'd never get
past them, never get out, she would stay here all her life. She*

knew this now: she was doomed to be trapped among the witches for all the years she had left. Suddenly, that thought weighed too much, suddenly she simply broke. Stupid woman, why not spare the poor wretch's life when she knew which life really needed to end...

Orovene launched himself across the antechamber without a word, trailing a hoarse cry in the air. Rede's arm was curling, coming around, her mouth opening to take the barrel of her pistol, until the preacher cannoned into her, knocking her sprawling and wrenching her gun-arm down. Rede squalled and struggled in his grip, fighting to get the pistol back up to her head. Somewhere, a klaxon started to sound, as Calpurnia punched the amulet on her torc a second time. Every other cullis around the chamber smashed down. Dechene was contained.

But she was contained in here with him.

'Otranto didn't need begging,' said Dechene, stepping daintily away from the brawl on the floor. His coat was rippling as if in a breeze. 'Otranto needed telling. Too many people think they don't need telling. I like telling.'

The air between them vibrated. The witchcullises rattled in their mounts.

'Had two long good years since this little talent woke up,' said Dechene. 'Otranto was the first time I really opened up and pushed it: stupid old man. Who'd have thought I'd give him a slap and he'd feel a punch?'

Calpurnia's grip closed on her gun, but then it hammered into her and her thoughts blurred for a moment, before *she fumbled and only managed to flip the pistol out of its holster onto the floor. She grabbed for it, comically, her co-ordination gone, and then Dechene's open-handed slap knocked her onto her back with her gun on the padded floor a metre away from her hand. A little woman like her had never stood a chance against someone like Antovin Dechene. She should have known never to stand up to someone like him. It was no use fighting him; she should just lie there and…*

…and the gun came free of the holster. Calpurnia realized that she was breathing in gulps, her legs shaking. Dechene's face was purple with the strain. A thread of blood ran from his nose.

'No good,' she managed to gasp. 'Arbitor senioris, Daughter of Ultramar: no good thinking I'll fold in a fight.' They circled each other. On the floor, Rede and Orovene fought on.

'Guess not,' he panted back. 'A pity.' He wiped blood off his lips with a creamy linen sleeve. 'So you can fight, can you? Well…' Then the wrecking-ball came through the front of her skull, and although she had raised her gun…

…against Dechene, now she heard the racking of the shotgun and she leapt, twisted catlike in the air and landed in a perfect roll. Spinning, she deftly shot the gun out of the astonished Bruinann's hands, and put the second round between his eyes. Orovene, standing, drew on her, but her maul was out and she crushed his skull. Then she leapt into the air and sent Rede choking with a lightning-fast flying kick into her throat. Calpurnia landed in a perfect warrior's crouch as the cullises raised and the other arbitrators poured in. She met a shouting Chastener Dast maul to maul. The big man tried to drive her back in a flurry of strokes, but she parried each one easily, numbed his arm with a skilful counter swing. She ducked under his clumsy riposte, destroying his throat and neck with the power-flare off the maul's tip. Before his body had even began to fall, she was turning a cartwheel, firing shot after shot with deadly accuracy as she pinwheeled upside-down through the air. The other Arbites flailed and fell back onto the polished floor…

What the…

'…hell is going on?' She was in front of him again, her vision dark with swarming spots and her mind blessedly her own again. As Guilliman help her, she could even feel a chuckle on her lips.

'If you wanted to lose me in some ridiculous battle-fantasy, Dechene, you never had a hope. Did you think that would sit properly in the mind of anyone who's ever really held a gun?' She put spite into the words, and tried to hold his attention on her voice while she shuffled forwards, 'A boy drooling over a Commissar Cain propaganda-poster, maybe, but me?' She saw a flash of anger in his eyes. Good: get him angry and stop him concentrating. Her gun felt lead-heavy, but it was raised halfway now.

'Oh, well, yes, little miss warrior, I should have known you wouldn't accept a dream of a battle you were winning: little thing like you, and not as young as you were, either, by the look of you, and oh, those scars, too. Ehh, look at those.' Calpurnia felt as if she was floating, her legs barely strong enough to hold her down. One knee shook and buckled and she half-staggered against a rough concrete wall. Dechene's laughter was ragged at the edges, rising into whoops and cries.

'Memories are harder than fears, harder to bend. Let's see how hard yours are.' She managed a step and started to raise the gun when a sick sensation welled up inside her, because she was back there. She was back in the place she sometimes dreamed about. She was wide awake and yet she was back there still, *back there behind her they all were, dead limbs tangled with the hard white lights coming off the carapace armour. The smell of their blood welled up and mixed with the stink of the gun smoke and the scorched reek where lasfire had hit the flaking metal walls. There was another smell, a weird sharp chemical stink as organic, but as inhuman as the voice in her ear and the limbs gripping her shoulder and her head. The sound of leather parting as a serrated dagger edge sliced through her chinstrap and the helmet dropped off her head. 'A little poetic, this,' says that voice, 'one and one, down to us with all the blood on the floor. That's the end of it. That's the end of the poetical little duel, and in a moment I'll be here all on my own…' and she knows the knife-blade is coming around to cut her throat, but it's shifted its balance to make the cut clean, and she can see the proctor's wide-bore stubber in front of her. She stamps backwards. The leg behind her is all wrong in the length so she misses the joint, but now the balance is gone and she drives herself forwards, wrenching her head forwards against the claw. The points are driven into her eyebrow, ripping three sizzling lines of pain up into her scalp. She's fallen flat. The gun is in her hand and she's rolling over, one eye already filling with sticky blood. She's firing, firing and her cries mix with the scraping shriek of agony from the shape above her…*

That flash in Dechene's eyes wasn't anger any more. It was fear. She wondered if he had even admitted that to himself yet.

'Didn't die then,' she said. Her voice seemed as strange and distant as her limbs. 'I won't die now.' Her chest felt cramped and her breath short, and she just had time to mutter *the Emperor is my–*, before it hit her again. It wasn't a blow, but something softer and more sickening, crawling over her like an amoeba. It found the chinks in her thoughts with sly little fingers and fanned her memories out like cards, searching for pain, searching for hurt…

…struggling up a silica slope on Hazhim under the hard low constellations of the orbital forges, until the shell hits her and cracks her carapace apart. She's airborne for whole seconds before she drops into the scorching dust and…

…and in the chilly claustrophobia of the drain ways. They know they're just mopping up and so they're too confident to stay away from the sieve-grate that's suddenly punched clean across the drain way. The thing comes out all glistening, without even breaking step, and before she can cry out an

*order, a great wedge of flesh has been scissored out of the
front of her hip. There's an artery in there somewhere and
she's painting the wall of the drain way red as she collapses
in shock. The shotguns open up behind her…*

*…and she's walking, trying to walk up the steps, the silent
bulk of the thing behind her. Its crusher-claw and the drills
and chainblades are slick with the gore of Arbites and Sisters.
Her arm and shoulder a slumped and wrecked ruin, in
agony. She can barely walk, but for the thing behind her that
has been told to bring her to the very top of the stairs to die…*

The gun was still only half-raised and the shot just
creased the side of Dechene's leg. He wasn't used to
pain, he didn't expect it, and he screamed and tottered.
The fear in his eyes was real. *Focus on that*, she told herself, forcing her mind through the last wispy dregs of
the delusion. *He's weakening, press him.*

'Pain is an… illusion of the… senses…' she said.
'Despair… illusion… of the mind.'

'What does it take for you?' hissed Dechene, panting.
A red haemorrhage was blooming in his right eye. He
seemed oblivious to the insanity of putting the question
to her. 'What does it take to… oh, now. Oh, wait.' He
managed a giggle. 'Oh, of course, it's not pain that
frightens you, is it? It's not hurt or fear. They're too *crude*
for you.' The crawling was starting again and his voice
was becoming flat and colourless in her ears. 'If I can't
make you afraid, then what is it, what is it, what is it
that can make you *despair*?'

Inside her mind those crawling, violating amoebic
fingers found their weak chink, slid home, and
squeezed.

*Shira Calpurnia Lucina grunted as she clambered off the
bunk, already nervy, and shooting her eyes around to see
what she'd missed. The morning shift alarms were already
half through – in a moment, the daily reading from the Book
of law would begin through the vox-horns. From there, she*

*had minutes to get to the mess before the reading was fol-
lowed up with the daily sermon.*

*She hauled on her uniform breeches – they were tight,
harder to get on than they should have been. She'd been disciplined for her physical condition already this month – and
shoved her feet into her boots. She scrabbled with her armour
as the sermon began, and someone dropped her helmet onto
her head. She didn't know who. Her barrack-mates had
received enough group punishments for her errors to have
learned to cover for her.*

*The reading was a homily against allowing seditious
speech to go unchallenged. It lasted four minutes, bellowing
over the vox-horns in every room, and from the boxes slung
under the arms of the proctors who prowled through each
barrack. Proctor Todzaw's gaze passed over her, and the man
kept moving down their hall and away. She was clear for the
moment.*

*She was half a pace behind as they ran out of the long bar-
rack halls, and three paces behind and out of breath when
they went up the steps into the mess. Half an hour later she
was trailing out towards the gate hangars and moaning softly
under her breath: she had spilled protein meal onto her chest
and onto the eagle embroidered over her heart. Staining a
holy symbol: two strikes from the proctor's maul on its lowest
setting, and she had been sent to the barracks to change. She
had a clean tunic, but she hadn't pressed it, she had meant
to, but she just hadn't. She hoped it wouldn't show with her
armour on top of it.*

*Hers was the last squad to climb into their Rhino: they had
been waiting for her. There were no oaths or complaints, and
no insults. They all knew that she knew what they thought of
her. She slumped down into her place as the engine gunned.*

*The ash-clouds were low this afternoon, and they turned
Drade-73's sky lush like a bruise. The pumice slicks on the
canals clicked and ground, and the sulphurous breezes blew
flakes of hot ash down the street.*

It was her squad's off day for formation and range drill, which meant a long patrol loop instead. First to the labour-gangs hauling slag panniers up towards the mills for a surprise inspection of the local enforcers' prisoner handling. Calpurnia handled that well enough, since all she had to do was stand in formation. They were back on the move before her arms had started to ache too much with the shotgun, on to one of the syndarchs' plazas where the detectives' pict-spies had shown too many citizens loitering without authorisation. A slow sweep of the plaza on foot, the city folk hurriedly finding ways to look busy, but then the handful who were loafing about the water-still in the central obelisk started eyeballing them. Calpurnia saw it first, and her mind froze: should she fire a warning shot? Fire at them? Warn someone? She had made up her mind to fire a warning shot, moved her gun, and then the proctor had pointed his maul at them and roared for them to disperse or face the consequences.

'Thank you for your signal, arbitor, but I saw them,' he had muttered to her as they had boarded the Rhino again. She hadn't known whether to be ashamed or thrilled – she had meant to fire, but had just waggled her gun. He had thanked her. He had thought she was doing well.

The thought of doing anything to make that compliment go sour terrified her, and so, of course, she did. She moved too clumsily when they were disembarking again, and got some-one's shoulder in the chest for it. She grabbed at the hull and steadied herself before she fell, and swallowed the humiliation: she had done that so many times that she barely noticed herself doing it. The shove probably hadn't been intentional anyway. The squad was past bothering to do things like that to her now.

A long foot patrol through the avenues and back streets of the Seventeenth District. Poor temple attendance and slip-shod labour performance had shown up in the courthouse compound's reports once too often, and it was time to put the record straight.

By the second hour, Calpurnia's feet were aching and her muscles were sore. She tried to disguise it, stopping and staring down alleyways while she shifted her weight from one bruise-soled foot to the other, or kneeling as if to check a sightline while she vainly hoped for the energy to return to her legs, when a voice came over her torc: 'You're not fooling us, woman.' After that, a little scrap of pride made her try to keep up for another half hour, but soon, even that was gone and she was walking flatfooted, her shotgun hanging from her arms. She was almost too tired to care that she looked such a disgrace, but not entirely, so that was one more thing that hurt when she caught up to the squad by the aqueduct steps.

'Punishment vigil tonight, Cal, forty minutes,' Nalbern muttered – a message from the proctor, who'd turned his back on her. She nodded. It had been about what she'd expected.

Back in the Rhino some of them risked jokes about what would happen to the officials who'd let Seventeen slide into that state. Two had already been arrested. The lead arbitor sprang a test on them, demanding that they quote the laws and citations under which the arrests could take place. The others shot out the passages of the Lex Imperica almost in unison. Calpurnia moved her lips randomly a moment behind them, pretending she remembered the answers too. She didn't think anyone was fooled.

On the range that afternoon, her body was clumsy. Her hit rate was tolerable, so no additions to her penance today. She looked at the other enforcers as the guns danced through their hands, out of scabbard, in, out of holster and in, fire, and reload. Their hands were quick and methodical, and she knew how she looked: the chunky woman with her feet planted wrong, never quite getting the knack of wearing the recoil-kick, the shells and magazines still apparently slippery in her hands. She stripped and cleaned her weapons with the rest of them, scrabbling to finish in time, and walked back to the barracks with her head down.

Her punishment vigil was on the chapel steps, where she knelt outside the doors with her eyes on the broad steel aquila inside. She wasn't so vain as to think that its eyes were on her, nor the eyes of the Emperor it embodied. Her own eyes blurred and stung and her voice hitched and stumbled over her prayers. In the barracks, they would be reading passages from law and scripture, arguing and testing one another: laws, weapons, Arbites history, tactics, and judicial theology. She wasn't missing much. She never tried to speak there any more, not when she struggled to remember the passages the others quoted, confused names, misquoted laws, in her timid little voice that so often got lost under someone else's anyway. They were better off with her out of their way.

Her vigil came to an end, eventually, and the preacher came to lock the doors as she clambered up off her raw knees. He didn't greet her. They were used to seeing each other here.

She stumbled on her way back into the barracks as she usually did, no matter how well she thought she knew the way. Tonight there was only one curse from someone down the hall who didn't know about old Calpurnia and the noise she always made coming in from her punishment details. She made her way through the others as they sat and talked and ignored her. She dropped onto her bunk, exhausted, knowing she should undress, that there would be trouble for it tomorrow, but all she wanted to do was sleep and not think about it, just sleep and maybe tomorrow it would be all right.

Anything was better than having to think about this place, this baking, ashy reeking world that she had always meant to be the first posting in her grand career. This first posting where she'd been for nearly twenty years, still an entry-rank arbitrator, no closer to even a lead arbitor's pins than she had been the day she left Machiun. No closer to joining the noble Calpurnii whose portraits and statues she'd stared at on Iax, no closer to bringing her own distinctions on her family. A dead-end, a cast-off, nothing to the Arbites and nothing to the Calpurnii: she was smart enough to know the truth of it.

For twenty years, whole generations of enforcers had come here, served alongside her, learned more than her and moved on. They had quickly learned to ignore her, ignore the dead-end woman stuck in the corner bunk. There was one like her in every garrison, man or woman.

She put her fists to her face. This was how it was and it wasn't going to change. If she'd had the power to change it, she would have changed it by now. So this was it, she told herself, this was her life, this was the place where this seed of the Calpurnii would never bloom. She wanted to drink to forget, but the others always drank her liquor ration, and she wasn't brave enough to argue when they took it and sneered at her. The last time she'd had a bottle in her hand was in the garrison festivities after Candlemas, when Nalbern had got drunk too and had come back to her bunk with her. She was years older than he was and the years had not been kind ones, she knew he came to her with no real desire, she had known as soon as they'd finished that it had only been sympathy. He had felt sorry for her, and nobody had even bothered teasing her about it...

She lost control then, and the worst of it was this: still nobody cared, because this happened so many nights that it was just another part of the joke, just another night of Fat Cal blubbering herself to sleep in the corner bunk, just another waste of space.

After a time, she sat up. Tears were still sticky on her cheeks. Talk and laughter from the other end of the room swirled around her. She looked dully down at the boots sitting by her bunk, the boots that never seemed to have as much of a shine on them as anyone else's no matter how hard she worked on them.

Fine, she'd work on them now. She wasn't going to sleep any time soon. She might as well give her hands something to do. She angrily dashed the tears away. She promised herself that it would be the last time, but she had promised that many times before.

Working the polisher over the boot felt odd. The sound of the others talking was flat in her ears, as if the pressure in the room had changed. She ignored it and concentrated, although the feeling only intensified. Just keep working, she told herself. You can at least do this much. You can work at this. Twenty years an arbitrator and you're just learning to polish a boot properly.

Fine, then, she snapped back at herself. Twenty years an arbitrator and learned to polish a boot. If it takes another twenty to master the Thirty Maxims and another twenty to do disembark drill without stumbling, then fine. The lights flickered for a moment. She ignored them. If those are all the skills I learn in sixty years, then those are the skills I learn, she told herself, and that will be fine, because I will have spent my life...

...she closed her eyes under a wave of dizziness...

...working at my duty. Working at my duty. The thought seemed to firm her and she thought it again, said it aloud. No matter what, I'll spend my life working at my duty.

She put the boot down without really looking at it. Her feet seemed to rest lightly on the floor as she stood. The talk from the lit end of the room seemed forced, tinny.

I don't understand why I've been in such misery these twenty years, she thought. I don't understand why I haven't understood this before. The Emperor wants me here. The Emperor wants me doing this. My duty, my duty... however humble, how can I be unhappy if I am embracing my duty with my whole heart?

The shadows of the bunks and lockers were strange, the angles of the partitions leaning in a way she didn't remember, and why did her memories of this place feel so old? Why did she remember giving orders to Nalbern, not, not...

She walked slowly into the knot of talking, laughing enforcers. None of them paid attention to her; she might have been a ghost. The room seemed to spin lazily around her. She closed her eyes and spoke to herself again, made it a prayer.

God-Emperor on your Throne, if it is my duty to live and die here, then hand me the cup and I will drink from it. Your laws: your will.

The words were coming into her head as if she had newly thought of them, but even as she discovered each concept afresh, it was as if she had embraced it all her life.

My place is where my duty is. My achievements are what my duty provides. My life is what my duty makes it. I am Shira Calpurnia Lucina of Ultramar and I will do my duty with all my heart, I am Shira Calpurnia, I am... I...

I am not this woman.

The floor seemed to be heaving under her, and when she opened her eyes the lamps and the other men and women, and the shadows, and everything were just a blur, ghost-weak, a meaningless pattern turning around and around her. A poor stage-backdrop was painted around her, painted on eggshell, and it seemed that all she had to do was reach out to push against it...

...and she felt this shell-world lurch and spin...

...and then... it...

...CRACKED.

EPILOGUE

THE ORDO HERETICUS came first, and Calpurnia wasn't surprised, riding aboard a sleek Battlefleet Pacificus cruiser that they had commandeered at High Septacian. Inquisitorial troopers in stern grey cloaks filled the hangar – everything that moved did so under the scrutiny of red-eyed targeters and pale ceramic face-plates, like the ones Lohjen's chameleon-armoured agents had worn.

After the storm troopers came the Sisters, nine of them, in the white livery of the Sacred Rose, faces rigid with disapproval that they had been ordered to come to this place. Two stood back with long ceremonial saris-sae crossed over the ramp; the rest surrounded the stasis-cage that carried Antovin Dechene onto the ship. Within the field, light grew murky, but Calpurnia could just make out Dechene's face. His mouth was still in the gape of horrified denial that he had worn when she hatched out of the fantasy. 'You can't,' he had said, and

'No one could,' and 'No one has *ever*…' before she shot out his brains.

'They say that not even the Black Ships see every one of them,' said Rede from next to her.

Rede had ceased to hide her rank. She wore the black arbitrator uniform she always had, but with her red collar, and a red sash, lanyard and epaulette, openly displayed. Calpurnia, somewhat to her amusement, had been able to tell which of the Navy contingent knew about Arbites ranks by the way they had started to shy away from her. Ylante had been indifferent, but then Ylante had a lot on her mind, marshalling the concordiasts and counselling Dast about the astropaths who might ascend to the Mastership. She and Calpurnia had avoided one another for the most part. None of the astropaths seemed to care about Rede's rank, and that hadn't surprised Calpurnia at all.

'I've heard stories of witches who make it into the Administratum, the Guard, who knows where else,' Rede went on. 'They can go for years without being discovered. How do you think they do it? How do you think they believe they'll get away with it?'

'I'm no inquisitor, detective,' said Calpurnia with a shrug, not taking her eyes off the cage and the ring of white-armoured Sisters around it. 'All I care to point to is experience. It seems to me that the power in Dechene was starting to work on him by the end.'

'That does trouble me,' said Rede with a shudder. 'The idea that that could happen and the watch-hall not register a single note of it–'

'I understand you, but it's not what I meant,' said Calpurnia. 'I don't believe anything, any kind of… shadow entered him. I think that when a power like that grows in your mind it pushes other things aside to make room for itself. Your own reports show that Dechene was always a cruel man, a criminal bastard in the making, but when that power in him woke up, it expanded his psyche like a balloon. It distorted him even further. It's no wonder Renz wasn't able to control him in the end.'

'Huh, Renz.' There hadn't been any need to hold Renz's trial over for conducting at the Wall. Rede had sat him in the execution range and simply read from her dossier, DeMoq had interjected with the formal citations for his crimes, and Calpurnia had pulled the trigger. The whole affair had taken less than two hours.

However, Calpurnia had gone straight to the chapel afterwards, and Rede had gone with her. The two women hadn't spoken to each other, but they had both prayed there for a long time. The trial and execution – and the knowledge that there would be more to follow as Rede uprooted the rackets that Teeker Renz's little clique had been running – had focused their minds.

'Arbitor senioris, I...' Rede began, and faltered. The wheeled cage with Dechene's remains had reached the bottom of the ramp, and a man in a grey cloak like the storm troopers' was talking with the Sister Palatine leading it. Calpurnia watched as the man finished and walked towards them.

'I'll be coming to Hydraphur myself when my work here is finished,' said Rede, 'to account for the shortcomings in my own work here.' There was regret in her voice, but no rancour. It would be hard for Rede to sound wounded about going on trial for failure given who she was talking to, Calpurnia thought ruefully. 'I shall see you when I'm called by the arbitor majore to testify about you, I think. Dast and Orovene have both gone into detail about that. They're having several of your actions here added to the trial charges.'

Calpurnia allowed herself a little smile. Dast had regained consciousness a day before. His first action had been an order that he be wheeled into Rede's room so that he could start going through the reports. His second had been to declare the investigation over and hold his hand out for Calpurnia's arbitor senioris pins. Handing them over had hurt far less than she'd expected.

Dast's old bed in the Precinct apothecarion was taken by Bruinann, brain-burned by one of Dechene's strongest attacks, and barely coherent. When the Arbites ship arrived to take Calpurnia away, Bruinann would ride with them to the apothecarion at the Wall.

'Orovene says he hated working to add to the charges on you,' Rede said, 'if you can imagine that. I wanted to say that I'll tell the arbitor majore–'

'The truth,' said Calpurnia. 'You'll tell him the truth exactly as you recall it from the events that happened here.'

She saw the other woman turn to stare at her.

'I'm not afraid of my duty, detective-espionist, not any more. I'll meet my duty no matter what it requires of me, because that's the Emperor's will. It took a strange kind of teacher to teach me that, but I'm holding onto the lesson with both fists. My duty as an arbitor... it's what I am. Good or bad.'

'Arbitor Calpurnia?' said the young man in the grey cloak. A black velvet cap on his head didn't quite hide the augmetic inlays, and one of his eyes was a clear green graft that shone like glass. A rosette was pinned at his breast.

'We are passing on now, arbitor. Ah, Arbites,' he corrected himself with an easy smile and a nod at Rede. 'We've got the body and our agents are already at work within the Tower. We'll have cause to confer with Detective Rede before long, but for now–'

'I understand, sir. Thank you for coming to appraise us.' Calpurnia gave a click of her heels and a small bow. The man returned it, still smiling.

'Forgive the departure from protocol, but I'm specifically charged to say this. Inquisitor Stefanos Zhow extends his commendation for your work, and declares that although he will by no means press the matter he would be pleased to offer you passage to Hydraphur aboard the *Aeon Aquilifer*.'

Rede's eyes widened, but Calpurnia only smiled.

'Please present the inquisitor with my thanks and my compliments in return,' she told him, 'but my duty commands the protocol of arrest, and without duty…'

'…what are we?' said the man, and bowed again. 'I am pleased to have spoken with you, arbitor. I understand an Arbites cruiser is closing to dock when the *Aquilifer* casts off – reinforcements for your purge, I believe, mamzel detective? – I doubt you'll have too long to wait for your departure. For what it is worth, I hope that your duty will not call you to the execution cell quite yet, and I speak on more than my own behalf.' He spun on his heel and marched away without looking back.

'You have work to do, detective,' Shira Calpurnia said. 'I won't keep you. For the moment I think I'll just wait here in peace.'

Rede started to say something, but thought better of it. She saluted, and walked away without looking back. Calpurnia turned and watched the Sisters walk up the ramp. The airlocks began to stamp closed.

It wouldn't be long now. She would take ship for Hydraphur, and she would stand her trial. Her trial no longer frightened her, and nor did anything that might come after it. She didn't doubt herself any more. She had seen herself stripped down to the core, and she knew better than to be afraid.

I'm ready, she thought to herself. *I'm ready to go home.*

ABOUT THE AUTHOR

Matthew Farrer lives in Australia, and is a member
of the Canberra Speculative Fiction Guild. He has
been writing since his teens, and has a number
of novels and short stories to his name,
including the popular Shira Calpurnia novels
for the Black Library.